BOBBIE HAMLETT

Dark Skies

First edition

ISBN: 9798338105467

Cover art by Jeannine McCloskey
Illustration by Brian Reedy
Editing by Catherine Morriss
Editing by Ventta Schang

This book was professionally typeset on Reedsy.
Find out more at reedsy.com

I dedicate this book to my husband for putting up with me during my writing process and to my amazing beta readers, editors, and proofreaders, who give me all the feedback I need to keep me going. To my bestie, Christy, I hope everyone is blessed to have one of those once-in-a-lifetime friendships like ours.

To anyone who has ever fallen in love with an Oliver or a Josh.

AuthorBobbieHamlett.com

Trigger Warning:
sexual behaviors, sexual violence,
rape content, stalking, murder, and death

Contents

Prologue

Oliver

I should be happy tonight. I graduated. I should be celebrating with all my friends and my girlfriend. Yet here I am, sitting by myself, looking into the flames of a beach bonfire and watching everyone enjoying themselves. Everyone I have known for what seems like my whole life. I pick up a small shell from the sand surrounding me and turn it over and over in my hand before I toss it into the fire.

"Hey there, stranger. I never get to see you anymore." Avery sits down next to me with two beers in her hands. She tosses me one.

"I think I am gonna head out and check on Khloe." I shake my head no as I start to stand up.

"Oh, come on, you just got here. I hoped you could have at least one drink with me to celebrate. Please," she looks up at me, pleading.

Avery has always been a good friend and my lab partner more times than I can count throughout high school. She's a pretty girl, but we have never had any chemistry.

"Okay, one drink." I sit beside her, pop the top on the can, and raise the can towards her.

"Cheers!"

We tap our cans together, and we both take a long drink. It feels good just to let loose for a minute. So much has happened lately to this small town. So much loss. I take another long drink and look over at Avery. She is trying to keep up with me, chugging her drink. I smile at her.

"Round two?" I ask.

She nods her head. The moonlight shimmering off her golden hair. I jump up and head for another round of drinks. Passing other classmates along the way and saying hey to a few of them. I grab two more beers and a few Jello shots from the table. Maybe I will stay and celebrate, feeling my mood shift.

"We did it!" Tristan says as he grabs one of the beers from my hand.

"Let's shotgun a few of these, and then let's go skinny dipping." He says as he starts to laugh.

The crowd standing around him yells with excitement. A few others have joined us by now, including Avery. I smile slightly at her, and she grabs a beer as I move back over near Tristan.

"Let's go!" Tristan shouts as everyone gets their drinks ready, including me.

Josh

I lean against the rail of the back patio overlooking the bonfire party. I remember my senior bonfire party on this beach just a few years ago. Man, I have known some of these kids their whole lives. I grew up with some of these families. I see Oliver among them. He is smiling and laughing. I have known the Jenkins for as long as I can remember. His brother Caleb and I were in the same small graduating class.

I scan the crowd for Khloe. If Oliver is here, she has to be close by. I don't see her. I do see another girl starting to hang on to Oliver. I wonder if there is trouble in paradise. I turn my back to the party. I should go for a ride and clear my head a little. Why can't I get this girl out of my head? What is her hold on me, I wonder. She's probably too young for me anyway. I close my eyes, and I see her. I remember tasting her on my lips.

The sound of yelling and splashing pulls me from my little fantasy. I turn around and see a group throwing clothes and running into the water. I walk down towards the beach. I see Nicole and walk towards her.

"Hey, I think I will head out for a little while. You good?" I ask her.

"Oh yeah, I am fine. Wear your helmet." She smiles at me, showing her dimples.

"Always. Hey, who is that girl with Oliver? Everything with him and Khloe okay?"

"Oh, that's Avery. She has had a crush on him forever. I told her to give it up; he's with Khloe." She says before she starts walking towards the beach.

I nod as I look out at them in the water. I watch them dunk one another underwater. I start to feel upset with him. Knowing what he has waiting for him. Maybe I am jealous because he has what I may want. I turn and walk back towards the house. I go to my room to grab a hoodie, keys, and my helmet.

I stand there for a moment. I picture him holding her in that hospital bed. I put my hands on my dresser. I close my eyes and take in a long breath. I want to wrap my arms around her. I wanted to be the one holding her. I want to be the one she smiles at. From the moment I met her, there was an instant attraction, but it's so much more than just physical. She is the light that shines to light up a dark room, which has been my life for the last year or so. She is confident but also shy in some ways. More is going on in that pretty little head of hers than she is letting anyone know. I want to know everything about her, but she loves him. I push away from the dresser and leave the bedroom.

As I walk back into the kitchen, I see Oliver and Avery enter through the back door, laughing. They are wrapped in beach towels and carrying their clothing, dripping water everywhere. I see Oliver stumble a little. I walk over to him.

"Hey, you okay? Do you need me to give you a ride home?" I ask him.

"Josh! Hey, no, I'm fine, but I am happy to see you. I need to talk to you." Oliver is slurring his words some.

I could tell he had too much to drink. He points his finger at my chest as he speaks.

"Do you have something going on with my girlfriend Josh?"

"You, my friend, are drunk. Maybe we should talk tomorrow when you are sober." I say, slightly irritated with his tone.

"No, I want to talk right now!"He demands.

I let out a long breath, feeling the frustration rising in me.

"Look, Oliver, I love you like a brother, but if you're not gonna let me take you home, you need to go upstairs, dry off, lay down, and sleep this off."

Avery pulls him away from me as she talks in hushed tones close to his ear.

"Oliver, come on, I'll go upstairs with you. I can help you get dressed."

I stare at her, knowing this is going to cause trouble for him if he goes upstairs with her.

"I think you need to get dressed and call for a ride home, Avery. I would happily get you home safely if you don't have one. Oliver can take care of himself."I tell her with the frustration coming out in my tone.

"Hey, don't tell her what to do. Do you think you can have all the females in this town, Josh? Come on, Avery, let's go upstairs and dry off." Oliver chimes in.

I walk away from them towards the kitchen sink. I hear them go upstairs. I hear a door close. I shake my head and feel the anger setting in for so many different reasons right now. I set my helmet on the counter with a little more force than necessary. I sit at the small kitchen table and kick my feet up on another chair. I better stay here and ensure these fools don't return downstairs and try to get in a car and drive anywhere. I shake my head, thinking what a fool he is.

I sit there for about twenty minutes before I see Khloe enter the Kitchen. I look up at her beautiful face and feel the heat rush through my body at the site of her. Then, the panic sinks in as I look towards the staircase.

Lucas

I sit here watching Danielle pace back and forth as she talks on the phone with someone, but I'm not sure who exactly. I can tell she is getting upset as the conversation goes on. I wonder what is going on. She looks in my direction, and I give her a tight smile.

I pause the movie and walk over to the large picture window in the living room. I look out over the dark front porch. The darkness always reminds me of Khloe. All the nights, I would see her leaving the school at dusk and admiring her from afar. The night I drove her home from the movies when we shared our first kiss, the time I saved her in the Outer Banks at that club. There is always chaos and darkness around her. Yet there is this flicker of light about her. The kind that pulls you in like a moth to a flame. You cannot deny the pull to save her somehow.

Danielle comes up from behind me and wraps her arms around my stomach. She rests her head against my back. I move my hands to hold hers. There is something different I feel for Danielle. There is no darkest around her. There are only colors and sunshine. She has this contagious energy, and you want to be near her. My feelings for her are growing stronger. There is just so much about me she doesn't know, so many burdens I carry. The secrets I know that I wish I could tell someone and have them understand where I am coming from.

"Everything okay?" I ask as I turn to face her.

"You will not believe what happened tonight. Oliver went to that seniors' party, and I guess he drank too much and was messing around with another girl named Avery when Khloe showed up. She caught them."

"What! Is she okay?"

"That's the thing, no one knows where she is now. She ran out of the house and drove off. Sidney found out from Jen, who was there and saw it. You know, word travels like lightning in this small town."

That old obligation to save her tugs at me slightly and I want to suggest we get in the car to look for her. But I need to let that go. I am with Danielle now, and trying to save Khloe all the time needs to stop.

"I am sure she is just trying to process everything. She will probably be walking through that door any minute. Let's finish our movie while we wait." I tell her.

Danielle nods and softly kisses my cheek before she turns and walks back towards the sofa. I sit next to her and start the movie again. I softly caress her shoulder as I keep my eyes on the door, hoping Khloe will walk through it. Trying to keep the panic I feel inside at bay.

Khloe

As I travel down the highway, I feel the phone vibrating on the seat next to me. I would throw that thing out the window if I didn't need it for directions. I have been driving for hours, and the lines on the road are getting blurry from exhaustion, and the tears are making my eyes sore. I don't think I have any more tears left to cry. I need to stop soon and get some rest so I can continue this trip safely tomorrow.

A few miles later, I spot a hotel, and I pull off at that exit. I find an empty parking spot and look at my phone. Oliver has been blowing me up since I stormed out. The thought comes back to mind of what happened earlier tonight. Tears swell up in my eyes again.

"Enough!" I scream in the cab of the truck. I am so over crying over him. Is he even worth it? The pain in my chest makes it hard to breathe. I pull in a shaky breath. I delete the texts from Oliver without reading them and block him. There were texts from others, including two from Josh.

Josh: Please tell me you're okay. I can meet you, so you're not alone. Where are you?

Josh: Khloe, please.

Khloe: I'm fine. I need time to think alone right now.

I toss my phone away from me to the other side of the seat. I can't stand either of them right now. He knew what Oliver was doing, but he didn't tell me. What kind of friend is that? I shake my head as I exit the truck and enter the hotel lobby.

As I walk back outside to find the door of my room, a dog was sitting by my truck. I think of Buddy. I miss him; he was such a good dog. I walk slowly towards my truck, and the dog sits there, slightly panting. He doesn't move as I approach; he sits there looking up at me with his tongue sticking out. He looks like he is mixed with a husky, with thick fur and blue eyes. I slowly bend down next to him. He sniffs me.

"Hey there, little guy. What are you doing out here." I start to pet him. He was so soft. He starts licking my arm, which makes me smile.

"You better get back home, boy," I tell him as I stand and walk toward my room.

I open the door, and as I walk in, the dog runs past my legs and jumps on the bed. I sit on the bed, and he lays beside me, putting his head on my lap. I feel around for a collar; but I can't find one. I start to pet him behind his ears.

"Do you want to be my new friend? Are you a boy?"

I lift his leg to see if he is a "he" or not. It's a male. He looks up at me with his piercing blue eyes. "You want to travel with me, so I don't have to do all this alone? Well, you are gonna need a name." I lay back on the bed, and he snuggles up next to me with a heavy sigh.

"You may be my new favorite, everything." I cuddle up next to him, and just as I am dozing off to sleep next to him, I slowly run my hand through his thick fur. "I will call you Beau because you are my new guy from here on out."

One

Wildflowers

I stretch out my legs and cross them at my ankles. I can feel the cool metal on the back of my legs as I look up at the sky.

"You ever look at the stars, looking into the abyss, just wonder who else is looking up at the same stars at that exact moment, that very second, in that single breath? Is he looking up at the sky tonight, too? Is he thinking of me in that single breath? Is my name hanging in the air on his lips as he exhales?"

Beau starts to snore. I chuckle a little. I guess he got sick of listening to me ramble as we took a break at a rest stop. I woke up today and took Beau to a vet to ensure he had no chip. I couldn't just kidnap someone's dog that may have run off or gotten out of a fence. I reach over and start to pet him. He makes this better somehow, though. I don't feel so alone.

I don't know what my plan is yet. I cannot just show up at the home where Katie is. I honestly don't even know where it is. I have only been there once with my family years ago. I don't know how I will get in touch with her. So much is running through my head. I need somewhere to stay and some way to get in contact with Katie.

"Come on, Beau, let's go."

He lets out a big yawn and stretches before he stands up. I jump down out of the truck bed and turn to lift him down. We get back in the truck cab. I check my phone for text messages.

Sidney: We are all worried about you. Oliver told me what happened. I am so upset with him, but he is not doing good. Could you call me or let me know where you are? Maybe you guys could work through this. Danielle and I are here for you if you need us.

Khloe: I'm okay Sid. I am going to see my sister, Katie for a while. I am not sure when I will be back as of right now. In time, I will be able to talk to Oliver. Right now, it just hurts too much. Please let him know I need time. I will reach out to him when I am ready.

As I drive through my old small hometown, all the memories of living here with my family come back to me. My parents, Katie, and places like the ice cream shop and the small bookstore. The parks Katie and I played at. Hangout places my friends and I used to gather. It all feels so different now. I drive down our old street. I pull the truck over to the curb in front of our old house. I let out a deep sigh. I feel the hole that is never filled in the pit of my stomach.

It still looks the same. I look up at my old bedroom window. I close my eyes as the tears roll down my cheeks. The little girl that lived in that room is not who I am today. I put my head on the headrest. Beau starts licking my tears away. I smile and start to pet him.

"You are the best, Beau. I love you so much already." The thought returns to the memory of Buddy, Oliver's dog, and what happened to him, what Linda did to him. The sadness is slowly replaced by anger. I see Linda Coffman's face as I grip the steering wheel tighter. All the pain that whole family has caused. I shake my head and put the truck in drive.

I drive on all the familiar streets I have known my whole life. The ones I walked on with Katie and rode my bike down. I reach a street I've only been down once. The one that leads to the cemetery where my parents are buried. I stop by the little field before the entrance. I see all the beautiful wildflowers growing. My mom would always stop and pick wildflowers whenever she saw them. They sat in glass vases all around the house growing up. The thought makes me smile as I get out to pick her some.

I walk through the tall grass and pick flowers, as Beau chases bugs. I feel more connected to my mom here than I will when I walk through those iron gates. I run my hand across the tall grass and flowers as I walk around. I feel the sun's warmth on my skin. I stroll and pick flowers, letting my mind drift until I have a little bundle to take with me.

I lay the flower bundle near the gravestone with my parents' names forever etched in stone lettering. It is so permanent looking. I take a deep breath. I sit on the grass and then lie with my head near the flowers I laid there. I look up at the blue sky. Beau lays down by my feet.

"What is heaven like? What does it look like? Are you peaceful and happy there? Everything is so different here without you. So much has happened. Can you see it? Do you know everything we have been through since you left? Can you see our pain?" The tears roll down into my hair.

"I hope the angels know what they got when you both arrived. I would give anything to have both of you back here to help me through all this."

I ramble on and on about the Coffman's and what has happened since I left Indiana. I tell mom about Katie and Oliver. I even mention Josh. I talk for so long that my voice feels raspy. I sit up and face the tombstone. I pause and close my eyes.

"So, don't get mad, but as you can tell, my life is kinda a shitshow now." I can hear my mom saying my name with disappointment for cursing. That thought makes me smile a little. I look at the words "Loving parents" on the stone before me. I sit there in silence, thinking. I am all out of words and tears. Beau comes and puts his head in my lap. I need to come up with a plan. I need to find Katie.

"Love you guys and miss you beyond words. Please pull some strings up there and send help. Lord knows I need it right now." I stand up and return to the truck with Beau on my heels. I drive back towards the downtown area. There is only one place I can think of to go right now. I need to see Gavin. I think back to the time we first met.

I sit there with a book in my hands as class is about to start. I got a jump start on the book list for this English class over the summer. I hear a male sighing next to me as he sits down. I didn't look up right away. I finish the page I'm reading first. I fold the corner of the page I am on, close the book, and look up to see who sat next to me. He has dark brown, almost black, hair that is a little longer on top and shorter on the sides. He pushes his hair back out of his eyes with another dramatic sigh.

"Can you believe how hot it is in here? My moisturizer is about to melt off my face." He starts to fan his face with a folder as he closes his eyes.

I guess I didn't notice how warm it is in the room as I am pretty used to school starting in August, and of course, our school has no air conditioning.

"I'm Gavin." He says as he continues to fan his face.

"Hello, I'm Khloe. Is this your first day here?" I ask because I have never seen him and have been with these kids since kindergarten.

"Do I stand out that much already?"

"It's a small school, and it's not hard to stand out when you're new to the area."

He stops fanning his face and opens his eyes as he looks at me. He has such handsome features and blue-green eyes with lashes to die for. His skin tone is just beautiful, a permanent sun-kissed color. It makes me want to pull my shorts down my ghostly white legs to hide them.

"My Mom was transferred here over the summer, so here I am in, all my glory, living it up in New Harmony."

I start to chuckle at his comment. He began to laugh with me.

"Do you have a car Khloe?"

"I do; why do you ask?"I stare at him, trying to guess what he may be thinking.

"Because we might have just become besties with places we gotta go. And I need a ride to school tomorrow because I cannot with this bus situation."

I smile at him and catch him smiling back at me as he begins to fan his face again before I look away.

Two

Little Miss Sunshine

I pull up to the cafe, where, last I heard, Gavin works. I sit in front and look at the building, hoping to see a glimpse of him as I look through their big windows. I pet Beau as we scope out our mission. I feel the nerves deep in my stomach. I have lost touch with everyone I knew and loved besides Katie over the last year or so. I couldn't face anyone from my past life. I still feel that deep, ashamed feeling for what has happened to me and for how I cut everyone in my life at the time off.

I see him behind the counter, talking and laughing with a co-worker. I can hear that laugh in my mind. It warms my heart, just as it did before another lifetime ago. I close my eyes and take a deep breath. I am not ready for the wrath I am about to get from him, but I am anxious to run into his arms for the biggest hug ever. I close my eyes and think back to memories of our friendship as they play like short movie clips behind my eyes. I feel the tears coming to the surface and the ache in my chest as one plays for me.

I pull up in front of Gavin's house to pick him up for school, as I have been doing since the beginning of school when we first met. His twin sister Blakeleigh has been riding with us, too. She is just as beautiful as Gavin, with as much spunk as he has too.

They get in the car, and Gavin gets in the front seat. He hooks up his phone to my stereo.

"Good morning, sunshine! Let me start our day right, as DJ G starts this party on the way to school." He says with a wink.

I chuckle at him. I already know what song he will play. We listen to the same song every day on the way to school. Might as well call it our theme song. Rihanna voice fills the car as he turns it up. We look at each other, smile, and start singing "Umbrella."

I find a small table outside. I nervously sit there, waiting as Beau starts to lie down at my feet. I hear the door open as someone walks out, and I look up.

"Oh, Khloe!"

It was not the voice I was expecting. It was Blakeleigh, Gavin's sister. I stand up as she moves closer to me and go into her open arms for a hug.

"Does Gavin know you're here?" She asks.

"No, I was going to surprise him. I just got back in town." I tell her as I sit back down.

"Oh, Khloe, he is going to flip. Want me to go get him?"She turns her body slightly towards the door.

"Yeah, but don't tell him it's me yet."

She smiles so big you can see it in her eyes.

"It's so good to see you. Let me tell him someone has requested him to be their server." She winks and walks back inside.

A few moments later, I see him walk out smiling and holding a menu. He sees me, and the shock crosses his face; the smile disappears.

"I know my ex-best friend did not just walk in here after almost a year and request me to be her server after she has just done up and ghosted me all this time." He looks down at Beau as he begins to talk to him instead of me. "You, Sir, are hanging out with shady company."

Beau makes a whimper as he lays his head back down near my feet.

"Gavin, I am so sorry. Please forgive me. I have so much to tell you." I pull out my phone and lay it on the table. I look up at him with pleading eyes.

He cocks out his hip and crosses his arms in front of his chest like he is debating my words. I push play on my phone, and Rihanna's voice fills the air around us. He lets out a puff of air as he looks up.

"I cannot believe you just brought Rihanna up in this. Get over her sunshine." He opens his arms, and I crash into them, hugging him as tight as possible, like he may slip away if I don't hold him tight enough.

I begin to cry onto his shoulder as I hold onto him. Being here with him is a piece of me I didn't even realize I was missing until this very moment.

"I was so worried you wouldn't be working here anymore," I tell him, slightly pulling away to look at him. I take him in and notice all the little changes from the last time I saw him.

"Well, I haven't found a sugar daddy yet, so."

"Good luck with that around here," I say back to him.

"Girl, you're not kidding. I gotta get out of this town. The men in this town are ghetto."

We both start laughing. We sit down at the small table. He reaches for my hand, and we hold hands on the table.

"Where have you been, Khloe?"

"I was here for a while after my parents passed, but I have lived in North Carolina for the past few months. Did you hear about what happened?" It's a small town, and I thought he had to have heard about the shooting by now.

"I did, but mostly rumors. I tried to text, call, and message you on social media, but you were just gone. Honestly, I thought you may be in the slammer, girl living that thug life now."

We both look at each other and start laughing.

"Could you imagine?" I said as I shook my head, realizing that was a real possibility after what happened.

"Girl, no. But I still need to know all the tea. Let me talk to my boss so I can get out of here. I will be right back."

I sat there, waiting for him to return, and thought about the night everything went down with Jared. I see the blood traveling down the hallway again. I close my eyes tightly, trying to will the memories to leave me, rid myself of him and the memories that still taunt me. My skin starts to crawl, and goose bumps cover my skin as I almost feel him touching me again. I feel the pain spread through my body. I am instantly back in that bedroom, scared and crying, falling into the darkness.

Three

Jared

I take a deep breath, calming my nerves as I wait in a small chair in the school office.

"Hello, Mr. Coffman. Thank you so much for coming in on such short notice. We greatly appreciate you helping us out. Ms. Parker went into labor early, and it was so unexpected." The assistant principal of New Harmony High School says, as he extends his hand to shake mine.

"No problem at all. I hope she is okay." I say as I extend my hand to accept his handshake.

"Oh, She and baby are both doing good. She may need some extra time away. Our substitute teacher who will be taking over for her maternity leave will be here next week. If you could fill in the remainder of this week, that would be wonderful." He tells me as he pulls out of our handshake.

"Yeah, that shouldn't be a problem at all. I have been trying to get a full-time position, but it seems there are not many openings around the area currently. My wife and I just moved to Evansville. She was transferred, and the school I was teaching at was moving in a direction I was uncomfortable with, so it was just the right time to have a fresh start in a place near family." I say to him as I wipe my hand on my pants. I start to feel my palms getting sweaty.

"I am happy that worked out for you then. Seems the timing was great. Evansville is a great district. Do you have children in the school district in Evansville?"He asks me.

"No, not yet. We were thinking about adopting at some point. My wife has some infertility issues that we have been trying to overcome." As soon as I said it, I thought I was probably already telling this man too much. I need to stay more tight lip.

"Oh, I see. I am sorry to hear that, Mr. Coffman. Let me show you the classroom before it gets too late." He holds the office door open for me.

"Sure. Please call me Jared."

We begin to walk to the classroom. The halls are filled with students, and their voices and laughter fill the air. It reminds me of the last school I taught at. Immediately, I think of her. How painful it was to fight the urge not to touch her, not to take her. The agony of trying to stay away from her. The nights I spent thinking of everything I would do to her if given the chance. How she taunted me. How Myla was the real reason I had to leave that school before I did something I would regret. It became too hard to continue to fight the demons inside of me. Then Linda found out. The nagging and fighting, I couldn't take it anymore. How I really slipped up and let the urges win. I hope that this move will be good for us. I can get control over the urges I feel inside. I clenched my fist, feeling a tightening in my chest. I try to take a deep breath.

We continue to walk the halls, going down different wings. The assistant principal continues to talk as we walk. I was halfway paying attention to what he was saying. I am looking around and taking in my surroundings when I see her. She looks so much like Myla, and I was taken aback momentarily. I held my breath without even realizing it, waiting for her to turn around. She is talking to a boy with black hair. They are laughing near the lockers, and I was instantly jealous of this young man with all her attention given to him. She begins to turn around. I stop and feel my breath catch in my chest with anticipation. She has many similarities to Myla. She looks older. My heart begins to race. I feel the heat throughout my whole body. I have a surge of excitement in my lower gut.

"Mr. Coffman, Mr. Coffman, Jared!"

"Oh. I'm sorry. I thought I saw someone I knew; my apologies." I smile at him as I look at the door of the classroom. I walk in and thank him for showing me the way. I am sitting my items on the desk in front of the class and watching the door, hoping and praying she is in this class. My palms sweat as she walks in with the young man from the hall and sits in the middle of the classroom, dead center down from me. I cannot hide the smile on my face.

For two days, I teach this math class as a substitute. I have been trying to have conversations with Khloe. I have noticed she keeps to herself, besides that one boy who is always with her. I have one more day. I fight the urge every day not to do something I will be sorry for later or cause more trouble after just moving here, running from the issues at the last school with Myla.

At night, I have relentless fantasies about this young girl sitting here in front of me. I dream of how she would feel in my arms. How sweet she would taste. I go home and fight with my wife, Linda. I can hardly stand that woman anymore. I think she knows the demons I battle. The monster I can be at times. She reassures me that I am a good man and that I need to have a fresh start.

I look at Khloe working at her desk. This fresh start is starting great, I think, as I stare at her. I feel the smile tug at the corners of my mouth.

"Khloe, could you come to my desk, please?" I call to her to have her near me.

She looks up, and a moment of shock crosses her face before she relaxes and walks towards me.

"Yes." She says in the sweetest voice I have ever heard. She is fidgeting with her hands.

I didn't have a plan thought out. I take a deep breath to smell her scent while she is this close to me. I tighten my hands into fists, fighting for any control I have left inside me.

"Can you do me a favor?"I ask her

"Sure, what do you need?" She says softly.

"Could you show me where the teacher stock room is? Is there somewhere I can go to get more supplies?"I ask her in a low voice to keep this between us so others do not hear me.

She looks back to the boy she sits with every day.

"Umm, I may know where that is, but I'm not sure if the closet I am thinking of is the one you are looking for. Do you want me to show you now?" Just then, the bell rings. She looks up at the clock.

"Oh, maybe tomorrow. You better get to your next class." I tell her, knowing there are too many in the hall now that the bell rang. I would not be able to take my time with her.

She nods to me before gathering her things and leaving the classroom. What am I thinking? I must find another way to make her mine. I can't stand it. It's making me crazy. I have one day left to come up with a plan.

The next day at school, I wait for her. Today is the day, I tell myself as I feel the uncontrollable ache in my groin. Everything is set and in place, I made sure of it. She's not in her seat, though. I look out into the hall before I close the door. I stand in front of the class.

"Before we begin, has anyone seen Khloe?"

The boy who is always with her looks up with a sad face and puffy eyes.

"Her parents were in a car wreck last night."

Four

Hear The Thunder

We drive towards Gavin's house. This should feel more like home, but it feels so foreign.

"I think I miss your old car. Where did you get this truck?" Gavin says as we sit in the cab with Beau between us.

"This is what I could afford at the time. Josh cut me a deal on it."

"Josh? Who's Josh?" He says with a smirk.

"Oh, I have major guy issues right now. I need time to tell you about it, but I am still upset with them."

"Wait, there is a "them" as in more than one guy we are upset with?" He asks with amusement in his voice.

"I am sitting first class on the hot mess express right now, Gavin." I shake my head, not believing this is the mess I still need to deal with.

"Choo choo! Well, I am now very intrigued to hear about your little love triangle it sounds like. I cannot believe my little sunshine has guy issues. So glad we are over the Lucas character."

"Oh, well," I say as I am just realizing he probably didn't know he was there, too.

"Oh well, what? You still have a thing for Lucas, too?"He asks. He watches me like he is waiting for a reply.

"No, I don't, but did you know he moved down to where I was staying? He just showed up one day and thought I was his girl or something. It was awkward."

"Khloe Pierce, you mean to tell me you are just living your best life at the beach with all these guys, and I have been stuck here doing what? Nothing, that's what."

"Well, I haven't even told you about all the other stuff yet. My life is so different now. So many things have happened, Gavin. Do you think I could stay with you for a few days? I could use a friend right now, and I need your help. I need to get in touch with Katie."

"Mom will be so happy to see you. Of course, you can stay with us. We can have one of our old Thelma and Louise movie nights and discuss all this. I am off for three days and could use a little excitement in my life." Gavin said with his dreamy eyes.

The thought of reliving all the details of everything that has happened makes me uneasy. What will Gavin think? I know he will never judge me. He is my safe place, but still, just having to relive it again is sickening.

The thought of something happening to Katie also causes me to panic a little. I take deep breaths and try not to get too worked up over it. I am here. I will get to her and get to the bottom of this. I want her to be with me. I am 18 now. I have the funds with the trust to take care of both of us. I want Katie to be with me. I start developing a plan in my head as we continue to drive to Gavin's house.

I cannot get comfortable on the sofa. I keep tossing and turning. Beau is snoring on the floor next to me. I roll over to my back. It was a great evening here with what feels like family. I felt the love and acceptance as soon as I got here. To hear all the laughter and banter over dinner.

I smile just thinking about it. I pull out my phone to see if I can busy myself until I fall asleep. I have so many unread texts. I start to go through them. Dee, checking if I made it okay and if there is anything she can do. I quickly reply, to let her know I made it safely, and that I will keep her posted. Sidney, Danielle, Nicole, Lucas, and Josh. I roll my eyes. I tap on Josh's name.

Josh: Are you gonna tell me where you are? Maybe I can help or keep you company.

I read that text ten times, trying to determine how I should reply. Do I want him here? Do I just let that mess stay there and worry about it later? I close my eyes. I picture Josh's face. How I felt so tiny and safe in his arms on the beach the night he kissed me.

Oliver instantly comes to mind. All the times we were together. That smile he would give me with one eyebrow raised. A tear escapes my eye. How could he do that? I put my phone down and stare at the ceiling. I remember Avery and what I saw just a few nights ago. Am I any better than him all the times I messed up with Lucas or fantasized about Josh? I let out a sigh.

I pick up my phone, ignoring all the red flags that are waving in my head, and unblock Oliver. I send him a text.

Khloe: Hey

He replies almost instantly.

Oliver: Are you okay? Can I call you?

Khloe: I'm fine. No, I can't talk right now.

Oliver: There is no excuse for what I've done. I am so sorry! I want to talk to you or see you in person. I have been going crazy knowing I have messed up what we had because I let my feelings get the best of me the other night, and I drank too much. Please believe me when I say I didn't mean to do that or hurt you or Avery.

Avery! He is sorry for hurting Avery. I sit up with anger heating my face. I start to type a reply, then delete it, then type a new one, then delete it again. I could scream right now. I hold the pillow over my face and let out a low, muffled scream. I am not replying. No reply is the reply he deserves right now. Yeah, let's save face for her, Oliver. I go back to Josh's text and reply.

Khloe: New Harmony, Indiana. It's a small town, text me when you get here.

I am not being petty, right? I do care for Josh. I could use his help anyway. No one here knows who he is. At least, that is what I am thinking to myself as I tell him to come. My phone vibrates with a text message.

Josh: See you soon.

A smile comes automatically. I lay my phone down. I feel a little better, yet I am still uneasy and restless. I roll over to my side. My phone vibrates again. I check to see what Josh said. It was not Josh.

Private number: I know you are in New Harmony

I feel immediate panic, and I shoot up off the sofa. I feel a million eyes on me. Is it someone helping Linda? I look out the front window and check if there is anyone outside or any cars. A flash of lightning bolts across the sky as I look out. The loud clap of thunder fills the home. I sink to the floor with my back to the window. I wrap my arms around my knees as my phone vibrates again. Beau nudges me with his wet nose.

Private number: I want to help you as much as I can. You will have to trust me. Remember, I am a friend.

I can't trust anyone these days. I do not want to be alone anymore. I run up the stairs to Gavin's room. I lightly knock on the door before I open it.

"Gavin," I say softly.

He looks up at me from his bed. He lifts the covers and waves me over.

"Come on, sunshine."

I rush to his bed and jump under the covers just as the sound of loud booming thunder fills his room. I start to cry as he wraps his arms around me and holds me until I fall asleep.

Five

Three's a Crowd

I wait at a little table outside the café where Gavin and Blakeleigh work. Starting to feel helpless about how I will get in touch with Katie. I can't just walk up to her door and ring the doorbell after what they said to me. With how fast gossip travels, they may already know I'm in town.

I sit there in my thoughts, just going over and over it, trying to devise a plan. I wish school was still in session. I would wait there for her. I have been waiting for Gavin to get off work at this little table with Beau for about an hour. I have been waiting at his house the last few days for him to get off work, but today, I felt a little stir-crazy.

I have been feeling a little jumpy lately. Every motorcycle makes me look, thinking it is Josh. My heart races, and then I'm let down each time. He is probably not coming. I haven't heard from him in days. It's crazy to think he would come all this way for me. Oliver has texted a few times, but I have not responded. I still don't know how I feel about everything that happened with him and Avery. I shudder at the thought. I pull up his social media account and check for any new posts. Nothing since the night I left. The last photos are from the bonfire. I feel my face heat up. I put my phone down on the table with more force than I should have.

"What are we to do, Beau? I am just a hot mess." He looks up at me with pleading eyes."No, we cannot have another pup cup," I say as I reach down and rub him behind his ears. He gives a big sigh. He makes me smile. Just then, Blakeleigh comes out of the café. She sits a smoothie in front of me and bends down to Beau with a pup cup. I shake my head as I chuckle.

"You have to stop spoiling him," I say to her as I smile.

"No way, he is my favorite customer here, no offense." She smiles at me.

"None taken," I let out a small laugh. "Blakeleigh, while you are out here, I have a favor to ask." I open the straw and put it in the drink she gave me. I take a sip as she finishes with Beau. I look down at him as he licks around his mouth to avoid missing one drop of his little treat."Thank you for the drink." I say with a heavy sigh.

"Of course. You must be getting hot out here." She sits down across from me. "So, what's up? What's the favor?" She asks as she leans on the table to get closer to me.

"You know my sister, Katie, right?" I smile as I picture her.

"Yea, sporty mini you." She says with a smile, pulling at her lips.

"Would you be willing to stop by the house she is staying at and ask for her? Maybe they will let you see her, and you could slip her a note from me or tell her privately that I am here. Somehow, set up some time or place we can meet." I put my head down, looking away from her eyes. Thinking she may say no. Maybe I am asking too much, getting her involved. "I don't know what to do. How to contact her." I let out a frustrated sigh.

She reaches over and puts her hand on mine.

"Of course I will. We are family. I am off work tomorrow. Let's do it then."

I squeeze her hand. In that single moment, I feel just a little bit of hope. I will be able to let Katie know that I am here. She's not alone.

"Thank you so much. It means the world to me."

She winks and smiles at me as she stands back up and walks back inside the café. I sit back in my chair and look up at the blue sky. Not a cloud in sight, matching my mood, feeling so much weight lifted off my shoulders. Tomorrow Katie. This is will be fixed in no time.

The sound of the café door brings me back from my daydream. Beau jumps up quickly, bumping the table. I grab the smoothie to save it from spilling as Gavin walks towards us. Beau is excited, thinking another pup cup is coming his way. He sits down in front of Gavin, wagging his tail and making it swish along the ground.

"Look, Beau, I am not trying to give you diabetes. My sister has given you a year's supply of them." Beau kept his pleading eyes on Gavin, as he reaches down to pet him.

"Better watch out, Khloe; I think my sister is out to steal your little man." I laugh, as I think about how much Blakeleigh really does love Beau.

"She has agreed to go to Katie's house tomorrow, on her day off. I am so thankful for her. I don't mind sharing him a little."

"Well, speaking of sharing, have you heard from yours truly yet?" He laughs a little and sits down with me.

I let out a sigh, knowing I really don't know which guy he is talking about. I shake my head at how my love life is so messy.

"I have no new news on either of them."I tell him.

"So, all that spying on their social media is not paying off for you yet?"

"I am not spying."I feel my face heat up with embarrassment.

"Sunshine, do not lie to me. I know you are." He looks at me, raising one of his eyebrows.

I put my head in my hands. He knows me too damn well.

"So, what is your plan when Prince Charming shows up in New Harmony? What are you going to do with all this yumminess?" He is looking at something on his phone.

I pull his phone away. He has a photo of Josh pulled up.

"What are you doing? How did you get this photo?"

"You think you are the only one spying? Girl, what kind of friend would I be if I didn't do my own investigation? But facts, this is the best eye candy investigation I have participated in." He lets out a laugh.

I look at the photo of Josh on the beach with no shirt and start to feel some type of way. I give him back his phone.

"I am happy to see you are amused with my troubles." I say with a smile.

"Oh honey, I will take this kind of trouble any day of the week." We both laugh.

"What does his dad look like?" He gives me a devious smile.

My mouth drops as I shove him on his shoulder.

"Stop!" I say as I give him a punch on his arm. Sometimes, his jokes are too much for me, but he knows how to get me out of my moods.

"So, we need to talk about a bigger issue here for real." He says to me as he puts his phone down. "You honestly cannot let that man see you in these two outfits you keep rotating. You need to go shopping. You need to be looking snatched when he shows up." He says with a grin.

"I don't even know what that means." I look down at my tee and shorts, which are all loose on me. I was still healing some when I wore these. I think back to all the bruising and pain I was in after my run-in with Linda.

"I am off work now. Let's go shopping, and I will show you exactly what that means. Blakeleigh is off too, and she can hang with Mr. Blue

Eyes here while we have a night out." He reaches down and pets Beau.

"I could use a little night out shopping with my bestie." I tell him as I smile, feeling excited about doing something other than obsessing about everything running through my head.

We swing into all the stores in the mall and hit up all the little shops. I let him talk me into some ridiculous outfits. They did look good on me, just wondering if I can pull them off. Not to mention the bathing suit I let him convince me to get; there is barely anything there, but I'll admit it was nice to have him hype me up on how beautiful I am. I was starting to believe it.

I look over at Gavin as he talks to a group. I think everyone needs a hype man like him in their life. I am blessed to have him in mine. I do know why I pushed away from him for so long. He has healed my soul a little in this last week. It was so hard to look at anyone after all those dark days with my parents and then the Coffman's house. I finally feel like once I get this Katie issue worked out, my life will be back to normal and on a better path.

I see Gavin walking back over to the table where I am sitting in the food court area. He stands in front of me, snapping his fingers.

"We have plans tonight. We need to get home and get ready, quick."He tells me all excited.

"What kind of plans?" I ask.

"There is a barn party out at the Cooper's. No protests, little miss, we are going." He said with firmness.

I heard about the parties out there during school, but I've never been invited to one. The Coopers own a large farm on the edge of town, and a few times a year, they have a huge party out in the field in an old barn. I used to hear all the stories of what went down at them.

"We better go get ready then," I say as I stand and grab my bags.

He took some from me and linked his arm with mine. He starts to sing as we walk towards the door.

"It's our party. We can do what we want. It's our party, we can say what want. It's our party; we can love who we want!"

I chime in, and we sing Miley all the way to the car, laughing and looking obnoxious the whole time.

A few hours later, we pull up to the Cooper's. Blakeleigh volunteered to drive. I sat in the backseat with Beau. It felt good to get all dressed up with Blakeleigh. I wore my hair down with some long curls. Blakeleigh loaned me some cowboy boots, which she insisted I wear. A crop top and shorts with a belt finish my barn party look.

The music is blasting, and people are all spread out everywhere. Some pickup trucks backed up with the tailgates down and people dancing in them. We weave our way through the various groups of people. Playing a mix of country, rap, and everything in between. I stop and say hi to people I know, and they are shocked to see me. Some greet me with happiness. Some are hesitant. I can tell they have heard some things about me since the last time they saw me. God only knows what they heard.

Beau stays close to my legs. Gavin grabs my hand to give it a little squeeze for encouragement.

"What do you want to do first?" Gavin asks.

I look around. There are coolers open with drinks in them. There is a barn swing, dancing, and a lot of mingling. I shrug my shoulders. I was starting to feel a little uncomfortable.

"Let's get on that swing. It looks like fun," he suggests. He smiles and pulls me with him, and then he starts to walk towards the swing.

We both get on the swing from an upper loft in the barn. We start swinging over an area with piles of hay. We both start laughing and yelling, as it goes faster and higher. I lean back like I used to as a kid and hold the ropes, almost upside down looking at everything moving fast past me, checking out all the faces in the crowd. I see him standing there. I jerk up and look back at that area of the barn. I don't see him. I swore I saw him, though. I start looking everywhere, but the swing is moving so fast that I can't see faces clearly.

"What is it?" Gavin asks as I start looking everywhere.

"I thought I saw Josh in the crowd."

"How would he know about this Khloe?"

He is right. Only locals know about this. It can't be him. I keep looking for him. Feeling a little dizzy after jumping off, I fall in the hay, and Gavin starts to laugh with me and helps me up.

"That was so much fun," I say to Gavin. "Want to get a drink?" I ask him.

He nods as we head back towards the coolers. I get two bottles of water and hand one to him.

"This is my song. Do you want to dance with me?" Gavin asks.

"No, you go ahead. I still feel dizzy. I am going to step outside and get some air with Beau."

"Suit yourself," he says as he moves towards others dancing.

I watch him for a few seconds before I head toward the doors.

Soon as I get outside, the cool air gives me a brief chill. I wrap my arms around myself. There are so many different kinds of music playing; it all meshes as just noise. I start to walk a little further out, away from the barn and the cars playing music. Beau runs out into the field. I watch him chase fireflies and I think about how long it has been since I saw a firefly. I remember catching them as a kid. Lost in my memories, I do not hear anyone coming up from behind me.

"The swing looks fun." His voice pulls me out of my thoughts immediately. His breath barely touches the side of my neck and ear as he leans in when he speaks to me.

I close my eyes and take a deep breath. I knew I saw him in the crowd. I turn to face him. He reaches up and pulls a piece of hay out of my hair. He gives me a small smile, showing one dimple. I wrap my arms around him and hug him hard. He wraps his arms around my lower back. I take a deep breath, breathing in his scent. He leans down to my ear.

"It's so good to see you cowgirl."

I smile, not letting go or moving.

"I have to tell you something, Khloe. All I want to do right now is kiss you."

I pull away, looking up at him, giving him the invitation to do so, and feeling the excitement in my stomach. I start to get on my toes, moving closer to his lips.

"But I am not here alone." He says instead of taking the invitation.

"What do you mean? Who are you with?" I lean back to look at him.

"You think I could find this place alone?" He says as he looks around.

I guess that's right. How would he know everyone would be here?

"How did you know I would be here?" I give him a quizzical look.

"Lucas."

"Lucas! Lucas came with you?" I shout.

"He was heading down here already to finish a few things to finalize his move he said. He showed up at the restaurant the day I was leaving to come here. I asked if I could catch a ride with him."

"Yeah, I guess it makes sense. Where is he?" I look around, checking to see if I can spot him.

"There's more. He also brought Oliver."

"What! Why?" I pull away from him altogether.

"I am pretty sure that once Oliver found out Lucas was coming here, and there was a possibility that he could see you, he would not take no for an answer. Looking at you right now, I do not blame him." Josh looks me up and down. His eyes burned through me.

My skin is heating up. I feel myself blushing as he looks at me.

"So, is this the kind of stuff you guys do in Indiana?" He looks around and nods his head a little as he crosses his arms over his chest.

I notice how his chest muscles puffed out a little. Has he gotten bigger since the last time I saw him?

"I guess you could say this is our version of a beach party."

Avery and Oliver, and that night come to mind. I cannot believe he is here. I guess I will have to face him at some point.

"You want to go say hi? They are waiting over there." He pointed in the direction of the barn. "I am sure Oliver is watching our every move right now," Josh said in a low voice as if he could hear us talking.

"I cannot believe you came with them." I feel the stress already. I pinch my eyebrows together. I whistle, and Beau comes running.

"Who is this?" Josh asks as soon as Beau runs up to me. He knelt and began talking to Beau as he petted him.

I look down and see Beau eating it up. Trader, I say under my breath to myself.

"This is Beau. He is my new traveling buddy."

"Hello, Beau. You are a handsome fella." Josh stands up and starts walking in the direction he pointed. Beau and I follow him. I start looking for Gavin or Blakeleigh. I feel I need them right now. I pull out my phone since I don't see them. I text him.

Khloe: Help! Outside the doors, Hurry!

I slip my phone back into my back pocket. I look up and see Lucas talking to some other guys, but standing next to him is Oliver, watching me. I catch his eyes. In that instant, the anger rushes through my body, but I also feel the pain of my lost love for him. I am slowing my pace as I walk and feel conflicted. I stop following Josh. I stand there a minute, staring at Oliver. He is sending me pleading looks. I turn and walk into the barn. I need Gavin. I can't do this.

I hurry my pace through the crowd, looking down to make sure Beau is with me. I scan the people, looking for Gavin. I want to leave right now. I start to feel panic set in.

"Khloe!" His hand grabbed my hand as I was walking.

I stop. Close my eyes. I can feel his touch burn my skin. I turn and face Oliver. I can't keep running. He is here right in front of me. He doesn't let go of my hand.

"Khloe, I messed up, I messed up in the worst way. I can never tell you I'm sorry enough." He steps closer to me and puts his mouth to my ear. "But I will spend all my days trying." He let go of my hand and brought his hands to my face. His fingers slide through my hair.

I look into his eyes.

"I love you," he tells me.

I look into his eyes, getting lost in them, feeling myself starting to forgive him little by little.

"There you are!" Gavin says as he pulls me out of Oliver's embrace.

Oliver stands straighter and steps towards Gavin. I put my hand on Oliver's chest to stop him. I do not know what was about to happen, but I feel Oliver is being aggressive in that moment.

"Oliver, this is Gavin. He is my best friend."

"I thought you said you saw Josh?" Gavin whispered in my ear.

I look at him, rolling my eyes a little.

"Oliver showed up here in town with Lucas and Josh today," I say out loud so Gavin is up to speed.

"Oh," Gavin says, dragging out the word, looking at me and trying to read my face.

"I'm sorry. It's nice to meet you, Gavin," Oliver extends his hand to shake Gavin's.

I look at these two men, almost weighing each other up in front of me. I have never seen Gavin act this way with anyone before. They shake hands.

Just then, Josh and Lucas walk up. Blakeleigh walks up from the other side. Blakeleigh speaks first, breaking the odd silence with us all looking at one another.

"Lucas, it's been a while. How are you? And who are your good-looking friends here?" Blakeleigh asks.

Lucas hugs Blakeleigh.

"This is Oliver and Josh. They came up with me from North Carolina."

I watch Blakeleigh look at them both, smiling and batting her eyes. Just then, it registers with her, and she looks over at me and starts to cover her mouth with her hand.

"Oliver and Josh, wow! It's nice to meet you," she states as she looks at them and then back at me a few times. She walks over to me, puts her back to the guys, and whispers in my ear."Girl." Dragging out the "R" in the word.

"Hello Blakeleigh. And you are?" Josh asks as he looks at Gavin.

Gavin winks at him.

"I'm Gavin; of course, you have heard how wonderful I am from Khloe.

Josh looks at me, showing me that smile that made me slightly weak at the knees.

"Well, of course, I have," Josh says, winking back.

"Okay, so now everyone knows each other," I say.

"Not yet. Who's this?" Oliver says as he bends down to pet Beau.

"This is Beau. He's mine," I say as I look at Oliver. I think of Buddy.

Oliver looks up at me, and I know he is thinking of him at that moment, too.

Lucas steps forward to pet him, too. Beau backs up slightly and gives a low growl.

"Beau! I'm sorry, Lucas. He has not ever growled at anyone before."

Beau doesn't stop and watches Lucas carefully. Josh reaches down and pets Beau.

"Looks like he doesn't like you, Lucas," Josh laughs as he says it.

Lucas backs away a little. Beau stops growling. I reach down and pet him on the top of his head.

"It's okay," I say to Beau.

"Let's get some drinks," Lucas says as he walks towards the coolers.

Gavin and I follow the group last.

"Are you okay? Do you need me to get you out of here?" He asks me quietly.

"No, I think I am okay. It's just a lot, you know."

"I can tell. By the way, I'm not a fan of Oliver. I am team Josh."

"Gavin!"

"What? I can tell these things. He is better for you. And gawd, look at him. I want to order my own version but rich too."

I started to laugh, and it just felt good to do so after all the tenseness a few moments ago.

"But with my budget, I am gonna have to order from Shein, and it will probably get lost during shipping."

"Stop!" I bump into his shoulder as we walk and laugh.

"I am going to have to get down to North Carolina." He said, laughing, squeezing my hand. "All seriousness, let me know when you are ready. And I always knew Beau and I were kindred souls. Screw Lucas too."

"Crazy, he has never done that," I say about Beau's behavior.

I get another bottle of water and take a big drink. Then I pour the rest so Beau can drink. It's so crowded here that I want to go back outside almost as soon as we walk into the barn.

"Hey, I am going to take Beau back outside."

I start walking towards the large doors. I didn't look back. I knew at least a few of them would be following me. Once I get outside, I sit in the grass. I watch Beau sniffing the ground. Oliver sits down beside me. I look back, and I see no one else coming. I feel a little sad that Josh did not follow, too.

"Khloe," I stop him from saying more.

"Look, I cannot talk about that night over and over. I get it you are sorry, but please stop making me relive it over and over. I will let you know when I am ready to talk about it, okay?"

"Okay."

We sit there for a while, watching Beau. I am very aware of how close he is to me the whole time.

"So, this is where you grew up, huh?"

"Well, kinda. Though I never lived this far out. I went to school with a lot of these people. They all treat me a little differently, more so now than before. You know how small-town gossip travels."

"I do," he replied.

We both sat there for a while. I lean back, putting my hands behind me to hold myself up. He does the same but places one of his hands on mine. Rubbing his fingers against my hand. He put his chin on my shoulder.

"It's so hard to be this close to you and have to resist touching you, kissing you. It is taking all the control I have."

He moves and kisses my bare shoulder. I turn my head to look at him. We look at each other for a few moments. He starts to move in. I watch his lips getting closer to mine. So many thoughts race through my head. Do I want this to happen?

"I can't." I jump up and walk back towards the others.

I leave Oliver sitting there. I don't look back. I whistle, and I hear Beau running to catch up with me. I look ahead and see Josh, leaning up against a car, facing in the direction I was just sitting. I walk up to him and text Gavin that I am ready to leave.

"Where are you staying?" I ask him.

"With Lucas, at least for tonight."

I nod my head.

"You, okay?" He asks.

"Yeah, I am ready to get out of here. I am ready to go home." I look at my feet. I stare at the pattern on the cowboy boots. "Were you watching us?" I ask him.

"Yes. Does that bother you, Hon? I am just trying to see where your head is." He says as he pushes off the car.

"You can just ask me Josh. I will tell you."

He steps closer, closing the gap between us. I could smell his cologne in the light breeze.

"What are you thinking, Khloe? What is it you want?" He reaches up and tucks a strand of hair behind my ear. He runs his fingertips down the side of my face before he drops his hand back to his side.

"I want to see my sister. I want her to be with me, and I want Oliver to go back home."

"And what about me? Do you want me to go home too?

I turn and look for Gavin. I see him and Blakeleigh walking towards us. I turn back to face Josh.

"You scare me a little. I don't know what I am doing right now." I look down. I start to walk towards him to pass him and walk towards the car, but as I pass him, I turn towards him and talk to him in a low voice.

"No, I don't want you to leave. Stay."

Six

The Secrets

I'm standing in the field with Oliver. His caress is gentle as he runs his hand from my shoulder down my arm. He intertwines his fingers with mine and holds my hand. He slips his other hand to the back of my neck into my hair, pulling me towards him. My body touches his, and I feel the heat coming off him as my skin starts to heat up. He kisses me. I try to protest, but my thoughts don't catch up with my body in time, and I'm kissing him back.

I let go of his hand and bring my hands up to the back of his neck. I run my hands through his hair and grab his hair with both hands. I feel the hunger take over. I pull slightly, and he meets my desire and pulls my hair some, making my head pull away from his mouth and back some. I do not open my eyes. I feel his other hand on my hip squeezing. He moves that hand up my side, over my breast, up to my neck. His hand is on my neck while he rubs my jawline and chin with his thumb, pulling my chin down slightly and making me open my lips.

I let out a breath. I am burning from the inside out. He kisses my neck. He moves up to my ear.

"You want me, Hon? Tell me, I want to hear you say it."

That wasn't Oliver talking. My eyes pop open, and I look into Josh's eyes. I'm stunned for a moment, but it only takes a moment before I pull him back to my mouth. I kiss him with eagerness. He pulls my leg up, squeezing the back of my thigh with his hand before moving it to my butt. I can feel him push up against me. I can feel he is getting hard as he rubs against me.

"Say it. Tell me, Khloe."

I am having trouble finding my voice. I almost feel as if I am out of breath.

"I want you," I tell him.

We fall onto the grass. He is on top of me. I look up at the dark sky and see Katie standing before me.

"Katie! What are you doing here?"

She is looking down at us.

"Khloe, where are you? What are you doing?" She begins to turn and walk away. I try to push Josh off me.

"Katie!" I yell; I cannot get Josh off me.

He is too heavy. He starts licking my face. I turn to look at him and put my hand there to stop him. He begins to lick my hand. I blink my eyes and the bright light stings. I see Beau lying on top of me, licking me.

I throw my head back on the sofa. I close my eyes as I shake my head. You have got to be kidding me.

"That must have been a good dream," Gavin says from the kitchen opening, looking at me.

I sit up and throw my pillow at him. He throws it back at me; I take it, put it over my face, and scream in it. I hear Gavin laughing as he walks down the hall.

I wait in the truck at the end of the street as Blakeleigh walks towards the Mates' house. I take a deep breath as she knocks on the door.

"Come on, work, please, work."

The door opens, but I cannot see who opened it. I can see Blakeleigh talking to them. The door closes, and she walks back towards the truck. I rest my head on the steering wheel. I feel sick to my stomach. I start the truck as she gets close.

"She's not there. The lady said that Katie is at camp until the end of summer."

"You have to be kidding me. Did they say what camp?" I ask with more anxiety than I have felt in a long time.

"No, she was not very friendly. That is all she said before she closed the door in my face." Blakeleigh reached over and put her hand on mine. "I'm sorry, Khloe. We need to talk to her friends; they might know what camp. Maybe we can go there once we find out."

I nod, feeling defeated but trying to think of who she used to hang out with.

I sit in Gavin's room as we talk about Katie, Oliver, Josh, and my dream from this morning. I am no longer in the mood to talk about any more of this. I am starting to go stir-crazy. I lay down on the floor with my phone and try to block out my racing thoughts. I look at my text messages.

Private number: You should get the police report.

What is this person talking about? What police report? The Coffman's? I shake my head. Yeah, I am not ready to read that report. Maybe this person knows where Katie is.

Khloe: Do you know where Katie is?

Private number: No.

Khole: Do you know anyone who does?

Private number: I will see if I can find out and get back to you. Get the police report.

I let out a sigh. This person gets on my nerves as much as everyone else right now. I click on Oliver's name.

Oliver: Can we set up a time to meet up?

Khloe: Are you at Lucas'?

Oliver: Yes.

Khloe: I will come by tomorrow.

Oliver: I look forward to seeing you. See you then.

I may need Lucas' help. He knows everyone around here. He may know something, I think to myself. I roll my eyes. I guess I will talk to Oliver. I don't know what else is left to be said. I look over at Gavin. He's on his bed watching videos on his phone. He is not going to like the plans for tomorrow.

"Do you work tomorrow?" I ask him.

"Yes, I do. I close tomorrow night. Why?" He puts his phone down to look at me.

"I was just wondering," I say, trying to sound confident.

"Are you planning to go see Oliver?" He asks as he picks his phone back up.

"I need to see Lucas. Just happens Oliver is there and wants to talk too."

He lets out a humph sound.

"Team Josh," he says as he returns to watching his video.

I look at Josh's text message.

Josh: I checked into a hotel in town. I rented a bike. Let me know if you need to get away and want to go ride with me.

That must be the Inn. There is only one hotel around here. I think about the last time I rode with Josh.

"Can you watch Beau tonight for me?" I ask Gavin.

He put his phone down again to look at me.

"Where exactly are you going? Like for the whole night?" He raises an eyebrow.

I stand up and start to look through my new clothes. He clears his throat.

"Josh rented a bike."

"Did he? I approve. I can babysit for you," he says as he gets up and walks towards me with a mischievous smile. He starts to give his opinion on what I should wear. I take it and put on the jeans with a white crop top. I put on some sneakers before I leave the house. Once I get in the truck, I reply to Josh's text message.

Khloe: I'm on my way over.

Josh: See you soon, beautiful.

I pull up to the brick building and drive around the parking lot, looking for a motorcycle. I see Josh leaning against one near the back of the building. I pull in and park next to him. As I step out of the truck, the sun is just starting to go down, and the sky is full of orange, red, and pink coloring.

"Good to see that old truck is holding up for you."He tells me.

He gives me a little smile that makes me feel a flutter in my stomach. I try to ignore it and tell myself to act normal as I attempt to find my voice to talk to him. His dark eyes fixating on me. My palms start to sweat. I rub them on my jeans.

"It is a good truck. And I got it at such a bargain on it."

He lets out a laugh as he hands me a helmet. I take it and put it on, trying to adjust the strap under my chin. Josh walks up and tightens the strap for me. My skin tingles at the slightest touch of his fingers on my neck. He trails his fingertips down my neck, across the upper part of my chest, and back to the tops of my shoulders. I know he can feel my breathing picking up under his touch.

He turns around and gets on the bike. He puts his helmet on. He smiles at me and motions with his head for me to get on behind him. I put my foot on the footpeg and hold onto him as I slip in behind him. I don't know if I was this close to him when we rode together before. We are so close I can feel the heat between us. My legs and stomach are touching him.

He starts the bike, and it roars to life. I feel the vibration all around me. I wrap my arms around him as we pull away from the parking spot. I lay my head against his back. I take a deep breath and breathe him in. We start to get speed once we get on the road. He doesn't talk to me. He can sense I need the silence. I feel myself starting to relax mile by mile.

My hold on him gets lighter around his waist as we drive through town. He puts his hand on top of mine and gives my hand a little squeeze as he leans back into me. I am highly aware of every movement he makes under my hands and every part of my body touching his.

Time is completely lost on how far we have gone or for how long. We stop at a red light, and I see him put his hand up, feeling for rain. I watch a few drops hit his hand. He puts his hand down and rests his arm on my leg. He keeps it there as we turn around to go back in the direction we just came from.

The rain starts falling harder now. I let go of him, stretch my arms out to the sides, and feel the rain hitting my arms all the way to my fingertips. I look up and let it hit my face. I feel like I am flying in the rain. I feel free. I feel his grip on my leg getting tighter.

"Do you want me to pull over and wait for the rain to stop?" He asks.

"No," I tell him as I put my hands on his shoulder and move closer so he can hear me.

I run my hands down the back of his wet t-shirt. I can feel his muscular back. I can tell the bike is going faster. It made me chuckle a little. He let go of my leg to put both hands on the handles.

We pull into the hotel parking lot. You can hear thunder getting closer as we get off the bike. He grabs my hand and pulls me with him as we run toward the entrance. Thoughts are racing through my mind. What is going to happen once I get to his room? What do I want to happen, what should happen? I am torn as I debate what I want in my head.

He opens the door, and we step into the room. I lean against the closed door. My clothes were dripping water onto the floor. He takes off my helmet. I instantly move my hands to my soaked hair, thinking it probably looks like a mess, wet and tangled. He cups my face. My breath is catching as my breathing comes in and out faster the closer he gets. He puts one hand on the door next to me. My cheek is almost brushing against his arm. He moves in closer to me. I look into his eyes, pleading for him to kiss me.

"You should get out of those wet clothes. There is a robe in the bathroom." He backs up, making room for me to walk in the bathroom.

"Okay, thank you," I say softly, feeling slightly disappointed that he didn't kiss me like on the beach that night.

I walk into the bathroom and see two white robes on the back of the door. I close the door and look into the mirror, staring at myself. I pull my hair up since there is no brush, and my fingers can only do so much. I hang my clothes on the shower curtain rod, hoping they will dry hanging there. I slip the robe on over my bra and panties. I walk out and instantly notice that he has also removed his wet clothing. He is wearing only a pair of gym shorts. I stare at him, taking in his muscles. His broad shoulders, his biceps, his back, the six-pack on his stomach, how I can see his hips just above the shorts. My heart is beating so fast that I feel he can hear it in the room's silence.

He has a tattoo on the left side of his chest. It's writing, but I can't read it from where I stand. He sits on the edge of the bed and looks at me as I walk closer.

"You want to watch TV or something?" He asks.

"Not really," I move and stand right in front of him, looking down at him.

"You sure make it hard on a man, let me tell you," he groans.

I put my hands on his shoulders. I want to kiss him. I may have to make the first move.

"Can we talk? I want to know some things that need to be cleared up." He says as he motions for me to sit next to him.

"Of course," I tell him as I back up and sit beside him.

I look at the tattoo and read the writing. *"Follow your heart and nothing else, Mom."* It is written in a script font. I have the urge to touch it. I reach over and run my fingers across the writing. He looks down and watches me intensely run my fingertips over the writing.

"It's my mom's handwriting. She wrote that to me in a letter before she passed away."

I pull my hand back but stare at the writing. I study the way the letters are shaped.

"What happened to her?"

"She died from kidney failure. Something she suffered from her whole life. She used to say I was her miracle baby. She was a true Southern woman. She loved Lynyrd Skynyrd. She used to sing "Simple Man" to me all the time. This is from that song. She wrote letters to me and my dad while she was in the hospital after the transplant failed. I was 18 when it happened. So, a few years ago." He stares at the floor while he speaks. His voice was soft.

I soak in his words. I close my eyes and try to picture what his mom would look like. I instantly see a woman dancing with Josh as a little boy.

"I was a little rebellious for a while, maybe for a long while." He let out a little laugh."I was mad at the world. I couldn't stand to be around my father. He was so broken I thought he would shatter into pieces with a single word. I bought my first bike that year after I graduated and left. I rode all over; I had no plan. I just went from place to place, earning money along the way and doing all kinds of small jobs. I would earn enough to get me to the next place." He turns to look at me and continues.

"I learned a lot about life and myself during that time. I found out I missed what little family I had left. I went back home and helped my dad with his business. We started planning our move back to the coast. We left to get my mom better healthcare in a bigger city. My dad and I hated the city life, though." He pauses as if he is reliving a memory.

"Then I met this little blond that shook up my whole world." He chuckles.

I blush. He moves back on the bed and leans against the bed frame. I adjust to sit next to him.

"I'm so sorry. Both of my parents died in a car accident last year. I know how it feels to lose someone." I grab his hand and hold it.

"I am so sorry that happened to you, Khloe. I really don't know anything about you. I know you have a story to tell. I know there is a reason you ended up at Tara's. Everyone around there knows how she helps girls. I was so clueless about what was going on when you ended up in the hospital looking like that." He looks into my eyes as he talks.

"Did Oliver tell you that I came banging on his door thinking he had something to do with it? He wasn't home, but Caleb was, and they tried to assure me it had nothing to do with him. Then I heard about Tara and the other lady." He looks away and shakes his head as if he is remembering.

I think back to all the pain spread through that little town. Linda was there because of me. I look away from him. I feel as if I cannot look at him. Feeling the shame hit me like a truck.

"I don't want you to tell me anything you are not ready to tell me. Or hell, even if you do not want to discuss it again. I am okay with that, too. I understand that. Just know I am here if you ever do." He reaches over and squeezes my hand. He lifts my chin with his finger, forcing me to look up at him.

"What do you want to know about me? What needs to be cleared up?" I ask, looking away. I take a deep breath and get ready for the worst.

He moves down on the bed and rests his head on a pillow. He pulls me in to lay on his chest. We lay there a few minutes before he spoke again.

"I understand secrets, and there may be things you do not want me to know or even talk about. But I do need to know the truth about one topic. I need to know what is going on with you and Oliver. Are you still in love with him? Are you thinking about getting back together?"

I was thankful I was not looking at his face. I close my eyes as I speak.

"I still care about him. I am still upset with him. I am still figuring out the Oliver thing. I know that's not a real answer. I just don't know right now."

"Fair enough. Would you say you guys are a couple right now?"

"I would say no, we are not together right now."

"So, how do you feel about me then, Khloe? Where do I fit into this?" He puts his finger under my chin and moves my face to look at him as he wraps his arms around me and continues. "Because I know what I feel and what I want." He plays with a piece of hair that fell out of my sloppy ponytail. "I wouldn't want to be anywhere else right now." He says as he twirled the hair between his fingers.

I sit up and turn so I am facing him.

"I like you, Josh." I move my face closer to his. I want to kiss him. The desire fills me as I continue. "I feel free when I am with you. I can be myself. I am not just the victim girl that everyone else sees."

"You are stronger than you even know, Khloe."

I move to where our lips are almost touching.

"Can I kiss you?" I ask.

"What's taking you so long?"He says as he reaches for me and pulls me down to meet his waiting lips.

He puts his hands in my hair. There is such a need for both of us in this kiss. He rolls me to my side and pulls me closer to him. I think back to my dream. I let out a little moan accidentally. He pulls back and looks at me.

"I have a confession to make. I had a dream about you, a hot one."

He raises an eyebrow looking like he is enjoying this a little too much.

"Do tell." He replies, taking a finger and tracing little circles on my neck, moving down to where my robe is open.

"Never. But I will say I thought you were licking my face, and I woke up, and it was Beau." I smile at him.

"Oh, like this," he licks the side of my face. As I fight him off to stop him, we both laugh.

Seven

Questions

I walk into Gavin's house mid-morning. I already know what is coming since I did not reply to his texts, which he sent me last night and again this morning.

"Where have you been all night?" Gavin asks with a suspicious tone.

"Thank you for watching Beau." I bend down and pet him.

"Don't try to bypass the question." He says as he walks closer to me.

"I'm not. You know I was with Josh." I tell him as I stand back up.

"I didn't know you were spending the night. I need some details, please. I mean, come on, look at that man."

"We fell asleep watching a movie," I tell him.

He crosses his arms and kicks out a hip as he taps his foot on the floor.

"We went for a ride; it started to rain. We went back to his room, and we talked. Then we fell asleep watching a movie."

"Umm hmm?"He says impatiently.

"Okay, so we may have made out a little bit, but I swear that was it.

He told me he would not go any further with me until I figured out this Oliver thing."

"I knew I liked him. So, what is your plan with Oliver?" He asks with a grin.

"I really like Josh, but I was in love with Oliver; well, I thought I was, I thought he was. I need to see if I am going to close that chapter or not. I have so much going on right now."

"Speaking of that. What are you doing today besides going to Lucas' house?" He asks.

"I think I may go by the police station. That random unknown person said I should get the police report."

"What police report?"

"You know, I am not sure. I am assuming the shooting at the Coffman's." I pause to think.

"Oh. That sounds like it may not be the best thing to read alone. Maybe hang on to that, and we could read it together." He comes over and hugs me.

"We will find Katie and get this all worked out, sunshine."

"I know. It just makes me anxious." I whisper to him as I hug him back.

"I know, and now you have all your little boy toys here, too. How fun." He laughs while still hugging me. He pulls away.

"You know what we need, and we have not done in forever."He says with excitement in his voice.

"What?"I ask.

"A float trip. Yes, we need a river day in the worst way. Saturday. Let's do it. Hey, maybe you can invite your friends. I will get a front-row seat for the battle of the fittest." He starts laughing.

I put my head in my hands and shake my head.

"Team Josh!" He says as he leaves the room.

I look at Beau lying next to my feet. I sit down next to him and start to rub his belly.

"You ready to go for a ride with me?" I say to him."I need to shower first though." My phone goes off. It's a text message.

Josh: What time are you heading over to Lucas' house?

Khloe: I'm going to shower and I need to run one errand first.

Josh: Okay, text me when you are on your way there. I will meet you there.

Khloe: I will text you. May be about an hour or so.

A smile comes across my face, then fades away just as quickly. Oh no, Oliver will be there too. I am just going to have to tell Oliver. I get up and head towards the shower.

I walk into the police station. I head to the little desk behind the glass.

"Hello, I need to get a copy of a police report."

The man passes me a form on a clipboard.

"Fill this out and bring it back up here to me."

I nod and take it, grab a pen, and sit in the small, empty waiting room. I fill out all the information I knew. I take it back up to the officer behind the glass.

"Here you go. I do not know the report number. Can you look that up for me?"

He takes the clipboard.

"Yeah, give me a minute." I go back to the waiting room. I feel a sickening feeling coming over me. This place is so cold and depressing. I think back to the crime scene after the shooting. The officers were talking to me as I stared at the blood on the floor. What possibly could be in that report? I know everything about what happened, right?

I wrap my arms around myself and rub my arms trying to get rid of the chills that have overcome me. I look out the window, and see Beau sticking his head out of the window with his tongue hanging out.

"Ms. Pierce," the officer yells.

I walk back to the desk.

"I have two with your name listed." He tells me without looking at me.

"Two?" I feel the confusion coming across my face as I pinch my eyebrows together. I look at the man still looking at a computer screen.

"Yes, two. One is still an open case so I wouldn't be able to give you a copy, but you can talk to the detective on that one."

"Wait, I'm sorry, I guess I am confused. Which report is closed, and which one is open?"

The officer looks away from his computer for the first time since I have been standing here. He quickly looks away again to the computer.

"Looks like the one Khole Pierce vs Jared Coffman is closed. The State on behalf of Thomas and Jenna Pierce is open as it is an unsolved case still."

"Unsolved? The car accident?" I am trying to put this information together in my head. Why would their car accident not be a closed case?

"Would you like the detective's contact information?"

"Yes, please."

He starts writing the information down for me. He hands me a note with the name Aaron Graham and a phone number.

"Do you still want a copy of the other report?"

I am still staring at the paper he gave me.

"Umm, yes, please."

"It will be ready for pick up in 48 business hours. They will call you to notify you when it's ready."

I look up at him.

"Thank you, Sir."

I walk back to my truck in a state of confusion. Why is the accident not closed? I reach into my pocket and call the only person I know who may know something.

"Khloe! Is everything okay? I've been waiting to hear from you."

"Hello, Dee. Today, I went to the police station; well, actually, it's the sheriff's department. They told me that my parents' accident is still an open case. Do you know why it's still open?"

"I don't know a lot about it, honestly. I know initially they told us when there is adeath all accidents are investigated. That was the last I heard. I just assumed it was an accident. Do you need me to make some calls to see if I can find anything out?"

"Would you mind? I am just shocked that it is still open. I don't understand."

"I don't mind at all. Did you get in touch with Katie?"

"No, not yet. She has been sent off to camp. I don't know which one yet."

"I am so sorry to hear that, sweetie. I can try to make some calls on that, too. I will let you know if I find anything out."

"Thank you, Dee. How's Tara?"

"She has good days and bad days. Today is a good day. Jake is here helping today. She seems to be nicer to him." She lets out a little laugh.

I feel the pain in my gut from all the pain she has suffered because of me. All of them have suffered. I take a deep breath. I look over at Beau. Even Oliver suffered because of me. Maybe I should cut him some slack.

"Tell her I say hello and I miss her. Hopefully, I will work this out here and get back to help you both."

"You don't need to worry about that right now. We are doing just fine. You let me know what you need. I will call you tomorrow to tell you what I find out."

We say our goodbyes, and I hang up the phone.

I call the number on the note the officer gave me and left a voicemail. I start the truck and head back through town. I see people walking down the streets of the downtown area, couples drinking coffee at little tables out in front of the café, and others running on the trails.

All these people are just out here living their best lives, and I am barely keeping my shit together. I am in tears by the time I pull into Lucas' driveway. I look for Josh's bike. I remember I forgot to text him; I was on my way to Lucas' when I left the police station.

Khloe: I'm sorry I just pulled up to Lucas' I forgot to text you before now.

Josh: No worries. I will leave now.

I wait a few minutes to pull myself together. Beau and I walk up to the front door and knock. Lucas opens the door. He moves to the side to let us in.

"Um, Mom will freak out about the dog being here before we sell the house. Can he hang out in the backyard?"

"Okay, that's fine. I don't think I will be here long."

I walk in and see Oliver sitting at the kitchen table, looking at his phone. He looks up and stands when he sees me.

"Khloe! Hey, Beau."

Beau runs up to him. Oliver bends down to pet him.

"The back door is over there," Lucas says, pointing towards the kitchen.

"I have to put Beau in the backyard," I tell Oliver as I walk to the door.

"I will get him some water. It's hot out there." Oliver tells me as he moves towards the cabinets.

"Thank you."

I open the back door, letting Beau out, and see a table and chairs on the patio. I sit in one of them, thinking, why am I even here? He will not even let my dog in his house. I would leave right now if I didn't need to ask Lucas to help me.

"Here you go, friend," Oliver says as he sets the bowl on the ground for Beau.

Lucas comes out the door. They both sit by me at the table. I notice Oliver looking at me. I move my hands across my cheeks to make sure there are no more tears from crying when I first arrived to the house.

"Everything okay?" Oliver asks.

"Not really. I just found out my parents' car accident is still an open case."

Oliver reaches over and puts his hand on my knee. I see Lucas stand up. I look over at him.

"I will be right back," Lucas says as he walks back towards the house.

I nod at him. I look out in the yard, watching Beau sniff around.

"Khloe, what can I do to help? I feel so helpless here. I just sit here listening to Lucas and his mom fight all day."

"There is nothing you can do for me right now. I need to get this figured out by myself. Why did you come, Oliver?"

"I had to see you. I want to save us."

"I am not sure there is an us to save, Oliver."

"Please don't say that. I am willing to fight for you. Fight for us."

He puts his phone on the table and puts his other hand on my knee, moving closer to me.

"Please let me prove to you that it will not happen again. I can't lose you," he begs.

I put my head down.

"You're not going to forgive me, are you?" He says with a sharp tone.

He stands up and walks out into the yard. His phone vibrates on the table. I look up out of habit. I see Avery's name pop up on the screen. I stand up, pushing my chair back harder than I expected, almost knocking it over backward.

"Are you still talking to her?"

"Who?"He asks.

"Are you kidding me? Who? I don't know what game you are playing here, Oliver, but you need to take it back to North Carolina." I start walking towards the door. I need to talk to Lucas and get the hell out of here. "Might want to call Avery back," I say as I storm away.

I look for Lucas once I am inside. He is standing in the living room talking on his phone. I wait in the kitchen. I'm trying to give him some privacy, but it's hard not to listen.

"Danielle, come on, don't be like that. Danielle!" He tosses his phone down on the sofa. I watch him as he brings his hands to his hair.

"Everything okay?" I say just to let him know I am here.

"Not really. Danielle has been all worked up since I left. Maybe you could reach out to her for me?"

"Yeah, I will talk to her to see what's going on."

"Thanks," he says as he picks up his phone.

"I like her. I have to get all this stuff done up here. Help Mom out, you know."

I nod my head. I can feel the stress rolling off him. I remember Oliver just saying that he has been listening to him and his mom fight.

"I was wondering if you could do me a favor. I understand if it's too much right now, Lucas,"

"What do you need?"He asks as he looks over at me.

I study him for a brief moment. He looks different, almost older. His voice sounds different, harsher somehow.

"I need to get in touch with my sister Katie while I'm here. I'm sorry I forgot your sister's name, but I think they are friends."

"Brittany." He tells me as he looks out the window overlooking the front yard.

"Yes, Brittany, sorry. Could you ask her if she knows where Katie is?"

"I'll ask her. I may be able to help, too. Mrs. Mates and my mom are best friends."

I smile at this news. I may be able to use that if Lucas is willing to help me out.

"If she doesn't know, maybe you can find out for me from your mom or something?" He walks closer to me. I stare at him. Something is different, for sure.

"I will see what I can find out, Khloe."

"Thank you."

He nods and walks out of the room. I don't think I have felt him be so cold towards me before. I brush it off as stress getting to him. I need to go. I walk back outside to yell for Beau. I see Oliver sitting at the table again. He stands and turns towards me as soon as he hears me.

"Khloe, I can't help that she called me. I've told her I want to be with you. Come on, please."

He walks up to the doorway, but Beau gets there first. I close the door and start walking to the front door to leave.

"Khloe! Wait. Go on a date with me. Let's start over. Let me show you day by day. I want only you." He walks towards me.

He is standing next to me at the front door now.

"I will block Avery right now." He picks up his phone.

I let Beau out the front door. I watch as he runs to the truck. I need to figure out whether I want to be with him or not. Do I feel like I owe him this? I feel like he gave me so many chances when I was trying to figure out what I wanted and what I was feeling for Lucas.

"Tomorrow. I will text you." I say to him as I walk out the door and don't look back.

As I reach the truck, I hear Josh coming down the street. I open the truck door, let Beau in, and start it up to get the air conditioner running for him. I roll down the window before closing the door. I wait outside for Josh. He pulls up next to me. He shuts the bike off and puts both feet on the ground, standing and holding the bike up.

"Are you waiting to go in or leaving?" He asks.

I walk towards him.

"Leaving." I look back at the house. I can feel eyes on me. I don't see anyone in the windows. "Want to go on a walk with me and Beau?"

"Lead the way," he says with a grin.

I give him a little smile and walk back to the truck as I hear him start the bike. I drive towards the trail that goes through town. Josh parks next to me. Beau is so excited, running all over the truck after seeing him beside us.

"Okay, okay!" I say to Beau and open the door so he can run over me and jump out of the truck. "Beau, calm down," I say as he jumps all over Josh before he even gets off the bike.

"At least you're happy to see me huh?" Josh tells Beau, winking.

He pets him behind the ears.

"Hey, I am happy to see you too. It's just that it's already been an interesting day."

"Tell me about your day so far, then." He says as he walks towards the trail with Beau at his heels.

I hand Josh Beau's leash to put on him as we walk towards the trail. Josh listens as I ramble on about the private number text messages, police reports, Lucas acting different, and Lucas and Danielle possibly having some drama. I told him about Oliver and about Avery calling while I was there. I watch him closely as I let him know I agreed to meet with Oliver tomorrow to talk. He didn't seem to react at all. I watch my feet taking steps. Why does that bother me? Why do I want him to react to that statement? Why am I even meeting Oliver? I stop walking. He stops and looks at me.

"You are okay with me meeting with Oliver?"

"Do I like it? Not really. But I understand that you must figure out how you truly feel." He walks towards me, stopping when he is right in front of me. "I told you I need you to figure this out. It would be pretty shitty of me to say that and then get upset when you try, don't you think?"

"Yeah, I guess so," I say, still looking down instead of at him. I do not want to hurt Josh. I am starting to feel something for him.

He cups my face with his hands, lifting my face to look at him. His hands are almost the size of my face. My cheeks warm under his embrace.

"Do I want you to pick me over him? Every day I do. For you to do that, I know you must make that decision, not me making it for you." He bends down and softly kisses my lips.

He wraps his arm around my lower back and pulls me into him gently. I close my eyes and feel how he holds me, how my lips move with his. I get this rush every time I am with him. It almost makes me lightheaded when he kisses me. I am so aware of his body next to me, as well as mine reacting to him and his touch.

When I open my eyes, I see a field of wildflowers with an iron gate.

"You want to meet my parents?" I ask.

"I would be honored," he whispers in my ear.

Eight

See The Truth

Josh and I ride in the truck through the downtown area with Beau sitting between us. We drive up to the café to see Gavin and get a coffee. Then, I will take him back to his bike. It is nice to be a passenger as he drives. He insisted on driving the truck to make sure everything was good with the old truck. I didn't protest too much. As Gavin would say, it is nice to be a passenger princess now and then.

As we pull up, I can not believe my luck. Josh notices it as well. He looks over at me. I give a little smile to let him know it's okay, but honestly, I am feeling a little nauseous. Lucas and Oliver were sitting at a little table outside the café. There is no way to avoid it. Everyone sees us now. We walk up to the table and sit next to them. I see Oliver watching Josh. Lucas is just looking at his phone. Gavin comes outside and breaks the awkward silence.

"Oh good; look, the gang's all here," Gavin says with thick sarcasm.

I roll my eyes at him.

"I want to talk to all of you gentlemen. We are going on a float trip on Saturday. I would like to personally invite you all for a fun-filled day on the river." He says as he looks over at me, smiling.

I know what he's doing. Both Josh and Oliver are looking over at me.

"It would be great to have you guys come," I say to try to break the tension filling the air.

"Sounds like we will see you there then," Gavin says.

He winks at me and walks back into the café. I sat there trying to think of what to say since we were sitting here silently. Lucas still has his face buried in his phone.

"Lucas, I sent a text to Danielle. I haven't heard back yet," I tell him.

He looks away from his phone for the first time since I sat down.

"Thanks. I also asked my sister to see what she could find out."

I grin and nod at him. He stands up and pulls out his keys.

"I gotta run. Oliver, are you coming?" Lucas says as he heads towards his car.

Oliver doesn't answer. He looks at me and then at Josh.

"Yeah, I guess so." He tells Lucas as he stands up next to me. He puts his hand on my shoulder. "I will see you tomorrow." He bends down and kisses my cheek.

I look up at him and give him a slight grin.

"Tomorrow," I reply.

I watch him follow Lucas to the car. He looks back and sees me looking at him. At that moment, I see his hesitation. What am I doing? Why can't I get it together and decide between these two men? I turn and look down at my phone and see I have a couple notifications. I put my phone on the table. I will check them later.

"You want anything?" Josh asks me.

"No, I am fine, thank you." I turn towards him. "Josh, I'm sorry."

"For what?"

"Just everything. The float trip, my confusion. I feel like I am just dragging you along because I don't know what I want, but I also do not want you to leave either."

"I am just here being a friend and watching," he says.

"Watching?" I ask confused.

"I am just seeing what happens. When it comes to us, I want you to be so sure that you will never second guess it. So, I'll watch and wait. I'll watch how you act with me and him. But I do not want you to think I will wait forever, Khloe."

"You don't deserve that. It's hard for me because Oliver knows everything. I worry that you may feel differently once you know everything that has happened."

"Do you trust me enough to try me?" He asks.

I'm getting nervous and want to busy myself. I look at my phone. I read a text message.

Gavin: Let the battle begin on the river.

I shake my head. Of course, he so planned this float trip and in some way it worked out in his favor to ask them all at once. I text him back.

Khloe: Do you have a break? I could use you out here.

For some reason, it may be easier to tell Josh with him by my side. At least I will have his shoulder to cry on once I tell Josh the truth about me and he walks away. As soon as I look up, I see him walking out the door. I smile at him so he doesn't think it's something bad. He comes and dramatically sits down next to me.

"They're overworking me in there. What are you guys talking about out here?"

"I was just about to tell Josh all about my past. Good and the bad."

"Oh honey, I can tell you this girl was so introverted until she met me." He smiles as he tells Josh.

"You already know about my parents. That is when my life turned into a nightmare that I do not wish on anyone. My sister and I were sent to a girls' home. We did not have any family to take us in. Then, a few months later I was fostered by a family. Jared and Linda Coffman." I pull out my phone to google his name.

A story pulls up about his death. There he is, looking back at me from his picture with the story. I put my phone on the table so they can see it.

"This is Jared. They were great at first. He was great until he wasn't." I stare at him, looking back at me in the photo on my phone. It looks like a yearbook staff photo.

"He started raping me." I close my eyes. I did not want to see his reaction. I hear someone move my phone.

"That went on for some time. His wife knew. I tried to get help. Every time I tried to get help, it took so much to speak up. I thought I was to blame in some ways." I take a deep breath. I see the blood on the floor. I squeeze my eyes shut tight.

"I shot him."

"Khloe!" Gavin yells.

My eyes pop open.

"This man was our teacher at school. He was a substitute. I remember him; he asked about you the day after your parents' car accident. I will never forget that day. It's the day I lost you, too." He takes the phone and studies the photo closely.

I have no memory of seeing him before the day he showed up to visit me at home.

"He was creepy. You really don't remember him. He would stare at us?"

I shake my head no.

Josh stands up and walks away from the table towards the sidewalk. I turn and watch him. Tears start to fill my eyes. Beau rests his head in my lap. I start to pet his head, trying to calm myself.

"I heard the rumors around town when this happened, I never looked it up though. I was so hurt at the time that you ghosted me. I just thought it was all just a bunch of lies, no way you could do something like that. I did not hear about what he was doing to you. I bet this man planned something. I swear this was planned in some way, not just an accident Khloe. I swear I feel it."

Gavin goes on and on next to me with his theories. I watch Josh. His back is to me. He turns and walks back towards the table.

"Linda, his wife is that who attacked you and others in North Carolina?" Josh asks.

I nod at him. I close my eyes and remember everyone who lost their lives because of her. Tears overfill and fall down my cheeks.

I look up at Josh. He is standing in front of me. I am not able to read his face to figure out what he is thinking or feeling. He puts his hand out and I take it. He pulls me up to him and he wraps me in his strong arms. He just holds me and he gives the top of my head a gentle kiss.

"I am so sorry Khloe. I am sorry that they crossed your path and caused all this pain in your life." He whispers into my hair as he still holds me.

I look up at him as he continues to speak to me in hushed tones.

"You are so strong. You are the strongest person I know."

"I do not feel strong," I tell him.

He cups my face in his hands.

"I have always known that about you." He tells me, his voice still low. He bends down and kisses me right there in the open.

I was lost in that kiss. So much was spoken in that kiss. He didn't think any less of me now that he knew. I pull away but am still lost in his eyes. It was that moment where something changed between us. Something just changed for me, my feelings for him. I look away and notice Gavin was no longer there. He probably went go back to work.

"You ready to get out of here, hon?"

"Where will we go?" I ask him.

"Stay with me tonight." He pleads.

"I have Beau."

"We will sneak him in." He smiles at me and then looks at Beau.

"Okay, let me say bye to Gavin first." I walk towards the door of the café. I see Gavin behind the counter.

"Hey, we are going to leave in a minute; I just wanted to say bye."

"Girl, I am so shaken by this Jared thing. I cannot shake the feeling he may have done something to your parents." He walks around the counter and pulls me away to the side so no one can hear us.

"You need to call that Detective. Maybe this is why that case is still open. Something is just not right here."

"Gavin, I cannot think that I was a target and I am the reason my parents are gone."

"Girl, stop that. You know damn well you had nothing to do with what sick people do. If you do not stop blaming yourself for these things I am going to have to ring your neck, I swear it."

I look at my shoes. I know he is right. I cannot fight that feeling sometimes.

"I will tell them once they call," I tell him.

"Good, but if you meet him, I want to go too if I am off work. Your problems are my problems bitch."

I smile at him.

"I love you, but you know you are causing so many many problems and trouble with this float trip." I put my hands on my hips.

"Oh, that is my kind of trouble; that is entertainment. I get to watch all this eye candy fight over my sweet little bestie." He begins to laugh.

"I am staying with Josh tonight."

He raises one eyebrow.

"It's not like that." I tell him.

"It could be like that, though, if you wanted. I see how he looks at you."

"He said until I decide only him, he wouldn't anyways."

"What are you waiting for?"

I shrug my shoulders.

"I hope you get the answers you need soon. Because I will be needing some details on all the things. I am ready to live viciously through you."

"Me too," I say, and we both chuckle.

"See you tomorrow. Love you."

"Love you back," I say as I start to leave.

"Oh! Your phone." He hands it back to me.

"I was sending myself screenshots. I am researching this. I have my FBI skills ready to go."

"Thank you," I say as I take the phone. I already know he is not going to drop this.

"So, what is the plan to get Beau past the desk in the lobby?" I ask Josh.

"I was thinking I could distract them as you just walk past and go to the room."

I smile at him. I glimpse into the lobby and see the sweet-looking older lady at the desk.

"She doesn't stand a chance to your charm," I chuckle at the thought.

He looks into the lobby.

"Let's go, Cassanova." I joke with him. I watch him start talking to the lady. I see him flash that smile.

"Alright, Beau, that's our queue; let's go." I walk in and keep walking without looking back. As soon as we are out of sight, I pull out the key card he gave me to look at the room number on the card envelope.

I open the door. The room smells like him. I walk over to the window and look out; Beau jumps up on the bed and starts making little circles, trying to find the perfect spot to lie down. I hear a light tap at the door. I hurry over to let Josh in.

"That was not so bad," he says as he walks in. He hands me take-out menus.

"What's this?"

"Our dinner choices. That's what I asked her."

"The choices are slim around here," I tell him as I look at the pamphlets he handed me.

"We have to eat something. We could order food, watch a movie, and chill."

"Chill?" I ask.

He walks over to me. He has a mischievous look on his face as he looks at me.

"Yeah, chill." He gave me a crooked smile that made my heart race slightly. It has me thinking if the plan really was to hang out or if he has more in mind.

"Sounds like a plan, but I will have to start leaving some clothes in the truck. What am I going to sleep in?"

"Hmm, such a dilemma," he says with sarcasm.

I nudge him with my elbow.

"I'm sure we can find you something, beautiful. So, what's for dinner?"

I wake up in the middle of the night. Josh is sleeping and hear Beau lightly snoring from the floor. I roll over and tap my phone to see the time, 2:35 AM. I see a text notification.

Private number: He is not here for the reasons he is telling you. You cannot trust him.

Who are they talking about?

Khloe: Who is "he"? Who are you talking about?

I am waiting for a response, but there is nothing. I look at the ceiling. Who are they talking about? Oliver? Maybe this is someone who knows what happened at the bonfire. Maybe it's Avery. Frustration takes over as I convince myself it is Avery this whole time. She knows I'm in Indiana because she has been talking to Oliver. Would she know about the police reports, though? I roll over with more force than needed.

I watch Josh sleep as my mind races. I reach over and put my hand on his bare chest as I move closer to him. I lean towards him and kiss his stomach; I make a trail of kisses to his chest and neck as I make my way to his lips. By the time I reach his lips, they are waiting for me. I straddle him as I begin to kiss him. He never opens his eyes to look at me but kisses me back.

He moves his hands to the back of my thighs and squeezes them, and I begin to rock my hips to rub against him. I feel him with every sway of my hips. I feel him getting hard beneath me. I feel the desire growing between my legs. I hear a small, low moan escape him. I pull my mouth away.

"I want you," I say to him in a raspy voice as I still rub against him.

He rolls me to my back and lays on top of me. I arch my back to be closer to him. I squeeze my legs against his sides.

He kisses me as his hands explore my body. I feel as if I am on fire everywhere he touches. I move closer, trying to close any space between us. I want more. I want it all. My body is almost begging for it. He moves from my lips and lifts the t-shirt he gave me to sleep in to expose my stomach. He begins to kiss my stomach as he moves lower. He kisses on top of my panties. I feel the heat from his breath. He moves lower between my legs. He kisses me again over my panties; I feel the hotness of his mouth on me through the thin layer. I buck slightly at the sensation and move closer to his mouth, uncontrollably wanting more.

He moves to my thigh and kisses there, then to the other one. I put my hands on his shoulders, then move them to his head, digging my nails into him slightly. I want him so bad it actually hurts. He tightens his grip on me. Both of us are fighting for control of our desires. He moves back up to my stomach, moving the shirt higher until he can see my bra. I again feel his mouth's heat through the thin layer of fabric. He brings his mouth back to my lips.

"Please," I beg him.

"I want you so bad. I want to taste you, devour you." He tells me in between kissing me. "I need the Oliver situation to be completely finished, and for you to be sure you're not going back to him before I go any further, Khloe."

Frustration kicks in instantly. He senses it immediately.

"I need you to know for sure," he says to me as he moves away from me. He lays on his back next to me. Breathing heavily, he says, "Don't be mad, beautiful."

I am mad, though. I do not say anything, but he is picking up on my mood and the silence.

"I am about to have no self-control left in me. Come here, hon; I want to hold you." He says as he reaches out for me to come into his arms.

I give in and move into his embrace. I lay on his chest, with his arms around me, until the sexual frustration fades, and I fall asleep.

Nine

Date Night

I leave the hotel after taking Beau outside. I don't think I can sneak him back in. I text Josh to let him know I'm heading back to Gavin' since he was in the shower when I left the room. Driving back to Gavin's, frustration overtakes me about what happened last night. Josh is right. I need to decide, and soon.

I pull over to the curb and park the truck in front of Gavin's. I rest my head on the steering wheel. I miss Katie. I want to find her. I wish I could have the old days back. I close my eyes and see her sitting in my room, painting our nails and giving me advice if I wanted it or not.

"Don't stress Khloe, it's not so bad." She would say to me.

If only we knew it would get so much worse. My phone vibrates. Danielle is calling me.

"Hello,"

"Hey, Khloe, sorry it's taken me a minute to get back to you."

I hear a sniffle on the other end.

"Are you okay? Lucas said you guys are having some issues. I just wanted to check in with you." I say, trying not to pry too much.

"Yeah, I will be okay. I just thought he was different. Silly of me to think that." She says with a little chuckle.

"What happened?" I ask.

"I really don't know how it started. He started acting different with me as soon as you left town. I should have known better, you know, with how he acted all crazy with you. I thought he was over you. He accepted you were with Oliver."

I shift in my seat, feeling a little uneasy. I thought Lucas and I had worked through all this already.

"He started asking questions all the time. If I heard from you? On his phone all day and night. It just started to make me feel some type of way. I am not blaming you at all, but I think he still has a thing for you, Khloe."

That doesn't make sense. He has not even paid attention to me when I talk to him lately. He is so distracted.

"I don't think that is it, Danielle. I don't know exactly what it is, but he is acting slightly off. He did seem distracted even when I saw him yesterday. Maybe his mom is stressing him out. Oliver said they have been fighting a lot."

"Maybe, I just know he was treating me differently, and look, I don't need him. I am not going to be a second choice or treated as if I do not matter. I am not some little girl he can just be present with when it is convenient for him."She says it with a firm tone.

"I get it. I think something is going on. Maybe I can talk to him and let you know."I tell her, trying to save anything they may have left.

"No, he can come to me and tell me what's going on. But I am not going to be the one to message him to be ignored. I am not the one for that."

I love how strong she is. She is so sure of who she is and what she is worth.

"How are things there with you? You get in contact with your sister?" She asks.

"No, I haven't. I have Oliver here, dealing with that after all that happened. I have Josh here, not to mention the new stuff I am finding out about parents. I really thought I was just going to drive up here, get Katie, and drive back home."

"Most things do not go as planned in life, Khloe."

"Tell me about it." Nothing in my life does these days." I let out a little laugh.

"Hey, I need to get to this appointment. Doing a photo shoot for a baby announcement."

"Okay, it was good to hear from you. I miss you."

"Miss you too. Be careful looking for the answers you seek." She says before she ends the call.

What am I seeking? What am I doing here? I may never find Katie this summer, but then what? What is my plan here? I lay my head back on the headrest. I picked up my phone and called Dee.

"Good morning." Dee answers.

Dee's voice is always so calming in a way I would think an aunt is. Her tone relaxes me a little.

"Good morning, Dee. I just wanted to see if you found anything out?"

"Well, I did find out some things, but I'm still waiting to hear back on others. I found out that the adoption has not been processed for your sister. They only have guardianship under the foster care paperwork. They do have a court date in August to finalize the adoption."

In my head, I am thinking I have two months to stop that.

"I was not able to find the camp. I contacted a few camps to see if they would tell me if she was there; I either left a voicemail or they could not release the information. I also tried to find out why your parents' car accident was an open case. I really haven't gotten any information on that yet."

"Thank you. I know you have a lot going on, so taking the time to try to help me means a lot to me, Dee."

"Khloe, I am always here for you. I do want you to know you could show up to that adoption court date and protest the adoption. You will most likely need a lawyer. If you want to go that route, I can see if any of the family lawyers I know can help you."

"Please, if you could get me in touch with one while I am here, that would be great. That may be my best route. I was unsure what I would do if I found out about the camp she was at. Go kidnap her?"I tell her as I let out a little laugh.

"Yeah, let's not do that. I think this would be your best route. You are 18 now; you have a steady income with the trust. You have somewhere to live, here with us. There is room for Katie to be here, too. I think this is the best way to approach this situation. You would need to get that ball rolling soon, though, so they have time to get your case together."

"Thank you, Dee."

"I will start on that and let you know the next steps. Do you need me to come there and help?"

"No, not yet anyway. Maybe you can plan to come for the court hearing." I say, hoping she will come.

"I will be there. You may want to try to get something temporary to rent while you are there. It will look better for your case and be more mature than couch surfing."

"Okay. That's a good point. I will start looking. Talk to you again soon."

"Yes, I will send you the info as soon as I get it set up," she tells me.

"Thanks, Dee, bye."

"Call anytime. Bye, Khloe."

"Break! Break! Break!" My mom yells as we drive to my dad's office in the town neighboring New Harmony.

"Mom, don't yell; it stresses me out. I was stopping."

"Khloe, you have no idea what stress is until you teach your child to drive. When that happens, let's have this conversation again." She softly laughs. "When you get the green arrow, turn left."

"Mom! I know." I swear driving with my mom is almost not worth it.

Dad is so chill when it comes to this stuff.

"Park in the back." She says as we pull up to the office building.

I do as she says. I cut the turn too short and am in the middle of two parking spots. I look over at her and smile. She puts her head in her hands and shakes her head. But small laughs are coming out.

"We made it in one piece," I say, as this feels like an accomplishment since I have only been driving for a few weeks.

I am one of the last in my class to get their permit. I am already seventeen. I wanted to do it when everyone else did at fifteen, but my parents wanted me to wait. I still feel some frustration with my parents over it when I think about it. They baby me in some ways. I just want to grow up and start my life away from them. I am so over feeling as if they are holding me back. Katie acts like them in some ways, too, always giving their advice whether I ask for it or not.

"What do we need to come here for anyway?" I ask her.

"Your dad has some papers I need to sign so he can get them filed today."

I nod and start getting out of the car. I have so many childhood memories of this office building, I think as I look at it. It used to look so much bigger than it does today.

"Mom, what exactly does Dad do? I don't think I understand what he does."

"Investments pretty much. He sets up investors with companies to invest their money. He does a few other things, but honestly, that is even more difficult for me to understand. Whenever I ask questions, I need to be ready for the hour-long conversation on markets, bonds, and numbers. So, I have learned over the years to no longer ask." She lets out a laugh.

I know he must do well since Mom was able to stop working when I was born.

"Do you miss working?" I ask her.

She holds the door for me.

"Sometimes. I did in the beginning. Now I enjoy helping with charities, volunteering, and my hobbies."

"Have you put in much thought into what you want to do? Do you want to go to college?"

"I want to work in a lab somewhere. I just don't know what research I want to do yet. I want to go to college for sure. I want that whole college experience, too."

She smiles at me. We walk into my dad's office. His secretary greets us.

"Hello, ladies. What are you two up to today?" Naomi says.

She has worked for my dad for a few years.

"Hello Naomi, is he free?" My mom asks.

"Yes, he should be. You can go on in."

"You okay with waiting here, Khloe? My mom asks me.

I nod and sit in one of the chairs. I pick up a magazine from the table.

"I heard you are driving now," Naomi says to me.

"I am. But don't judge me by my parking job out there." I say, blushing slightly and smiling at her.

"I was awful forever. I still can't parallel park that great." She tells me.

"Naomi! Please have the conference room prepared by 9 AM sharp tomorrow. We have the Baker's coming in." Seth Mates says to her as he walks out of his office.

"Absolutely. It will be ready." She replies to him shyly.

Seth is a real go-getter, according to my dad. He is younger than my dad. Maybe thirty-something. He has brown hair and an immaculate, neat beard. He is always in a suit when I see him. Even when we go to his home for dinner with his wife. My dad brought him into the company a year or so ago, and from what I have overheard, he made him a partner in the business my dad started.

"Hey there, Khloe. How are you?" He asks me as he looks away from Naomi.

"I'm good, thank you," I tell him.

"Good. How's school?"He asks as he starts looking at the papers on Naomi's desk.

"It's good," I say, realizing how much I hate small talk with adults.

"Enjoy it, I sure miss my high school days." He says as he looks up at me and smiles.

"Yes, sir," I say, looking back at the magazine I picked up.

"Are you here to see your dad?"

"Oh, my mom is with him." I tell him.

"Oh, okay. Well, it was good seeing you."

I smile at him.

"Don't forget Naomi. I mean it."

I didn't look up, but I could hear the anger in his voice when he talks to Naomi. I wonder if he doesn't like Naomi. Or if she forgot to have the conference room ready once.

"Khloe, can you come here for a moment?" My mom yells from my dad's office door.

I get up and walk into my dad's large office. Leaving the tension I feel in the lobby area with Seth and Naomi.

"Hi, Dad," I say as I go in.

He walks over to me, puts one arm around my shoulder, and gives me a little squeeze.

"Do you remember playing at my desk when you were little?"

"Yeah."

"So, you remember the secret place where you would put little notes for me?" He asks.

"Yes." I walk over to the desk, open the top right drawer, and push on the back left corner; the bottom of the drawer lifts in the front. I pulled the bottom out, and there was a little secret compartment. There are papers in there with a couple of little notes from when I was little with a heart around the word DAD.

"Good. I am going to keep certain things in there. Important things, if you ever need certain information about us, me, you, and your sister, okay?" He tells me with a serious tone I rarely hear from him.

I nod my head.

"If there is ever a time you need to get information, you know to come and look there, right."

"Yeah, okay," I tell him, thinking he is acting weird. "Everything okay?" I say since I am getting strange vibes from him.

"Yeah, everything is good. I need you to know. Only us three know about it. So, our secret." He winks and grins at me.

He always says that line to me, like when we get ice cream when Mom and Katie are at home.

"Okay, ladies, I got to run to the courthouse quickly. See you for dinner." He kisses my mom's cheek as she smiles at him.

"Bye, Dad."

I look in the mirror and roll my eyes as Gavin throws himself on his bed dramatically.

"I don't think you need to look good for this date." He tells me.

"I am wearing shorts and a T-shirt. I wouldn't say that's looking good." I say as I turn away from the mirror and look at him.

"You did your hair, girl." He says so matter-of-factually sounding.

"Really?" I turn and laugh at him. I sit down next to him.

"What are you doing tonight?" I ask him.

"I have a date, too, if you must know." He says with a grin, showing a small dimple.

"Oh, do tell." I raise an eyebrow at him.

"He is so good-looking, from out of town, and maybe he will wear those sexy gray sweatpants I hear he has."

I shoot him a look. I was telling him about my night with Josh and how he looked in the sweats he slept in. I also told him about my frustration with him when I woke up in the middle of the night.

"Josh?" I ask, confused.

"If you must know. Yes," he tells me, smiling big.

"Wait, what? My Josh? You are going out with my Josh tonight?"

"He's not your Josh if you have a date with another man, girl."

I push his shoulder.

"No, really. What are you two doing?" I ask.

"He is helping me get ready for the float trip tomorrow. He came by the café today for a coffee, and I asked him to help since I knew you would be out and he would be lonely. Plus, someone needs to help me be Betty Crocker up in here getting snacks ready for tomorrow."

I let out a laugh, thinking about the two of them cooking.

"What are you and Mr. Player doing tonight?" He asks.

Blakeleigh walks into the room, shaking a bottle of white nail polish. She sits on the floor at the edge of the bed and starts painting her toenails.

"Umm, breaking and entering," I tell them.

They both stop what they are doing and look at me.

"Excuse me? You are doing what, sunshine?" He says, confused.

"I am going to have him help me break into my dad's office. I want to see if his desk is still there."

He tilts his head and looks at me. He grabs the nail polish from Blakeleigh and starts to paint my toes on the bed.

"And what exactly will you two do with your dad's desk?" He asks. He pinches his eyebrows together and looks up at me.

I roll my eyes and watch him go back to painting my toenails.

"Not that. There is a secret drawer compartment. I want to see if there is anything in there."

"Don't you think Josh would be the one to ask for help with this secret mission instead of Oliver?" He asks me.

"Possible, but I have to do it tonight. I must know."

He leans back to look at my toes, admiring his work as he twists the bottle close.

"Well, you let Oliver know these toes are a signal for Josh, not him."

I look down at my toes and wiggle them a little.

"What are you talking about?" I ask as I reflect on how long it has been since I've done my toes.

Katie used to paint them for me all the time. I look over at Blakeleigh as she starts to giggle a little.

"White nail polish means you are single and ready to mingle," Blakeleigh winks at me as she tells me.

I start to laugh a little and shake my head.

"I better get ready to go. Say hello to Josh for me. And if he is wearing those sweats, I need a pic, or it didn't happen." I wink and smile at him.

"Don't be a ho on your daddy's desk. Love you."

I laugh as I walk out of the room.

"Love you too."

As I pull up, I think about going inside to tell Lucas I talked to Danielle, then decide against it. I honk the horn instead. I will keep my eye on you, Lucas, to see what is going on with you. I see Oliver come out; he runs his hands through his hair as he walks to my truck. I look at him, and I feel my heart race a little. He still does that to me. Our whole relationship flashes in my mind. I take a deep breath. I hope to tell him how I feel about Josh tonight. I look in the mirror, feeling a little nervous for some reason.

"Hello, beautiful." He says as he gets in the truck. He leans over and kisses my cheek.

"Do you have something in mind you want to do tonight?" I ask.

"I just want to spend some time with you. I want to be able to talk about us and see if we can work this out. But you know what I would love to see? I would like to see where you grew up. Where you lived, went to school. Show me your life here."

"Okay," I say as I put the truck in drive and pull away from the curb.

We drive all over town. I show him my old house. I tell him stories as we drive by landmarks that trigger memories. We drive by the elementary school and tell him about Jon, who used to eat my hair when we stood in line, and when I chopped it off to my shoulders, he didn't like me anymore and how it broke my heart.

We go by the middle school. I tell him about the embarrassing school dances I attended, about my crush on Zach Wilkens, and how he asked my best friend to the school dance. I cried in the bathroom the whole night because life was over as I knew it.

We drive by the place my parents took us for ice cream, and I always ordered a birthday cake milkshake with extra sprinkles. The parks where I spent so many days swinging on the blue swing. The city pool where I learned to swim. I gave him a private tour of the whole town and my life here. We laughed and talked. It felt like old times, when we would go for drives in his car. When he took me to see his and his mom's little private place on the beach with the horses. I stop and park in the high school parking lot. I shut the engine off and turn in my seat to face him.

"This is my high school, where my life forever changed." I look down. "It's not all bad, though. I met Gavin here. I had happy memories, too."

He moves closer to me and puts his arms around me. I put my head on his shoulder. I breathe in his scent. I feel a pain in my chest.

"I messed this all up. I know I did, Khloe. I feel I already lost you." He rests his head on mine. "It is so hard to see you get closer to Josh, right in front of me, knowing what I did push you into his arms. I knew there was already something there since graduation. I could see it on his face. Now I see it on yours."

I don't say anything. He's not wrong.

"I just want us to talk about it and end it the right way, if that's what is about to happen. I need to know I have done everything I can to try to get you back, and at the end of the day, if you still choose him, then I must accept that. Do you love him?" He asks with a low tone.

"No, I am not in love with him. I do care for him. But if I am being one hundred percent honest here, Oliver, I'm not even sure what love is. I thought I knew, but now I am not so sure."

"Did you think you loved me?" He asks with pleading eyes.

I pull out of his embrace and look him in the eyes.

"I will always have love for you, Oliver. In my mind, you were my first for so many things."

"But you are not in love with me anymore?" He asks with a frown, pulling at his eyes.

"You hurt me. In a way, that love was shattered, and it makes me question if I even know what it is. Maybe I am too broken to love anyone right now, truly."

He put my face in his hands, still holding my gaze.

"Are we over?" He asks as he searches my eyes.

"I think so, Oliver. At least for now, I do not want to get back together right now."

He puts his forehead against mine, still holding my face gently.

"I want to stay friends, but for now, that may be a distant friendship while this is so fresh. But I need your help with something tonight." I say as he takes a deep breath.

"I'd do anything for you, Khloe."

"I need to get into my dad's old office. I need to see if his desk is still there." I tell him, speaking with anxiety in my voice, which makes my words come out quickly. I am trying not to lose my nerve to even attempt to try this.

"Do you have a key or code or something?" He pulls away to look at me.

I shake my head no. He takes a deep breath and moves back to his side of the truck.

"Let's go." He says without looking back at me.

I smile at him. I put my seat belt back on and start driving towards Evansville.

We drive by the building in the old part of town. This is the first time I have done anything like this. I am trying to figure out what I am doing. I drive by slowly. I see the name on the door. It makes me cringe.

Seth Mates Investors and Financial Advisor

"Is that it?" Oliver asks.

I nod and start to pull into the side parking lot where I always park.

"No, don't park right next to it. Let's drive around and find another place. What is the street behind it?"He tells me.

"Oh, good idea." I drive around the block. I look over at him, confused. I wonder if he has done something like this before.

There is an oversized parking garage not far from the rear of the building.

"There. Pull into that parking garage." He tells me as he points towards the garage.

I start to get nervous, and my palms sweat as I grip the steering wheel. I cannot believe we are about to do this. I park in the first empty place.

"Let's look like we are just a couple taking a walk." He says before he gets out of the truck.

I nod in agreement as we both get out.

We meet at the back of the truck. He reaches for my hand. I squeeze it now that I am beyond nervous. The adrenaline is pumping. We start walking from the front to the side of the building. I am looking to see if there are people around. Oliver is looking at the building. I have no idea what he is looking for. Once we get to the side of the building, he pushes me up to where my back is against the wall.

"Act like you are about to make out with me." He says, putting his hand on my hip and the other on the wall beside my face.

"What?" I whisper as if someone can hear me.

"I want to look and see if there are cameras and how many people walk by." He whispers into my ear.

"Oh. That is probably a good idea." I tell him as I pull his face down to look at me. "Have you done this before? Or just watch too many movies. You are shocking me right now." I whisper as my lips almost brush against his.

"You don't know everything about me Khloe. I was not always a good kid." He raises an eyebrow as he looks down at me.

"Wait, what?" I say, shocked.

He looks at me again after looking around.

"You're shocked? I'm shocked you want to do this." He tells me.

I smile at him.

"There are no cameras from the front to the side. Is there a back door? Getting in through the front door will be hard. Is there an alarm?" He asks.

"I don't remember an alarm. There is a back door and a small window near the door in the break room and kitchen area." I tell him as I turn my head in that direction.

"Okay, let's walk that way." He says as he reaches for my hand.

I thought Josh would be better for this thug stuff, but I guess I was fooled. I quietly laugh to myself. What else do I not know about Oliver?

"The window is locked. We break in this door or break the window." He starts looking at the ground as he tells me. He picks up a large rock.

"The window will be loud, don't you think?" I suggest.

"Okay then." He drops the rock in his hand and walks over to the door. "If there's an alarm and it sounds, we have to leave. But back up a little to give me a little more room."

I move to the side of the building. I watch Oliver rattle the door knob.

"It has inside hinges and no deadbolt. I am going to kick in the door."

I watch him back up just a little and kick the door near the door knob. The first kick loosens the door, but he kicks it again, and it flies open. I move to go in, and he stops me. He puts his finger on his lips, making a shh sound.

"Wait a second." He whispers to me.

I stop and look into the dark room and listen. I hear nothing. I look back at him. He nods, and we go in. He closes the door behind us. He pulls out his phone and turns on the flashlight. We walk past the front desk, and I see a name tag. Naomi's desk now has a tag that says Julia Mates on it. Does he have his wife working here now? I wonder if he fired Naomi. I continue to walk towards the office door, the office that belonged to my dad.

Oliver follows behind me, staying close with the light. I walk in;

the layout is still the same. The desk looks the same. I walk behind it and open the drawer. It is full of papers; I move them to the top of the desk. I hit the back corner, and the bottom pops up. Oliver is watching me silently. I pull out the faux bottom. I see a heart with DAD in the middle. I grab all the contents, I put the bottom back, put the papers that were in there back, and close it.

"I got it," I say, relieved and excited.

Oliver nods, grabs my hand, and leads the way back out.

He closes the door as best he can. My heart is racing. I am so excited that it worked; we got the papers. I am amazed by Oliver, too. My heart races as we start walking faster back towards the parking garage. I feel almost giddy by the time we reach the truck. The papers were still there. He stops at the back of the truck.

"So, what are those?" He asks me.

"My father's papers he left for my mom or me. We are the only ones who knew about them." I was happy he helped me. I feel like I could run a mile around this parking garage right now. "Thank you for helping me," I say as I throw my arms around him and hug him.

I pull back, and the urge is there, and before I can make sense of it, I kiss him. I push against him. He doesn't waste any time meeting my urgency and kisses me back. When I finally pull away, I am out of breath.

"We should go," I say as I walk to get in the truck. I get in and put the papers on the dash.

Oliver gets in the truck next to me. I watch him close the door. I still feel that desire. I think about last night and the rejection I felt. The desire at this moment grows stronger. He looks over at me.

We stare at one another for a minute. He moves closer to me. I see everything happening in slow motion, yet I have all the time in the world to stop this. Stop this from happening, from going any further. He puts his hand on my thigh and starts to move his hand up. He never breaks eye contact. He is asking for permission from me with his eyes. His scent fills the truck. I bite my lower lip. I can taste him on my lips. I let out a big sigh before I make the decision I may regret later.

I move over to him and straddle him. I put my hands on his shoulders and move my mouth to his. I move my hands to the back of his neck into his hair. I close my fingers in his hair and pull it slightly. I feel him put his hands on my hips as I move them against him. I feel the pressure from his hands as they grip me harder.

"Khloe," he says before I stop him.

"Shh." I bring my mouth to his lips to stop him from saying anything else.

He moves his hands under the back of my shirt. I break the kiss, and he moves me down onto the truck seat and gets on top of me. I feel him rub against me, I welcome it by moving my thighs wider. I feel the stiffness straining against his jeans as he rocks into me. He lifts my shirt, his mouth on my skin as he lifts my shirt higher until it is over my head. He slides a hand down the front of my shorts. As soon as I feel him touch me, I am on fire. I move closer to him. His mouth crashes onto mine with a hunger.

I pull him closer to me, digging my nails into him. He pulls his lips from mine. I pull his shirt up and over his head and reach to unbutton his pants. He stops me with his hands.

"Are you sure?" He asks.

I sit up just enough to pull his lips back to mine.

"One last time," I tell him and kiss him again.

Ten

The Float Trip

The sun filling the room seems so bright. I pull the covers over my head. They get pulled back down. I jerk up to see what is happening. Gavin is standing over me with a coffee mug. I sit up on the sofa and rub the sleep out of my eyes.

"Beau, did you ask your momma where she was all night?" Gavin asks Beau.

Beau looks up at his name being called; he stretches out on the floor next to me.

"It was not that late," I say in my defense.

He sits down next to me.

"How was it?" He asks.

I move over to the end of the sofa and grab the papers on the end table.

"I got 'em," I say as I fan myself with the folder and two large envelopes.

"How did it go with Oliver? Did you tell him?" He asks.

"It was good. We talked, and I told him I was not going to get back together with him right now. I told him I had feelings for Josh." I pause, thinking about last night. "Then," I stop and look at Gavin looking at me.

"Then what?" He asks.

I put my head in my hands.

"No!" He shrieks.

I feel the guilt take over me.

"You didn't!"

"I did." I sigh and give a slight grimace. "In the truck after we got the papers. Maybe it was adrenaline. I just wanted him. He tried to stop several times, but I made him keep going." I bring my pillow to my face.

"Girl, I'm shook. Now, what are you going to do?" He says with his big eyes in disbelief.

"Nothing. I'm not getting back together with him. I just had a moment. It can just be sex. Nothing more? Right?" I ask.

"I don't know. Can it be that for you? Can it be that for him?" He asks me.

I cover up with the blanket.

"I think so," I say softly, almost doubting myself now.

He pulls the covers down and hands me the coffee he is holding.

"Here, drink this. You are going to need it more than me today."

"The float trip!" I groan. I close my eyes tight.

"Here's what we're going to do. We are going on this float trip with these clowns. But we are going to look fierce doing it." He says as he turns towards me.

I take a drink and listen to him tell me what the plan is.

"You are going to wear that red bikini and let them drool all over you. You are a young single woman. You can do as you want. You don't belong to either of them. So, let's go have a fun time and worry about this mess another day."

I stand up after Gavin hypes me up.

"That's right. I can do whatever I want with whomever I want."

"Yes, girl!" He shouts at me.

I take a long sip of coffee and feel the empowerment vibe Gavin just gave me.

"Now your skank ass needs to go shower." He says, laughing.

I look at him with my mouth making a big "O" shape and throw my pillow at him from the sofa.

I slip a t-shirt over this ridiculous bathing suit. It's almost a thong with a string bikini top. I pull my hair up in a sloppy ponytail. Grab some sunglasses and walk out of the room. I see Gavin in the kitchen leaning against the counter. He is wearing light blue swimming trunks, showing off that six-pack.

"So, you didn't tell me, how last night went with Josh?" I ask.

"Not as exciting as yours," he lets out a laugh.

I bump into his shoulder. I am not going to live this down for a while.

"It was good. We just went to the store and came back here for a couple of hours getting everything together. He asked me a lot of questions about you. And let me tell you, if you don't want him, I am pretty sure Blakeleigh will take him off your hands."

"Off, who's hands?" Blakeleigh says as she walks into the room.

"Josh."

"Oh, he's the whole package." She says with a grin.

I smile at her. I know he is, which makes me feel even more guilty for my weak moment last night.

"You hear that?" I ask.

"What?" Gavin asks.

"I think Beau coughed. He must be sick. I better stay here with him."

I say.

"Girl, negative. You are going. You will have to face them both at some point. Might as well be today." I feel nauseous. I hear a motorcycle outside. I close my eyes and take a deep breath.

"I'm going to go outside and say hello," I say as I take a deep breath.

"Here, carry this with you on your way out," Gavin says as he hands me a small cooler.

"Come on, Beau," I call to him as I walk towards the door.

I see Josh get off his bike as I walk towards him. He takes off his helmet and runs his hand through his hair. He has a backpack on that I have never seen him wear before.

"Good morning," I say as I walk towards him.

He reaches down, takes the small cooler out of my hand, and lifts it into the back of my truck. He turns back to me and slowly runs his fingertips along my arm before he hugs me, giving me chills.

"Good morning," he replies as he gives me a light kiss on the lips.

A car door pulls my attention away from Josh. I see Oliver looking at us as he and Lucas pull up.

"I'm going to go inside and change," Josh tells me as he winks at me.

"Okay," I tell him as I nod and smile.

I watch him walk back towards the house. I see Oliver leaning against Lucas's car. I head towards him.

"Good morning," I say, feeling a little nervous.

"Good morning," Lucas replies as he walks by.

I turn and watch Lucas walk up to the house. I turn back to face Oliver. He didn't reply to me.

"You're not talking to me?" I ask him.

"You didn't say much to me last night," he pauses, "after I mean. We pretty much drove back in silence."

"I'm sorry, I was just in my emotions, Oliver."

"It didn't change anything, did it? You still don't want to be with me?" He asks with frustration in his voice.

"We are not together. Thank you for helping me last night. But what happened after was the last time. I let the adrenaline and excitement of the night get the best of me." I say, feeling a little ashamed.

"I was ready to let you go; ready to let you move on, try to move on myself. Be friends as you said." He crosses his arms over his chest and continues. "Then, after what happened last night, I'm not so sure I am ready anymore. I want you back so bad it hurts, Khloe." He moves closer to me. He put his hand on my arm. "You liked it too. I know you did."

"Oliver, sex was never an issue with us. It was always good. It's Avery. It's trusting you now." I pull away from his embrace.

"And what about you, Khloe? I had to learn to trust you with Lucas and Josh."

I step further away from him. I know my anger can be seen across my face as it turns red from the heat I feel inside.

I turn and walk away from him. I am mad. I feel anger rising in me. I know he's right, but it still angers me. I look towards the house and see Josh standing in the window watching. I smile at him as I open the truck driver's side door.

"Let's go, Beau." He jumps up in the truck.

Everyone else comes out of the house. Josh walks up to me. I notice he is wearing dark gray swimming trunks and no shirt. I stare probably too long as he walks towards me.

"Everything okay?" He asks as he pulls a shirt over his head.

"Yeah. You want to drive?" I ask him as I hand him the keys.

"Sure."

I slid into the truck and put Beau in my lap in the middle seat. As Josh closes the door and starts the truck, Gavin gets in next to me.

"Let's get some music playing; I made a whole playlist for today," Gavin says as he picks a song.

I am trying to escape the mood that the conversation with Oliver and last night's events have me in.

The old school bus drops us off at the first sandbar of the float trip. They give us a tube as we walk towards the water. Gavin gets in, and I follow him into the water. The cold water shocks me for a moment. I pull off my t-shirt and slip it into the bag Gavin brought. I adjust my swimsuit from sitting so long. I look up at Gavin sitting in the tube. He points behind me. I turn and look. I see Josh and Oliver just standing there staring at me. I already know my ass is hanging out of this suit. I look back at Gavin, and he is laughing. I turn and sit in the tube. I called for Beau to sit in my lap.

We have a great day. We float, swim, jump off the rocks, and eat the snack Gavin made at the sandbars. Everyone is getting along and having a good time. I notice I am red from the sun as I pull back my suit to check. We stop at the last sandbar before getting to the end, where they will pick us up.

Gavin is having so much fun talking to everyone on the river today. It's hard not to have a good time when he is around. He starts dancing to the music, grabs my hand, and we dance together. Josh joins in. I didn't even know he could dance like that until today. I soak him in. Oliver walks up, not looking happy at all. I watch him from the corner of my sight, getting closer.

"Don't be mad, your girl loves me," Gavin tells Josh jokingly.

"Don't be mad, your girl had sex with me last night," Oliver says out loud.

Everyone stops and looks at him. I am stunned. Josh looks at me. He looks back at Oliver.

"Why would you say that?" Gavin asks him, walking towards him.

Oliver is just staring at Josh.

"I'm talking to you!" Gavin says.

"He should know," Oliver says as he points at Josh.

Josh steps toward him.

"She's single last I knew; she can do what she wants. But you are saying it like it is only directed at me. Do you have a problem with me, Oliver?" Josh says to Oliver in a harsh tone.

"I do have a problem with you, Josh. You moved in on my girl while she was still with me." Oliver starts raising his voice.

They move closer to one another.

"I think you messed that all up at the bonfire. And if I wanted to take her from you, I wouldn't have tried to stop you that night. Even now, I still am waiting for her to be sure she is ready to move on from you." Josh tells Oliver.

"Maybe she's not," Oliver says.

"I told you Oliver, it's over. What happened last night is not something I am proud of. It shouldn't have happened. It will never happen again. It's time for you to go back home." I say to Oliver as I walk right up to him. I am furious and in his face. I feel Josh and Gavin close behind me.

"Let's go, Oliver!" I hear Lucas yell.

Lucas comes over to him and pulls him away.

Lucas looks at me and mouths,

"I'm sorry."

Eleven

Aftermath

We pull into the driveway of Gavin's house. It's a good thing Blakeleigh ran into some friends down at the river because she lost her ride after Lucas dragged Oliver out of there and left.

"Well, that was eventful," Gavin says as he opens the truck door. Beau jumps out with him.

I sit there next to Josh in the driveway; neither of us has said much during the whole drive back. I wonder what he is thinking. I am in turmoil in my head. Did he mean what he said back there at the river? I am single. I should be able to do what I want and with whoever I want. I want to tell him I do care for him. I want him to know that even if my actions lead him to believe otherwise.

"Josh about last night," I say in a low tone, not looking at him.

He starts to shake his head.

"You do not owe me an explanation. You don't owe anyone an explanation." He says in his naturally calm Josh voice.

I look down at my hands in my lap.

"And honestly, I do not want a whole lot of details about it. It happened. I understand there are emotions, and things happen." He turns to face me.

I feel him shift in his seat. I did not look away from my hands in my lap, though. I'm struggling to face him.

"I wanted you to get the answers you need to figure it out what you felt. I feel I pushed you to do it. I cannot be mad that when you tried to do just that, it didn't turn out particularly how I wanted it to." He moves his hand under my chin to lift my face to look at him.

"Look at me," he pleads.

I look up at him. I feel awful. How could I be so weak? How could I do this to him?

"I'm not mad." He whispers as he moves his hand to the side of my face, takes his thumb, and rubs my cheek.

I feel the tears welling up in my eyes. I fight to keep them from falling.

"Do you want to be with Oliver? If that is what you feel, I want that for you."

That broke me. Tears fall onto his hand. He wipes them away.

"No. I told him I couldn't be with him. I could only offer him friendship. He broke my trust. I also told him I cared about you." I close my eyes and take a deep, calming breath. I know he didn't want to know, but my selfish side had to tell him.

"I asked him to help me break into my dad's old office and get some papers I remembered he left for me. I was so worried we would get caught that after all the excitement and adrenaline, I made a decision I would regret later. I know you don't want to hear all about it, but I needed you to know it was not planned. I need you to know I do not want to get back together with him." I look away and pull out of his embrace.

"And I'm sorry," I whisper.

He wraps his arms around me.

"Why in the hell were you breaking into your dad's office? I bet Oliver knew just what to do, huh?" He says with sarcasm thick in his voice.

I think back to Oliver, knowing exactly what to do. I was weirdly shocked and impressed since it seemed so out of character.

"I had to see if the papers were still there. They were hidden away in a secret compartment in the desk drawer. My dad's partner took over the office, and the same family has Katie right now. I doubt they would just let me walk in there and check."

"What do the papers say?" He asks.

"They're in the house. I haven't read them yet."

He shakes his head like he is processing everything.

"Why did you say Oliver would know what to do?" I ask.

"Did you not hear that small-town gossip back home?" He asks.

"I guess not," I say, confused.

"After Oliver's mom left, he was a little rebellious and mad at the world for a while. It was around the same time we found out about my mom. So, we got a little closer during that time. Kindred souls, maybe. But he was younger and just making bad choices. He got caught doing a few break-ins around town with the wrong crowd."

I am shocked. I would have never thought that. I always had this image of who he was and what had been his whole life.

"Thank you," I tell him.

"For what?" He asks.

"For being you." I look over at him and put my hand on the side of his face.

"Do you want to come in?" I ask, hoping he says yes.

"Yeah, I need to change before I can ride back to the hotel."

Ugh, it's not really what I wanna hear, but I will take it.

We walk in together. Gavin is sitting on the sofa. I sit next to Gavin while Josh goes and changes in the bathroom. Beau jumps up to sit next to me.

"You good?" He asks and holds my hand.

I nod.

"I'm sorry about today. Oliver was out of line. Maybe battle royale was not the best idea." He says with a small chuckle.

I look over at him, shake my head, and smile. I love this man with all my heart, but sometimes, he stirs the pot in my life a little too much.

"It's okay. In a way, it helped me decide. I saw a side of Oliver that made me realize I couldn't trust him with my feelings and a side of Josh that tells me he has my back no matter what. I hate that it happened, but it's done now."

"I am team Josh forever," he whispers in my ear as he squeezes my hand.

We both look back as we hear Josh coming into the room and giggle. He sits his backpack down on the floor next to the sofa and sits down next to me.

"What are you two up to tonight?" Josh asks.

"I need a nap; too much sun for me," Gavin says.

"I have no plans but so much to do," I say as the stress of everything left to do comes to mind.

"Like what?" Josh says, putting his hand on my thigh just above my knee.

I sit here with two people who matter so much to me, both with a hand on me. Gavin is holding my hand, and Josh rests on my knee. At that very moment, I realize I do not have to do any of this alone.

"I need to speak with the detective, read the papers from my dad's office, meet with an attorney Dee is finding me, rent a place to live, and if I am going to be here a while, a job is probably a good idea too."

"How long are you staying here?" Josh asks.

"At least until August for the court hearing for Katie's adoption. I cannot let that happen."

"I may know of a place you can rent above the café; they have a furnished apartment that they rent out. You could swing by there and talk to the owner tomorrow." Gavin states.

"That would be perfect," I say as I squeeze Gavin's hand.

I look at Josh because he moves his hand and runs it down his face. I can tell he is worried about something. He looks at me, staring at him.

"Will you walk me out?" He asks.

I nod and stand up with him.

"I will see you later, Gavin." Josh reaches out to shake Gavin's hand as he walks past him.

I walk out the door first and head towards his bike parked on the driveway's edge. Suddenly, I feel dread come over me. I think back to his face as we sat on the sofa. I thought it was worry, but maybe it's something else. Perhaps the craziness of today has finally registered with him. With what Oliver said and knowing what happened between us, it may upset him; he has been trying to hide it all this time. I stop at his bike. The bad news is coming when I turn around and face him. I feel it deep down in my stomach. I take a deep breath. I try to steady myself.

I stand there still. I know he is right behind me now. I can feel him close to me. He puts his arms around my waist. I put my hands around his. I put some of my weight back and lean into him. Feeling the warmth with his arms around me helps with the anxiety I am feeling. He rests his chin on top of my head. I hear him take a deep breath.

"We need to talk about something. I didn't want to bring it up in front of Gavin." He says softly.

I close my eyes and turn around to face him.

"I'm not going to be able to stay at the hotel much longer. I thought my trip here would be a quick one. I was hoping we could go back together." He puts his finger under my chin and lifts my face to look at him.

"You have to stay longer than I had hoped. I don't want to leave you, but if I am going to stay, I need a side job and to find a place to stay."He says to me as he brushes a lock of hair that escaped my ponytail.

I look up at him, shocked. I was expecting him to say something completely different. The tension leaves my body.

"I have to find a place to stay, too. Why don't you stay with me?"

"I can't do that. I can't just freeload, Khloe."

"We can work something out; we can both pay half or something," I tell him.

"I am not sure how I feel about that. We are still getting to know each other. I don't want to move so fast and ruin what we have." He replies.

"I want you to stay." I plead.

I stand on my tip toes and kiss his lips softly. I am almost scared to kiss him now, after all that has happened. He pulls me closer to him. He deepens the kiss. When he pulls away, he hugs me and just holds me.

"I need you here with me," I say softly in his ear.

He squeezes me tighter.

"I mean, I am a sucker for you; I am here for you as long as you need or want me." He jokes.

I smile, pull away, and kiss him again.

"Thank you!" I say before I kiss him again. "I will find out about the place above the café tomorrow."

"I will see if I can find some temporary work and call Jake to let him know I'll be here for a while."

"Oh, I forgot about Jake's. You think he will be upset?" I ask.

"I think he will understand regardless of whether he likes it." He says with a smile.

I pull away. He slips his backpack over his shoulders. I watch him get on the bike, kick the kickstand back, and stand it up.

"I will see you tomorrow," he says before he starts the bike, and it roars to life.

I step back into the grass and watch him walk the motorcycle back to the road. He winks at me and shows me that sly, adorable smile that makes me weak in the knees, before he takes off down the road. I head back into the house and see Gavin still sitting on the sofa. I sit down next to him.

"What did you two talk about out there so long?"

"He's gonna stay here with me. We might get a place together, so he doesn't have to keep paying for the hotel. He will look for a temporary job and help pay for half the rent."

He nods with approval.

"You know, last night when he was here, and you were, well, we know what you were doing."

I flash him a warning look.

"We went through the old yearbook, and I showed him your photos. He wanted to know everything about you. I asked him why he wanted to know so much. He told me that he is kinda obsessed with you in the cutest kind of way, not the stalker kind of way." He chuckles. "I genuinely think he feels something for you, girl."

"I don't deserve that man." I wrap my arms around myself.

"The hell you don't. You deserve the best of everything." He wraps his arms around me and kisses my cheek.

"Love you."

"Love you more, sunshine."

"I'm going to go take a long shower. I feel worn out after today. I know you are, too; maybe we both call it an early night." I tell him.

I sit at the kitchen table and stare at the folder and the large envelopes in front of me. I look at the sticky note stuck to the folder. I trace the heart with my finger around the name DAD. Am I ready for what's in these papers? What could be so important, he had to hide them. Only two people besides him knew where they were.

"Oh honey, you okay?" Gavin's mom, Rochelle, says to me as she walks into the kitchen.

I look up at her with tears in my eyes. She sits down next to me. She reaches over and puts her hand on mine.

"I am terrified of what is in here and confused about what it could be."

"Do you want me to look at them with you? It may help not to feel like you are doing it alone." She says sweetly.

"Please." I grin at her, trying to show my gratitude for being here with me. I slide the small stack of papers over to her.

"Okay, let's see what we got." She says as she opens the folder first.

The first paper has a business card attached to it. She removes the paperclip. The business card is a Realtor's card. She hands it to me.

"Do you know him?" She asks.

I take the card and read the name. Wade Cannon. I shake my head. I lay the card to the side. I look over as she reads the paper in her hands.

"It's a title to a commercial property located in Evansville."

"It must be for the office building," I tell her.

"Your parents are the sole owners." She hands me the paper as she speaks.

I look at it. I stare at their names.

"If your parents own that building and no one claims ownership, it may be in probate for ownership." She tells me.

I think of the Mates. I am sure they are trying to get ownership of the office building. It makes sense since they run the business now.

"This is about the partnership of the business. I am no lawyer, so I may not be reading this legal jargon correctly, but it seems that your parents' temporarily partnered with Seth Mates in all business matters for a total of 5 years. At that time, the permanent partnership would be reviewed for permanent shares of ownership." She looks up at me, and I try to read her face.

"Khloe, the dates of this contract are up. This is not an active contract." She hands me the document.

I look it over, and it doesn't seem too important. I slide it to the side.

"The rest of the papers in this folder seem to be paperwork on a trust set up for you and your sister. Do you know about this?" She looks up at me.

"Yes, I found out about that a little while back. I have that all set up already." She smiled at me.

"Good. It looks like your sister has one too. It should kick in when she is 18 as well." She hands me all the papers on it.

"Oh, there is one more in here; it looks like stocks, maybe like a portfolio. I'm sorry, Khloe, I know nothing about this stuff. I am sure anyone who worked with your dad would be able to tell you more about these items."

I nod. I don't think I would be able to ask Seth anytime soon.

"Want to open this one now?" She put her finger on the yellow envelope.

I nod at her.

She opens the envelope, tilts it slightly, and pulls out its contents. Two small white envelopes fall out onto the table. One has Katie's name on it, and the other has mine. I put my hand on hers to stop her. I pick up the envelope with my name on it. I run my thumb across the writing. It's my dad's handwriting.

"We can stop for tonight," I tell her.

She puts her hand on mine again and smiles at me. She stands up and leaves the room.

I put all the papers back in the folder. I slide Katie's letter back into the big envelope with the other papers. I carry the one with my name on it to the sofa with me and lay down feeling exhausted. Beau jumps up and lays down by my feet. I put the letter on my chest and hold it there.

"What do you have to say to me, Dad?"

I want to read it, but something about reading it right now sounds so painful. I take a deep breath. Is this letter what is so important? Is this going to answer all the questions I have? I hold the letter close to my heart and think about my parents. I slowly drift to sleep.

Twelve

New Spaces

I wake up to Beau whimpering. I rub my eyes; it takes me a minute for my eyes to adjust to the brightness of the sun coming into the room. He whimpers again.

"What is it?"

I hear a light knock at the front door. I look over to the door. I look around; no one is coming out from the kitchen or the hallway with the bedrooms to answer the door. I stand up and look out the small window at the top of the door. Beau growls a little from the sofa.

I see Lucas standing on the small front porch with his hands in his pockets. I open the door and comb my fingers through my hair.

"Hey, Lucas."

He turns towards me with his hands still in his pockets. He looks nervous.

"Hey, Khloe. I um," he looks back towards his car parked in front of the house. "I am taking Oliver to the airport. He wanted me to stop by here to see if you would talk to him before he leaves."

I feel my face heat up as the anger overcomes me.

"I should tell him no after what he did yesterday."

Lucas looks at his feet and moves them around. I can tell he does not want to be here doing his bidding for him.

"I'm sorry, Lucas. You shouldn't be in the middle of this. Go tell him yeah, I will talk to him." I have a lot I want to say to him anyway.

Lucas turns and walks back to the car. I sit down on the front porch step. I rest my arms on my knees. I hear him getting closer. My mind is racing with the things I want to say to him. I feel so used and dirty after all that has happened. I don't look at him as he sits down next to me.

"Khloe,"

I hear the pain in his voice. Part of me is happy that it is there, and the other half is battling the pain of him saying my name with such agony. I close my eyes as I battle these emotions inside.

"I'm going home today. I wanted to say sorry for yesterday. I feel like I am just apologizing to you every time I see you."

"You think Oliver? How could you say that yesterday? We shared something special once. Now you're just thinking about yourself. I think you are just trying to hurt me." I stand up and start to pace around the porch. I take a deep breath before I speak again.

"You are trying to get back at me for not being a perfect girlfriend. I was confused with Lucas when he showed up there. You realize I'm messed up, right? And when I thought I could trust someone again, you went and ruined that. The other night, I don't know; I guess I had a moment. But truthfully, I wanted to see if my feelings were still there. Before I completely walked away. I needed to know if there was still a spark."

I think back to the night in the truck in the parking garage. I have never done anything like that. Where it was just sex, that's it. It wasn't forced upon me, and there was no emotion of love or deep feelings in it.

"Our love and trust are completely gone. I really thought we were endgame." He says as he stands up.

"How could I even think you give a damn about me after what you have done?" I say.

"My feelings are just all in a mess. I can't stand watching you fall for someone else after I know what we had. I can't stand watching Josh fall in love with you. It's more every time I see him near you. I can't deal with any of this because I am still in love with you."

I look over at him. I see the face I once thought I loved, the one I thought would heal me. But now I realize only I can heal myself. It was never going to be him.

"Bye, Oliver," I say before I turn and walk back into the house.

I shut the door and sink onto the floor with my knees tucked into my chest and my back pressed against the door. I let it all out. I cry for the love I thought I had once with Oliver, for what he did with Avery, for being weak and entertaining the idea we could get back together, for being a fool and sleeping with him again, for not being able to forgive him. I cry for being damaged.

"It's going to be okay, sunshine," Gavin says as he comes and sits by me and puts his arm around me.

He will never know how grateful I am to have him in my life. I rest my head on his shoulder as the tears continue to fall. Beau walks over with something in his mouth. He drops my dad's letter next to me. I pick it up and hand it to Gavin.

"Can you read it to me?" I ask.

"Of course." He slowly opens the little white envelope.

Hello, my sweet Khloe,

From the moment I first saw you, my life has been forever changed. I never knew I could love someone so much at first sight.

I knew I would never want to leave you and miss any moment of your life.

I wish I could live forever and always be here for you,

but that was not what was written in the stars for me or you, love.

I put my hand on the letter and push it down as the tears come harder now. I hear Gavin choke back sobs.

"I can't do this right now. I will have to read this another day." I tell him in between sobs.

Gavin nods and wraps his arms around me. We sit there holding one another and cry together.

I pull up to the café in the afternoon. Gavin told me the owner would be in today for a few hours. I want to catch her and ask about the apartment. I look in the mirror before stepping out of the truck, my phone shows a notification.

Lucas: I'm sorry about this morning. I wanted to let you know I heard back from Brittany. She doesn't know what camp she went to. She saw her the day she left, she said Katie didn't even know she was going until the day they took her. That's all she said.

Khloe: Thank you.

I sit there for a moment and think about Lucas. About what Danielle said about him when I talked to her. He seems to be acting so strange lately. Maybe he is just under too much stress. I make a mental note to check back in with him later.

I walk into the café and ask for Carrie. I sit at a small table near the windows overlooking downtown to wait for her. The town looks peaceful, with families walking along the sidewalks and cars driving by reflecting the sun. I think back to the beginning of my dad's letter about how life can go on without him here. I was so angry when they first died. Time didn't stop; people still smiled and laughed when the whole world changed. My world was darker without their light was not shining.

I was in such a dark place. I was furious with everyone who was still living life. I was so angry; I was consumed by it. I was mad at the world. How could this have happened to me? Maybe this is why I couldn't see the wolf in sheepskin clothing coming for me.

The Coffman's had me so fooled. I thought they were there to help me. I close my eyes and think about Katie telling me how she would live with the Mates. How excited she was. I can relate to the excitement you feel when you have a second chance at a normal life. Then you watch that picture in your head catch fire, burn, and fall to the floor.

I wipe the tears from my face as I hear footsteps walking towards me. I need to be strong. I must keep going. I am going to make this happen for Katie. For me. I need to have her beside me.

"Hello, Khloe?"

I turn and smile as I reach my hand out to the woman standing in front of me.

"Hi, Carrie. I am a friend of Gavin's; he said you may have an apartment available for rent."

"I do. Let me get the keys, and I will give you a tour."

"Thank you," I say.

I follow her through the café door to the small black metal staircase on the side of the building. She opens the front door, which has a large window on it. There is a small hallway when you walk in, but then you walk into this small space with so much light from the large windows that overlook the downtown area. I walk over to the windows and look down at the café sitting area. It was the same view I was just admiring, only higher now.

It had wood floors with an area rug in the living area, a leather sofa, and a small chair. The kitchen was right off the living area, and had a small counter with seating facing the living room. The walls had framed black and white photos of different landmarks. The bedroom was cozy and right off the living room. There's a bed, dresser, and a large window that faces another building. There was a small closet space in the corner. She shows me the bathroom with a stacked washer and dryer, and a large shower.

"It's pretty basic," she says as she walks back towards the kitchen. "It is furnished with all the basic items you would need." She continues.

"I will take it." I say was eagerness.

She chuckles a little.

"Don't you want to know the price first?" She asks.

"Oh yeah, what is the rent?" I ask.

"Let me ask you this: where are you employed?"

"I am not currently working; I just came back to town. I will only be here for a few months.I have some loose ends I need to take care of then I will be moving back south. Is it okay to rent it monthly until I know more of a time frame?" I ask hoping she will understand.

"I don't have a problem with that, but are you looking for work too since you're not working? How do you plan to pay the rent and deposit?" She asks.

"I have enough money saved, I can even pay you for a few months upfront and then monthly once I know how long I will need to stay."

She shakes her head in agreement.

"Okay, would you be interested in working at the café? I could use some extra help down there. Maybe you could pick up some shifts, and I can knock some off the rent, too. I would still pay you, of course."

"That would be great. Yes, I would appreciate that." Maybe my luck is turning around, I think.

"Perfect. Let's meet tomorrow and sign all the paperwork. Khloe," she pauses, "I gotta say you look like your mother."

I turn to look at her. The statement takes me by surprise.

"I was in a book club with her. We met here at the café on Thursday nights. We still do if you ever want to join us. We all loved Jenna. We would be honored to have you." She says with a warm smile.

She knew my mom. I feel the warmth fill my soul, hearing her say that.

"I will do anything I can to help you. She was a great woman." She says as she walks towards me and puts her hand on my head, stroking my hair softly. "So much like her. She would be proud." She smiles at me and walks back towards the door.

I look out the windows again behind the sofa, then follow her out of the door.

I'm driving back through town when I decide I want to see Josh. I want to tell him all about the apartment. I pull into the hotel parking lot. I don't see his bike park anywhere. I pull into a parking spot and send him a text message.

Khloe: Hey there, are you at the hotel?

Josh: No, I had an errand to run. I should be back in about an hour or so. Can I come by then?

Khloe: Yes. I have news to tell you

Josh: Me too. See you soon.

I head back towards Gavin's house but, at the last minute, decide to check on Lucas. I see his car parked in the driveway. I walk up to the door, and a woman answers it. She stares at me longer than I think necessary and never says anything.

"Hello, is Lucas here?" I ask.

"Lucas!" She yelled but never leaves the doorway or invites me in.

It starts to make me nervous. I begin to take a step back from the door.

"Khloe! What are you doing here?" He pushes past the woman and bolts out the front door.

She stares at us as she closes the door.

"I was just coming to check on you." I am still staring at the closed front door.

"Oh yeah, I'm fine." He starts to walk away from the house towards my truck.

"Lucas, who is that?" I ask as I start to follow him.

"That's my mom."

"She seems upset. Is everything okay?"

"She is just under a lot of stress right now."

I look back at the house, and I see her looking out the front window. It makes me feel so uneasy. Maybe I shouldn't have come here.

"Khloe, you should probably go." He says.

"I wanted to let you know I talked to Danielle."

"What did she say?" He asks eagerly.

"She is just upset. She thinks you are acting differently," I pause and look at him. "I have to say, Lucas, you are acting a little off. What's going on?"

He leans against my truck.

"It's all too much, Khloe. I am dealing with my mom and this divorce. She is freaking out about everything and just lashing out at me and my sister. So much so that my sister would not even come around anymore. She moved in with my dad. It's just me here dealing with all this crap."

"I'm sorry. Anything I can do?" I ask, feeling the stress coming off of him.

"No, just maybe call or text me. Just don't come by unexpectedly." He says.

"I'm sorry for just showing up. That was rude of me." Now, I'm feeling bad that I am just imposing on him.

He opens the truck door for me. I climb into the truck.

"So, I guess asking your mom to see if she could find out information about Katie is probably not a good idea," I say, looking back at the window of the house.

He chuckles a little.

"No, I don't think she will be the one to help you. To be honest with you, Khloe, she will probably tell Julia Mates you are in town now. I wouldn't put it by her. I'm afraid your coming here may have made it harder for you to contact Katie. I never told my mom that you were in town. I also lectured Oliver about it when he was staying here." He says with an uneasy feeling.

I feel the uneasiness hit me. I feel sick to my stomach instantly.

"Please see if you can talk to her. Please see if she can not say anything," I beg.

"Khloe, you think they won't find out that you are here. This place is so small; everybody knows everybody, and everybody talks. They probably already know." He says.

The panic sets in, and I feel like I am being watched.

"I better go," I start up the truck and just want to get back to Gavin's house as fast as possible.

My mind was racing for the few blocks drive. What if I went over there, making that impulse decision, I could have ruined everything. I can barely breathe as I pull in front of Gavin's house. I feel like there is not enough air in the truck cab. I get out of the truck to get more air. I am trying to catch my breath and get my breathing under control when I hear the roar of a motorcycle coming down the street.

"Khloe!" Josh says as he runs towards me.

I'm standing there with my hands on my knees, trying to get control of myself.

"Take in a long breath, then let it out real slowly." He says as he starts to rub my back. He squats next to me. "Now, do it one more time. I think you are having a panic attack. It's okay; I used to get them, too."

I did as he said. After the lightheaded feeling disappeared and I could breathe normally, I stood back upright. I lean up against the truck.

"Thank you. That came on so fast." I say to Josh.

"Yeah, they will do that. Do you know what triggered it?" He asks.

"I went to talk to Lucas. He told me how his mom would tell her friends, the Mates' that I was in town. That could cause me not to be able to get to Katie." I tell him, feeling that panic in my stomach again.

"I wouldn't let that get to you too much. I have faith that we will find a way. Come here." He pulls me close to him and wraps his arms around me.

I hold onto him. At that moment, I believe we can work out everything together. He is my safe place.

"Want to go for a ride?" He asks.

I nod, still in his arms.

As we drive through town, along the river. I watch the water flowing over the rock; it's so peaceful and calm, unlike my life. He picks up speed as we leave the city limits. I wrap my arms around him tighter. He puts his hand on my leg, just like before. I love it when he makes that simple gesture.

I lose track of time as we ride alongside the cornfields. He starts to slow down. We pull into a small shack-looking building.

"I found this place a few days ago."He says.

I look up at the building and can smell the scent of smoked meat in the air.

"It's not as good as Jake's, but it's not bad." He says with a smile.

I get off the bike, put my helmet down, and look at the restaurant. I never knew this place even existed. He walks over to me and wraps his arms around me. He kisses me softly, then pulls away slightly.

"Would you like to have dinner with me?" He says softly in my ear. "I haven't been able to take you on a proper date, which needs to change. Even with everything going on, I still want to build something with you, Khloe."

I pull back to look at him after he just gave me the chills talking in my ear. This man melts my heart sometimes. I feel all warm and giddy around him. It is hard to describe the butterflies I feel when I look at him.

"I would love to have dinner with you. I'm thinking Italian." I point my eyes up, pretending like I'm thinking of places.

"Country boy Italian, you got it, honey." He chuckles. He grabs my hand and starts walking towards the doors.

"Next date night, real Italian." He says as we walk.

"I think you are being presumptuous that there will be a second date before the first one is over," I say jokingly.

He opens the door, and as I pass by him to walk in, he taps my butt lightly.

It is getting dark by the time we pull into Gavin's driveway. He walks over to the truck after we get off the bike. He pulls the tailgate down, jumps up, and sits on the tailgate. I jump up next to him. I sit there just in silence for a minute, enjoying his company. We both swing our legs as they hang off.

"What is the news you wanted to tell me?" He asks.

"I got the apartment over the café. I will sign the papers tomorrow. It will be month to month. I also got a part-time job at the café. Carrie, the owner, was great. She knew my mom."

"That is great news. It will be nice for you to have your own space."

"Our space," I say, excitedly.

He reaches over and holds my hand.

"I have some news, too. But I don't want to upset you," He says cautiously.

I feel my stomach drop.

"I found work today, too. When I used to travel, I had jobs with different motorcycle clubs. I would work on bikes and repair the clubhouse as needed, among other things. Well, I reached out to some old contacts and come to find out, there is a northern chapter located here near New Harmony. I got a name and met with him today at their clubhouse. I start working for the club tomorrow."

I was trying to wrap my head around this idea. The only thing I know about motorcycle clubs is what I've seen on TV and I can't see Josh being involved in something related to crime and drugs.

"Is it safe?" I ask, feeling naïve.

"Of course. They seem like an upright chapter. But let me tell you, if I find out something different, I will no longer work there, okay?" He smiles at me.

I nod in agreement with him.

"They offered me a place to live; over the garage is a small loft."

I look over at him.

"I thought we were going to stay together?" I say, slightly disappointed.

"We will still have nights that we can stay together, but I want to take this slowly. I don't want us to rush into something until we are ready." He says as he reaches over to hold my hand.

I put my head down to look away from him. I know he's right and probably doing the mature thing here, but I still feel hurt by it. He moves closer. He lifts my chin to hold my face, and he kisses me.

"Trust me, part of me wants to be with you every minute of the day." He kisses me again. "But you may get sick of me." He kisses me again.

"And we cannot have that." He kisses me longer this time. He pulls away.

"I understand, and you're probably right. I expect dates then." I say excited about the future.

"Absolutely, I am ready to wine and dine you. Well, maybe not wine because you are just a baby." He laughs.

"I am not a baby," I say, pouting.

He jumps down off the tailgate and stands in front of me.

"No, you're not. But one day, I would like you to be my baby." He says with enthusiasm in his voice.

I smile at him. I wrap my arms around his neck. I move in and kiss him. I want to prove to him that I can be mature like him. I am aware of the small age gap.

"I better head back. I need to let the hotel know I will check out tomorrow. Do you need help moving to your place tomorrow?" He asks.

"No, I have like one bag and Beau," I say, chuckling.

"Okay, I will text you. I will see you tomorrow sometime." He cups my face with his hands. He rubs his thumbs along my cheeks. "Think of me," he says before he softly kisses me.

"Always," I say as I hug him. I soak in the moment, holding him. I take a deep breath, letting his scent swarm me. I feel the butterflies in my stomach.

I watch him walk back to his bike and leave. As I follow his path down the street, I notice a white car parked two houses down with someone in it. With only one street light, I can't see it well, but the person is definitely looking my way, watching the whole time as I start walking back towards the house. As I approach the door, it begins moving towards the house. I open the door and hurry inside. I quickly look out the window and see the car in front of the house. The driver is looking up towards the house and then quickly drives off.

Thirteen

Subconscious

Gavin plops down on the sofa, sitting on my feet.

"Good morning, sunshine!"

I will be so happy to have my own bed again. I roll my eyes as I sit up.

"It's moving day, yay!" He says happily.

"Yay," I say with less enthusiasm.

"I thought you would sound slightly more excited now that you get to play house with your little hottie." He says with a smile.

"He is not moving in. He found his own place at some clubhouse."

"Clubhouse? Like Mickey Mouse?" He asks.

"No, like a motorcycle clubhouse. He got a job at one." I hit him with my pillow, laughing.

"Girl, you got yourself a real-life biker. That's so hot." He says as he fans his face.

"Yeah, he wants to take it slow. Or at least that is what he is saying."

"You don't believe him?" He asks.

"No, I do. I think I do. I know the last man I trusted showed me that was misguided." I say, trying to convince myself.

"I trust Josh." He says.

"Oh, we already know," I tell him.

"Well, I actually have something to tell you. But first coffee." He says as he gets up.

While Gavin starts the coffee, I jump into the shower. When I get out, I start putting all my things together. I lay the stuff from my dad's office on top. I am making a mental note to finish going through those papers. I need to read the letter. I pick up the letter and hold it in my hands. Maybe I should wait to read it until Katie can read hers, too. I flip it over and look and start to pull it out.

"There you are. Here's some coffee." He hands me a coffee mug. "So let me tell you what I have found out from my research on that child molester."

"Jared?" I ask, surprised. I put the letter back down with my things.

"Yes, Jared."

"Don't say it like that. It makes me feel so dirty and like a victim." I tell him.

"Sweetie, no matter how you want to see it, you are not dirty but you're a victim. But you were not the only one." He pulls out his laptop.

I move to sit next to him. I take a sip of coffee and prepare to jump down this rabbit hole with him. I'm unsure if I'm ready to feel the emotions about the memories this may cause.

"While he was attending college in Michigan, there are reports where he was arrested for assault. The charges were dropped for some unknown reason. There are police reports. The police were called out to the home where he and Linda lived. The neighbors may have called for noise complaints. There are no arrests or charges from those calls."

"How did you find all this stuff? That is not just public record, is it?" I ask.

"Don't ask me to give away my secrets. But honestly, I paid for some of this stuff." He says proudly.

"Gavin. You shouldn't have."

"It was worth every penny I paid for what the investigator found."

"You paid for an investigator?" I say, shocked.

"Well, I may have to go on a date or two in trade." He says with a grin.

"What!" I exclaimed.

"Oh, it's fine, he's cute. Let's get back on track here. So, he became a teacher right out of college in Michigan. He taught there for a long time. Then, he started getting reported for stalking. He was terminated from his teaching job the same day one of the student's families filed a protection order against him. The student's name was Myla Phillips. I found her on social media."

He pulls up the profile. He swipes through her public photos. She is younger than us. She has long blonde hair, and she has many similarities to me. In fact, she looks like me in a lot of the photos.

"Do you see what I see? I about died when I first found her profile. Khloe, she could be your twin. She looks more like you than Katie does." He says.

"This poor girl," I say, feeling the sickness rise from my stomach. I see a photo of her looking down at the ground. Did she go through what I did? Did he touch her? I start to feel my stomach roll.

"Did he touch her?" I ask so softly it's almost a whisper.

"There are no reports of that. I am going to say he didn't rape her. But he was following her. He would sit outside her home; he would ask her inappropriate things in class at school. It looks like one time at school, he trapped her in a supply closet. After that, she told her family because they went to the police. That same day, the report was filed, and he was terminated. He also tried to run her parents off the road with her in the car." He says.

I just stare at her photos. It looks like there is one with her parents. They were all dressed up; she was in the middle, and their arms were around her. She still had her family. Did he take mine because I looked like her? I stand up and pace the room. I feel the panic coming.

"He was our substitute teacher like a month later. I have no idea how he could continue to teach after all that. Khloe, it's possible he came to our school, and the minute he saw you, you snapped, girl. Maybe he did something to your parents, maybe he followed you home after class? Who knows, but he was a sick, sick man." He says with disgust in his voice.

I couldn't take it anymore. I close the laptop. I try to sort out all the thoughts I have racing in my mind.

"He was looking for you when he found you at that girls' home. I am sure of it, Khloe. He knew the minute he laid eyes on you, he was going to hurt you." He stands up, walks over to me, and puts his hands on my shoulders to stop me from pacing and going into a panic episode. "Stop, stop doing what you are doing. You are not to blame for this. You were a victim. I think this was just more planned out than a random thing. Promise me you will tell the detective when you talk to him." He pleads.

I look up at him with tears filling my eyes. I can barely breathe.

"It may be because of me, Gavin. Is my family gone because of me?" I cry out, trying to catch my breath.

"No, sweetie," he pulls me into a hug. "Just breathe, we don't know why it was your parents' time to go. But I know one thing for sure: it was not because of you," he says as he rubs my back gently.

"Subconsciously, Gavin, I always knew he selected me. It was not just by chance. I knew it, but I ignored it at the time. I was so sad and lost. They entered my life at my weakest moment and made it worse."

"And you ensured he paid the ultimate price for crossing you, girl." He says.

"It was an accident, though," I say between sobs.

"Accident or not, you took a predator out. You took that gun for a reason. He was a disgusting human being, and you had been through enough. You are stronger than you give yourself credit for." He squeezes me tighter.

"I need to get ready for work. You, okay?" I nod and wipe my face free of any tears.

"Want me to give you a ride? I need to meet Carrie anyway." I try to smile at him, but my face is still full of guilt.

"Yes, please." He says softly.

"Maybe we will work together sometimes," I tell him, trying to change the subject.

"Oh, I am sure I will be training you." He winks at me.

I walk outside carrying my bag of belongings. I look at the cars on the street. Thinking about that car from last night. No one in any cars on the street. I just have that feeling of being watched. I put the bag in the truck cab. I watch Beau sniff around the yard. I pull out my phone to send a text.

Khloe: I hope you have a good first day. Text me when you get off.

My phone starts ringing just as I send the text. I pick up without looking, thinking it is Josh.

"Hello."

"Hello, is this Khloe Pierce?"

A man with a deep voice is on the other end of the call.

"Yes, this is," I say with a bit of worry.

"This is Detective Aaron Graham. I got your voicemail. I was wondering if we could set up a time for you to come into the station and talk." He says.

"Yeah, of course. I can come later today or any time that works for you." I tell him as I look at the time.

"Late this afternoon will be great. How about around three o'clock?" He asks.

"I will see you then," I say nervously.

The

Fourteen

Lucas

I pace around this bedroom that was once my place of solitude, my refuge; now, this room, this house, feels more like a prison. I can't stand it much longer. I can't stand her, my mother. I think as I try to call Danielle again.

"Please pick up, Please pick up." I chant as I still pace the floor. She answers, but I don't even give her time to say hello before I start talking.

"Danielle, please talk to me. Let me explain." I beg as I sit on the bed.

"Lucas, there is nothing else to say. We're done. It is too late for you to explain anything to me. You are battling something I want no part of."

The phone goes silent. I stand up and pace the room again. Why did I even come back here? It has messed everything up. Everything is so complicated now. I feel like I am just on edge and about to blow a fuse. I sit down again. I lay back on my bed, feeling defeated in life.

"Lucas!"

"What Mom!" I yell back.

"Can you come down here, please?"

I let out a long sigh. This woman is driving me crazy. I walk out of the room, slamming the door harder than necessary.

"What," I say irritated.

"How long will she be here?" She asks.

I see her on the phone. I already knew she was talking to Julia. All those two do is gossip and cause mayhem.

"I don't know, Mom." I day with anger in my voice.

"Is she here for her sister?" She asks.

"Probably," I say.

She begins to laugh and continue to talk on the phone.

"She will never find her, don't worry. By the time she returns, you will have the adoption in place. You have nothing to worry about. What is she going to do?" She says to the person on the phone.

I roll my eyes but listen in to see if I can get any information for Khloe. Why stop now? I have been spending so much time fighting for her. I feel like I owe her so much. I carry a heavy debt when it comes to Khloe. I thought if I could make her mine, I could make it up to her. I could show her love and make her life better. She, of course, had other plans.

"Okay, I will see you tomorrow," she says her goodbyes and hangs up the phone.

I sit on the sofa. My mom marches up to me on the sofa.

"You honestly think you are sly, don't you? You think I would slip up and say something you could go tell her?" She says as she laughs a little.

"I have no idea what you are talking about, Mom," I tell her while shaking my head.

"You do know what I mean. We already know what you have done. How you involved yourself in affairs that do not concern you." She retorts.

"Do they concern you, Mom? Seems like this is an issue with the Mates'." I say, already upset with her.

"Julia is like my sister. Yes, everything that concerns her or affects her affects me." She replies to me.

"Khloe is from here. This is her hometown. She can be here without being up to something." I snap back at her.

"Well, then you better get her back to NC. You owe me; you owe Julia that, after all you did." She says, raising her voice at me.

"You are insane. No wonder Brittany has nothing to do with you, and Dad left you." I say as I stand up and walk out the front door. I drive around town blasting music. I feel so mad it is raging deep inside me. I turn the music louder. I pick up speed as soon as I leave the downtown area. Suddenly, memories flash through my mind as I drive, and I'm back in high school.

I watch Khloe walk down the hall at New Harmony High School. I see her look up at me and smile as she tucks a strand of hair behind her ear. I know she likes me. I have heard the rumors. I can tell, too, because she gets so nervous around me. I have been paying more attention to her these days.

I even broke up with my girlfriend recently to try and make my move. There is some pressure I don't usually feel when I try to talk to a girl. I want, I need her to like me. I hope I am reading her correctly. I walk behind her into class. It must happen today. I am not in this class, but there is a substitute today. He probably won't figure it out.

I take a seat at the table behind her and Gavin. Those two have been together since he moved here. I look up at the teacher, and he seems to be distracted. I pretend I am on my phone, but I listen to her and Gavin talking.

"Is he even in this class?" I hear her ask Gavin about me sitting there.

"I haven't seen him in this class before, who knows. What are your plans tonight, sunshine?" He asks her.

"My parents asked Katie and me to see a movie with them." She answers.

"A movie, huh? You did hear your little crush boy over there is single now. Doesn't he work there?" Gavin says with a chuckle.

"Gavin, Shh." She whispers.

I look up and see her put her finger to her lips. I smile a little. I knew she liked me.

"What? Maybe he will butter your popcorn." He tells her.

They start to chuckle. I don't look back up; instead, I text the work chat. I need to pick up a shift for someone so I can be there tonight if she is going to the movies tonight. I am off tonight.

After school, I wait for my sister to meet me at the car in the south parking lot. Brittany gets in the car with a sigh.

"Rough day?" I ask.

"This is too stressful." She says as she sinks into the seat.

I laugh; school is rough for girls, that's for sure.

"It will get better," I say sympathetically.

"No, not school stupid. The other issue here." She says.

I knew what she was referring to. Our mom has put us in a difficult situation.

"Katie and Khloe are going to the movies tonight." She says in a high-pitched voice.

"I already know. I changed my schedule." I tell her.

Brittany and Katie have become really close these last couple of years.

"You need to make her fall in love with you. No pressure, but you have one shot at this, Lucas."

"No pressure," I say as I nervously laugh.

"Katie says she is crazy about you, so it shouldn't be that hard. Don't screw this up." She says with doubt in her voice.

"I got this, Brit, don't worry," I reassure her.

Later that evening, I get ready to go to work and slip out the door without my mom seeing me. I want to avoid going through the questioning session with her. I'm over it lately. It is a hard pill to swallow finding out the real person your mother is. I will never be able to see her the same again. It breaks my heart a little.

I remember how I used to feel so protected by her. She was perfect in my eyes. Then, as you get older, you start to see who your family and loved ones really are. How do you get past it when you see them in a different light? A dark light that will never see sunshine again in your eyes.

I pull up to the theater. I take a deep breath. I got this. She's just a girl. My palms are sweating as I walk in. I go in the back and clock in. I wonder what movie she went to. Some have already started. They sent me to clean theaters. I feel like I will miss her, so I ask if I can work the counter for the rest of my shift. I busy myself behind the counter, watching for a glimpse of her in the lobby when I see her walking up to the counter. I make myself available to help her.

"Oh, hey, Khloe, what's going on? I reach over the counter to take her cup and give her a little smile.

"Sprite?"I ask, but I already know the answer before she responds.

She nods at me.

"I didn't know you worked here." She says.

Oh yeah, she knew.

"Yeah, I just started at the end of summer. How are all your classes this year?" I ask, looking into her eyes.

"Good. Yours?" She asks.

I lean on the counter to get closer to her. I slide her drink back to her.

"They're fine, but they would be better if you were in at least one of them." I flash her my best smile as I talk. I see her blush.

"Well, we can't always get what we want." She says.

I laugh at her. She is spicy, I like it. I find myself watching her soft lips. I immediately want to kiss them.

"I get off in 30. I could give you a ride home, you know if you're not here with anyone special, or hell, even if you are, you would rather be with me, right?" I knew she was here with her family. I reach across the counter and reach for her hand on the counter.

I watch her face. She is blushing again. I rub my thumb on her hand, praying she will say yes. If she says no, I need a backup plan and fast. I look back up at her directly into her eyes, trying to will her say yes.

"If you don't mind giving my sister Katie a ride too?"

Perfect, I think; I don't even have to offer.

"Nah, that's cool. Where is she?" I looked past her to see if I could spot Katie.

"Oh, still in the movie. I'll meet you back here when it's over, okay."

I nod and watch her walk away. I smile and text Brit.

Lucas: She said yes, driving them both home.

I wait outside near the ticket booth for them to come out from their movie. I see her and Katie walking towards me. I smile at them. She is beautiful. Any guy would be lucky to have her. I see her parents walk to their car. My heart starts to race. Are they going to come and talk to me? I don't want to have that happen right now. I look over at them again. I watch them walk towards the car. Dread takes over me. I fight it and stay focused on the plan, but my heart sinks.

"Ready, ladies, your chariot awaits," I say with all the charm I can muster, feeling nervous suddenly.

We walk to the car. Khloe opens the door for Katie, and I catch her gaze over the car and wink at her. I put on some music and try to take the longest route possible to get to their house.

We get to their house faster than I wanted. Katie immediately jumps out of the car and walks up to the house. I linger back with Khloe, as we walk slowly to the door. I reach for her hand as soon as we get to the door. I tilt my head and look at her.

"Khloe, I don't know why you're not my girlfriend." I smiled at her.

She begins to laugh. I may be coming off too strong.

"I think there has to be an agreement with both parties for that." She says with amusement in her voice.

I let out a sigh. Is she going to make me work for this?

"So, are you saying you wouldn't like me to do this daily?" I say in a low voice as I pull her close and move my lips to hers. I kiss her.

She tastes sweet. I move one of my hands to the side of her face, down to her neck, then down her arm, and hold her hand. I pull my lips away.

It feels like she is a little shaky. I hold her tighter it seems as though she might fall. I raise my eyebrows, surprised at her reaction.

"Well. Good night, Khloe. Hey, think about that agreement thing tonight. You already have my vote." I say, smiling at her.

I lift the hand I was holding and kiss it. I turn and walk back to my car. I drove home that night feeling hopeful, but it was short-lived.

I come back to reality. Tears fall down my face. Tears from sadness and anger; I have failed her and many others. I close my eyes and see her face from that night. The night her life was forever changed.

I open my eyes and see a semi coming at me. I hit the brakes to slow down on the curve and turn the car.

Fifteen

Raindrops

I sit at a little table outside the café, waiting for Carrie to be free. I look down at Beau and hope she is okay with him; if not, it will be a deal breaker. I love him more than anything. At this point, he is an emotional support animal. I reach down and pet him.

"That's what we will tell her, huh." He looks up at me with that sweet smile he gives me.

"Tell her what?" Carrie says as she walks towards me. She sits down and puts some papers on the table with a carton of eggs.

"I was going to tell you I have a dog, and I hope that is okay."

"Dogs are fine by me. Chickens are not." She says with a chuckle.

"Chickens?" I ask in confusion.

"I have too many at home. Here, I brought you a housewarming gift." She pushes the carton of eggs towards me. "Fresh eggs. I got them today."

"Thank you," I say, thinking that was kind of her but strange, too.

"Okay, so here is the paperwork. It's pretty basic. You will sign here, then initial here and here after you read it." She bends over to pet Beau as I look at the papers.

I sign the documents and push over the money in the bank envelope with the rent and deposit money.

"Okay, can you start work this weekend? I thought I would give you this week to get settled." She asks.

"Yeah. Thank you."

"Okay, let me know if you need anything. I will text you your schedule as it gets closer; plan for the Saturday morning shift. Here are your keys."She slides over the keys.

"Thank you so much for everything, Carrie," I say, grateful.

"Of course, sweetheart." She stands and walks back into the café.

I stand up and walk over to the truck to get my bag. Beau and I take the stairs up to our new place. The keys dangle as I open the door. Beau goes in first and starts checking it out.

"What do you think, Huh? Not too bad, right?" I ask Beau as I take in our new space. My very first apartment.

"We need to get a few things, I guess. Like you a bed and some food. But at least we got some fresh eggs."

I put them in the fridge. Then, walk over to the window. I look down onto the street. I feel like one of those successful city women you see on TV shows, except I feel so alone and scared at this moment. It will get better, I tell myself. I will get used to it. I look over at Beau, who is making himself comfy on the rug in the living room. I walk into the kitchen, get him a bowl of water, and put it down for him.

"Okay, I have to run some errands. I will not be gone long. You will be okay here. I love you." I say to him, as I turn on the TV for him so that he doesn't feel so alone. I pet him and give him kisses before I leave.

I sit nervously in the police station lobby, holding the papers from my dad's office and the ones Gavin gave me from his person since he had to work and couldn't be here with me. I look out the window and watch some police cars pull out with their lights and sirens on. Then, an ambulance drives by. I stand up and look out the window to see where they are going.

"Ms. Pierce?"

I turn and walk towards the man that called my name. He was a tall, slender man wearing a black polo shirt and khaki pants.

"Hi, please call me Khloe." I reach my hand out as I shift the papers into one arm.

He shakes my hand and leads me into a small room with a table and chairs.

"This interview is recorded just so you are aware."

"Okay." I sit down.

"You are the oldest daughter of Thomas and Jenna Pierce, I presume."

"I am," I say nervously.

"Well, let's start with why you wanted to talk to me?" He asks.

"I came to the station to get a copy of a police report. The person upfront said there were two reports with my name in them. My parents' accident was one of those reports. I was unaware that it is still an open case. I wanted to come here to talk about why that is. And I have some papers for you to review that may be helpful." I push the stack of papers toward him across the table.

"Your parents' case is still open because we discovered foul play after the vehicle inspection. Khloe, your parents' car brake lines were cut. A car accident occurred because they could not stop at a traffic intersection. We also found that the fluid had leaked in the movie theater parking lot. We pulled video footage, but couldn't see anything. So, it either happened at the theater, but the person avoided the cameras, or it happened just before they arrived."

I look at him, trying to take in this new information. I try to keep my emotions in check and fight back the tears. As I suspected already, someone killed my parents. I think back to the movie night.

"We were at home before we went to the theater that night. My dad worked from home that day. Everyone was there when I got home from school. I was the last one home before we left for the movies." I tell him, trying to remember all the details of that day.

"Did you drive your vehicle there?" He asks.

"No, we all rode together."

"Is there a reason you were not in the car with them after the movies?" He asks.

"My sister and I rode home with a friend from school. I ran into him at the theater. He offered to give us a ride home. My mom said they had some errands to run after the movie." I tell him, thinking that was the very last words my mom had ever said to me. Tears start to well up in my eyes.

"Who was this friend?"He asks.

"Lucas Matthews." I watch him write the name down in a little notepad.

"Was there a reason I was never notified this was an open case?" I ask.

"At the time of the accident, you were a minor. We had no reason to believe you were involved. I spoke to your sister once."

"Katie?" I ask, surprised.

"Yes, she came in here once. She's a feisty one."

I sat there and processed this information. Katie was here. She didn't tell me. Why would she not say anything to me?

"What are these papers you have with you?" He asks, so matter of fact.

"My father left most of these papers for me; the rest is information on Jared Coffman."

He starts to look through the papers.

"This is a registered will and living will." He starts reading it.

That makes sense. That would be something my dad would leave. I should have looked through all of them before I came today.

"Can I keep these for a while to review, and then I will return them to you?" He asks.

"Of course. I don't know if you know about the Jared Coffman case. Do you think he may have had something to do with the car accident? Have you looked into that?" I ask.

"I do know of it. I am very sorry for all you have been through." He says with sympathy to his tone.

"Thank you." I look away.

"I have that report for you, if you want it." He tells me.

"Did you read it?" I ask.

"I did." He pushes the folder over to me.

"Is there any information you think I need to know from this report?" I ask.

"I am not sure what you may be looking for. I think you would know everything stated in that report." He states.

I nod my head.

"Then maybe you can hold onto it for me for now?" I ask.

"Yeah, I can do that. I can put all these together." He says with a little grin.

"Is my parents' case a cold case, or is it still being investigated?" I ask.

"I will tell you we have run into some walls on it. There are no other leads for us to move forward at this time. I hope some of the information you gave me today will help or give us new leads." He tells me truthfully.

I look at this man in front of me. I plead with him silently.

"I will do everything I can to find out who did this to your parents.

I make that promise to you and your sister." He says as he reaches across the table and gives my hand a little squeeze that rests on the table.

"Thank you," I say with a slight grin. I am still trying to believe this is my life now.

"Before you go, can you write down where you are staying? That way, I know where to find you if I need anything, and so I can return these files to you." He says as he pushes pen and paper towards me.

I take the pen and paper and write down my address. I don't know the exact address just yet. I put the street name, and I am in the apartment above the downtown café.

I drive home in a daze. I cannot believe Katie knew. It started to rain hard outside. I park the truck and run for the stairs that lead to my front door. I walk inside and realize I forgot to stop by the store to get food for Beau and me.

"Hey, Beau. I am so sorry. I got distracted. How about some eggs for dinner?" I ask him.

I go into the kitchen and look for a pan. I start to cook some scrambled eggs. Beau sits at my feet, waiting patiently. I look at my phone, and still nothing from Josh. He must be busy today. I look outside. It seems almost like nighttime with such dark skies during this storm. I hear the raindrops hitting the metal roof of the building.

I put the cooked eggs in two bowls. I blow on one to cool it down for Beau. He watches me intensely. I sit one of the bowls down in front of him and the other on the counter. I get a glass of water and a fork and sit beside Beau. As soon as I sit down, there's a knock at my door. Beau only barks once and then goes back to eating.

I walk over to the door, and through the glass, I see Josh standing in the rain. I open the door and see him looking down, soaking wet.

"Get in here," I tell him as I watch the water drip off his hair onto his face.

He steps inside. He does not look up at me.

"What is it?" I ask with an uneasy feeling.

"Khloe." He pauses. "On my ride over here, there was an accident holding up all kinds of traffic. I thought I recognized one of the cars. So I walked up to the scene get a closer look." He looks down. He reaches for my hand.

I jerk it away.

"Who was it, Josh?" Who? Gavin?" I start yelling.

"Lucas." He says softly.

"Is he okay?" I ask.

He comes closer to me. He wraps me in his arms as he whispers in my ear.

"He didn't make it. He was pronounced dead at the scene."

I think back to the police cars and ambulance that passed by while I was at the police station. I start crying and sink to the floor. Josh crumbles with me to the floor and just holds me while I sob.

Sixteen

What ifs

I have been moping around my apartment for the last few days. Josh and Gavin keep checking up on me. I feel trapped here. I let Josh use my truck for the previous few days since he returned the bike he rented. He bought a broken-down one from a club member and has been working on getting it running again while spending as much time as he can with me.

I still cannot believe he is dead. I keep replaying the last time I saw him in my mind. The last few times, really. He was so stressed lately. Not the same Lucas I knew from school, who was always laughing and joking around. I think back to when I would watch him from afar. Or the night I first kissed him when he came to North Carolina.

His whole life is gone before it even started. Tears stream down my face, and my heart breaks for his family and his sister, mostly. His funeral is tomorrow. Of course, I will be there, but after seeing his mother's reaction towards me, I may have to keep a distance between us.

I wrap myself in a blanket. I move from the bed to the sofa. I sit and stare out the window, looking out over the street and watching the people come and go. How much would life be different if none of this happened? What if my parents had made it home safely that night? Would I have had a romance with Lucas for the rest of the school year? Would we be preparing to go off to college soon? Spending our last days together around town. Would he have been my first love, my first everything? It's too late to think about all of that anymore. I can't keep driving myself crazy with the "what-ifs" in life right now. I am torturing myself with it.

A knock at the door pulls me away from my thoughts. Beau runs to the door. He is excited, wagging his tail at the person on the other side of the door. I get up and slowly make my way to the door.

"Hey Blakeleigh." I greet her.

"Hey, girl. How are you holding up?" She asks.

"Meh," I say in a mellow tone.

"I know, I get it girl. Gavin is off today, but he told me to bring you something before I left for the day. So, here is a salad and some peach tea." She hands over the items and bends down to love on Beau.

"Thank you. You know you guys don't have to keep doing this daily." I tell her. I walk the items over to the kitchen counter and sip the tea.

"Yeah, well, Gavin thinks you are not eating." She stands up and walks towards me. "I understand you have emotions about this loss. We all loved Lucas in different ways. But you have to snap out of this a little. Take a long shower and wear clothes that are not pajamas. Leave this apartment and go for a walk or something. Lucas would not want to see you like this either." She says encouragingly.

I nod and look down at myself. I have been wearing these clothes since yesterday. I am such a mess right now. She is right. I really need to pick up the pieces of my life and keep going.

"I don't know why this is so hard for me," I tell her.

"We all handle death in different ways. There is a history there with you two and a future you never had that you are just sitting here questioning, right? I think you are being hard on yourself." She says.

Just then, Josh walks in carrying groceries.

"Oh, hey, Blakeleigh." He says.

"Hello, Josh." She says with a smile.

I watch Blakeleigh light up at the sight of him. I watch her blush just a little. He walks over to me and kisses my cheek on his way to the kitchen.

"I had to get you some groceries. If I have to eat eggs another night, I'm going to start clucking." He says jokingly.

Blakeleigh laughs out loud. I turn and glare at her. I'm getting irritated by the feelings she obviously has for Josh. I always took it as a joke before, but today, I feel some other type of way about it. Blakeleigh is beautiful and exotic-looking. I am just plain; right now, I am a messy, plain girl. I roll my eyes. Ugh, why am I feeling so jealous?

"Thanks, Blakeleigh, for bringing that by," I say with more rudeness than intended.

"Oh, of course. I see you guys around." She says bye to Beau and lets herself out.

I turn and watch Josh putting the groceries away in the kitchen. He is wearing a white t-shirt that clings to his muscles and some black joggers. He has been wearing loungewear the last few nights, probably because that's all we have been doing. I am going to run this man off. It's not like someone couldn't snatch him up. I'm sure Blakeleigh wouldn't mind making him a smoothie with extra whipped cream and having him lick it off her finger. I shake my head; what am I doing? I am sitting here making up scenarios in my head and actually getting irritated by them. I let out a sigh.

"Thank you for the groceries. You really didn't have to. Do you need me to give you some money?" I ask.

He looks up and empties the last bag. He walks towards me.

"Absolutely not. I want to cook dinner for you tonight. We will call this an at-home date night. Then we can watch a movie or Friends, anything you want." He ran his hands down my messy hair. He kisses my forehead. He then wraps his arms around me and holds me tightly against him.

"I'm gonna take a shower, and then maybe I could help in the kitchen?" I ask.

"Yes, you can be my sous chef." He says as he smiles at me.

We cook dinner together. It felt so good to smile and laugh for a change. I didn't feel guilty for being alive as I had been the last few days. We take Beau for a walk after dinner. I breathe in the night air as I hold Josh's hand.

"I took off tomorrow to go with you to the service." He says.

I give his hand a little squeeze.

"I am almost done with the bike. Just a couple of parts I'm waiting for. Then we can go for a ride." He says with excitement.

"I would like that." I think about how I love riding with Josh. How fun it must have been riding across the states when he did it.

"I changed the oil in the truck today, too. You should be good for a while. Thank you for letting me use it this week." He tells me as we continue to walk with Beau.

"You know you can use it anytime. Thank you for the oil change. You know you spoil me. I'm not sure I deserve all this. Lately, I have been such a mess, yet you're still next to me."

He stops walking. He steps in front of me, so I stop.

"Khloe, in my eyes and heart, you are my girl. I would do anything in the world for you. I know we haven't really talked about it or made it official or anything, but I am one hundred percent invested in you, in us."

I look up at him. I feel the heat all through my body. Hearing this man say this to me after, I thought I was pushing him away.

"I'm your girl?" I ask.

He cups my face and kisses me. He kisses me more passionately than I have felt in a while. Not since I stayed with him at the hotel or the first time on the beach. He backs me up to the brick wall of the café, near the stairs to my apartment.

"Do you want to be mine?" He asks as he kisses my neck.

I bite my lower lip.

"Do you think you are ready?" He whispers as he moves closer to my ear.

"I want you to think about it. I want to be all yours, too. I don't want to fight for space in that beautiful mind of yours with anyone else. I am willing to keep going slow until you are completely ready." He says as he reaches down, grabs the back of my thigh, and lifts my leg so it's near his hip. He pushes my back into the wall more as he presses against me and kisses me deeper this time.

I'm on fire. I know what he is doing. At first, I was starting to think he was teasing me. The more I get to know him, the more I see it for what it is. He is battling himself within, trying to take it slow so he knows for sure I am ready to move on. But he also gives me little glimpses of what it would be like to be with him. The hunger he has for me and to see if I match his. I am so turned on by him. I am beyond ready to take this to the next level. I want to be his. I want him to be mine.

I have yet to respond to him. I want to say yes. I'm all in. Take me now. That is not what he wants. He deserves better than that fast half-ass yes. Knowing damn well he knows the last few days, all I have been thinking about is Lucas, yet here he is next to me, letting me work it out in my thoughts. He stands by me and allows me to work out my problems, but he is always there if I need him.

"Ready for that movie," I say instead of what he may have thought I would say.

He smiles at me and kisses the tip of my nose.

"Yes, ma'am."

Sitting on the sofa with a movie playing in the background. Neither of us is paying attention to it. We have been talking about anything and everything. I learn so much about him in moments like this. He reaches up and plays with a strand of my hair. He has been kissing me off and on since we got back from our walk. We have been touching in some form all night. I look at his hand in mine. I look at the veins that show in his hand and go up his forearm.

"Josh, have you had sex without being in a relationship with the person?" I ask him.

I can feel his eyes on me.

"I have."

"Who was it?" I ask as I continue to look at his hand in mine.

"I girl I met while I was traveling."

"Was it like a one-night stand thing?" I ask.

"No, I worked with her. One night, it just went a little too far. I felt bad after because she was not someone I would see myself with, and it was just sex to me, but to her, it was something more. It made things complicated and awkward, so I left and moved on. I ran from it instead of dealing with it. I learned a lot from that situation."

I look up at him. I put my hand on the side of his face. I can tell he is not proud of himself as he thinks back. He has such a high moral compass and high standards. I think back to the stories of his mom. Did she teach him how to take care of women? I wish I could have met the woman who raised this man before me.

"How about you? Have you?" He asks.

I felt uncomfortable answering. He could see it.

"You can share it with me. I am your safe place, remember. If you cannot freely share your past with me, I feel it might hurt our future." He says as he caresses my leg.

"With Oliver. That one night." I say, embarrassed.

"Was he your first?" He asks.

"Well. I count him as my first." I say with a sigh.

"He was, then. That had to be hard. You guys shared that experience. I also think it's a healthy thing. We should not be ashamed of it. I know with me it is better when I have an emotional connection to the person." He says as he continues to move his fingertips over my leg.

"Do you ever think about me that way?" I ask, hoping for the answer I want to hear but also just curious what he will say.

"Do I want to have sex with you?" He asks with a little chuckle.

I look at him and nod.

"Only every minute of the day," he says as he moves his hand to my arm. "This is how I see it. I am no expert by any means, but I don't want you to confuse sex with love. I want you to know I am in love with you first. We need that foundation. You can trust me, feel completely comfortable, and be yourself with me. Maybe your relationship with Oliver moved fast so you could replace the memories of what happened to you. You needed that. You needed to replace it with something better. I understand that. I am not interested in being a step to forget, though. I want the healing." He moves closer to me and continues. "I want all the days of the future."

I crawl over him to straddle him.

"Your answer was even better than I thought it would be when I asked you," I say before I kiss him.

"Trust me, Khloe. You drive me crazy. When it happens, all bets off you will be mine, and I will be yours." He says as he rubs his hands up my thighs on each side of him.

Beau jumps up between us and starts licking us both. We both laugh and give him our full attention.

Seventeen

Unsteady

Josh and I walk up to the graveside service. I see Gavin and Blakeleigh standing off to the side. I walk over to them. As soon as I approach, Gavin holds my hand. Josh stands behind me. I feel his presence and that gives me some peace as I stand here. I feel the eyes on me. I look up at the others gathered.

I see his mother sitting in a seat with her head in her hands, crying. Next to her is Brittany. Her face looks swollen from crying. She is just looking at the ground. She never looks up. My heart breaks for her into a thousand pieces.

The man sitting next to Brittany must be their father. Lucas looked a little like him. He is staring at the coffin. I see the same green eyes as Lucas; I have looked into them many times before. Life is so fragile. It can slip away so fast. The pain is earth-shattering.

I look past them and see my parents' gravestones. They will be so close together. I pull my attention back to everyone standing here.

My eyes caught hers, and time stands still. I stare at Julia Mates. She doesn't look away. I refuse to look away; I match her staring. Something in me turns, and my anger for this woman floods me. Next to her is Seth. He is looking down.

I am screaming in my head as I continue looking at her. Where is Katie? Why isn't she here? What have you done? If you have hurt her, so help me, God, I will not be able to hold back. She is the only family I have left. Gavin squeezes my hand, and Josh puts his hand on my shoulder.

I am building my own family. I don't stand alone anymore. She will not get away with this. I break my stare again to look at Seth. He continues to look down. He looks different. I cannot put my finger on it, but something is different about him. Maybe he has aged since I last saw him.

I have been so worried about running into this woman. I was so concerned that if she knew I was here, it would mess up everything with Katie. But as I look at her right now, strength pulls from deep inside me. I am not afraid anymore. I want her to know I am here. I am going to get Katie back.

"I have seen that woman before, but who is she?" Gavin whispers in my ear.

"Julia Mates."

"Well, you two look like you are about to have a showdown right here and now. I think you got Josh worried." He whispers.

I look over at Josh. His jaw is clenched. I see him staring at her. I put my hand on his chest. He looks down at me.

"It's okay," I say to him.

"I see how she is staring at you. I don't like it." He says through clenched teeth.

The preacher begins to speak, and we bow our heads out of respect for Lucas. I can hear the small sobs fill the air. I silently start saying my goodbye to Lucas. I will always remember the sound of your laughter. The way your green eyes lit up when you smiled. The friend you were to me when I needed help, teaching me how to defend myself and possibly saving my life by teaching me those skills. I will miss you forever, friend.

They start to lower him into the ground. Something about that moment breaks my heart. I cannot bear it. I feel my palms getting sweaty, and my breathing gets faster.

"I am going to walk over there for a minute," I tell Josh and Gavin.

I walk over to my parents' gravesite. I look down at their names. I can hear the birds and squirrels in the trees nearby.

"Hey there. Maybe you guys can keep an eye on my friend. He's new here. Maybe you can show him the ropes for a little while so he is not so lonely. Mom, he could use one of your hugs. Dad, maybe you can tell him one of your dad jokes to make him smile. Can you tell him I love and miss him so much."

I turn to see Brittany standing next to me. I open my arms, and she crashes into me. I hug her with all the love I can give. She begins to sob into my shoulder. I rub her hair back out of her face as I begin to cry with her.

"I know it hurts so bad. And you get so tired of everyone saying they're sorry. You just want people to stop apologizing. You just want to wake up from this horrible nightmare that has become your life. You want them back, and it hurts because that is never going to happen." I say so softly between sobs.

She is unsteady on her feet. I sit down with her on the grass. I continue to hold her as she sobs. I rock her softly. I would have held her as long as she needed. The sobs slowly stopped.

"I wish Katie was here," she says to me.

"Me too."

She sits up. I'm able to look at her now. She has the same green eyes and dimples as Lucas. I notice as she puts on a small grin. She reaches into her pocket and hands me a folded piece of paper. I take it.

"Khloe, it's me." She says.

"What do you mean? What's you?" I ask

"The texts from the private number. It's me. At first, it was Katie and me. Then they sent her away for the summer, and I continued to send them to you. I have so much to tell you, Khloe. But they are watching me right now." She looks back over to the crowd of people. I follow her gaze.

"Read this letter. Katie sent it to me last week. I will be in touch, and I will tell you everything. Lucas would want you to know." She says.

"Lucas?" I ask, confused.

"I will explain. I gotta go." She says as he gets up.

I nod and look at the letter in my hand.

"Be careful. I think they are following you." She tells me before she hurries off.

Following me? Who? What is going on right now? I sit there trying to wrap my head around all this information. I open the letter.

Britt,

Hey there. Has Khloe made it there yet? Are you still texting her? They sent me to Wonder Valley Camp. I am here until right before school starts. Everyone else has been here for about a week or two. But I'm here the whole summer.

It's not too bad, though; I made some friends, and there are lots of activities to do. I have been swimming, kayaking, rock wall climbing, and they have a zip line. It is better than being there with them for the summer. There are some cute boys here LOL. You can write to me here and tell Khloe to send me a letter.

I just want to make sure she is okay. Try to lead her to the information we found out before I left. Help her get all of the

answers. She will be better at it than we are, I bet.

Write me!!

BFF

Katie

I reread the letter a couple of times. She sounds happy. I let out a happy sigh. I was ready for the worst. I'm so glad she's okay, and she's having fun. Gavin and Josh walk over to me.

"Everything okay?" Josh says as he kneels next to me.

"Yeah, Brittany gave me a letter from Katie." I hand him the letter. He reads it quickly and then passes it to Gavin.

"What do you want to do now?" Josh asks me.

"Road trip?" Gavin says as he hands me the letter back.

"No, I think I am going to let her just enjoy her summer there. I will write to her, though. I do not want her to worry. I need to get everything finalized here before she comes back. I need to find out what she and Brittany were up to. Brittany told me she's the private number that has been texting me. She said it was her and Katie, then when Katie left, it was just her."

"We have company coming," Gavin says.

I look up and see Lucas' mom walking towards us. Josh stands up and puts his hand down to help me up.

"You have some nerve showing up here. He probably wrecked his car because of you. You have been stressing him out." She says, raising her voice at me.

"Excuse me?" I reply. I'm confused as to why this lady hates me so much.

"I blame you!" She yells at me.

Josh steps in front of me.

"Look, lady. I understand you are hurting, but you are out of line here. I suggest you walk away." He says firmly without raising his voice.

"Or what? Your little boyfriend here is going to beat me up?" She snaps back.

"I would never put my hands on a woman, ma'am. But I will not stand here and let you badger Khloe. I would advise you to go back and mourn with your loved ones." Josh pleads with her again.

"I will throw hands," Gavin says as he walks in front of Josh, facing her.

"Gavin! No." I yell and stop him.

Josh turns towards us and puts his arms out to motion for us to walk away towards the exit. Gavin huffs and puffs all the way to the vehicle. We get to the truck before Josh speaks again.

"She is mad at the world right now, I'm sure. She just lost her son. She needs to blame someone, anyone. We should give her grace this one time. But if she wants to start that again, please let me know. We will not be so nice next time." Josh says.

"Yeah, and I will beat her ass," Gavin says, all hyped up.

We both look at him and chuckle. Gavin couldn't hurt a fly, to be honest. He is a lot of talk.

"Calm down, Gavin. But I love you." I tell him with a smile.

"Love you, sunshine."

Eighteen

Customers

I wake up to Beau barking at someone knocking at the door. I jump up, disoriented, and run to the door. I open the door; Josh turns towards me with a bag and a coffee in his hands. He cocks his head and smiles at me lifting an eyebrow. I realize I jumped up too fast without grabbing a shirt or anything. I am standing there with just a bra and panties on. I start to blush.

I take the bag and fresh coffee. I take a sip of coffee while still standing in the doorway. I am fighting every thought in my head to not turn and run to put on clothes. I must be feeling bold today. I stand there and let him just stare at me. It's no worse than a swimsuit, right? I am still sipping the coffee when I feel his hands grab my hips, pushing me back. He closes the door and gives me a deep kiss.

"I may have to come by early in the morning more often if this is how you will greet me." He says as he digs his fingers tighter into my hips.

I look at him as I put my arms around his neck.

"Maybe you should," I say with a wink.

He gives me a soft kiss.

"I know today is your first day at work, and I wanted to come by and start your day off right." He smiles at me as my face heats up.

"Oh yeah?" I ask as I move my eyebrows up and down.

He laughs as he pulls me closer.

"Not exactly like that, but with breakfast. I swear you sure do make it hard for me, though." He says with laughter in his voice.

I smile at him, knowing he wouldn't give in to that yet anyway. I have almost given up trying to seduce him anymore. There was no budging him on his moral compass. My parents would have loved him. I pull away and set my items down on the coffee table. I walk into the bedroom and yell over my shoulder.

"Could you take Beau out real fast as I get dressed?"

"You want to go outside, Beau? Come on, let's go." He talks to Beau in a higher-than-normal tone.

I smile as it just warms my heart. We have settled into a routine. We have not mentioned anything about being officially a couple, but it feels like we are. After the funeral, Josh has been here for me as much as he can with work.

I grab a shirt, pull it over my head, and slip on some jean shorts. I look in the mirror, run my fingers through my hair, and pull it up on top of my head in a messy ponytail. I hear them enter the door.

"Thank you," I say as I walk over to the bag on the table. I open it and see two muffins. I take one and hand it to Josh as I take the other one.

"You don't work today?" I ask as I tear a piece of the banana muffin off.

"I am starting a little later today. I also wanted to come by and ask you something."

I chew the buttery, sweet bread before talking.

"What's that?" I ask as I take another bite.

"Well, I know you and Gavin have plans tonight. But I was thinking maybe we could go out tomorrow night?"

"Wait, I don't have plans with Gavin tonight," I say, confused.

"I just saw him downstairs getting the food and coffee, and he said that you do." He smiles at me.

"Oh well, it's news to me," I say.

"I think it would be good for you guys to go do something. There has just been so much going on. You two need a little bestie night." He says as he pulls his muffin out of the bag.

I smile at him. How is this man so perfect? No way I deserve him, I think to myself.

"Thank you. You know you are almost too perfect." I say as I walk over to him and sit in his lap.

"I have plenty of skeletons in my closet, too, Khloe." He reaches up and cups my face.

"You make me want to be better. You are changing me." He says before he kisses me.

I can taste all the possibilities of us. The hope of something great.

"Can I show you something before I go?" He asks.

I nod and stand. He reaches for my hand. He leads me out the door and down the stairs to where the truck is parked. In the back of the truck is a motorcycle standing with straps.

"I got her all fixed up. What do you think?"

I look at the bike. I do not know much about bikes, but it looks different than the one he has at home or rented.

"It almost looks like a racing bike," I say, admiring it.

He smiles as he jumps into the back of the truck.

"It is a sports bike. The person who had it laid it down, and it was all bent up. She's going to be so much fun." He says with excitement.

I smile at him. He looks so happy. I just now realized I like seeing him like this.

"Can we do wheelies on it?" I ask, thinking how thrilling it will be to be riding with him.

He jumps down.

"I am not sure that is the safest idea with you on the back. I'm not Steveo, and this is not the Jack Ass show." He begins to laugh.

I laugh with him and shove his shoulder.

"Will you help me roll it down this ramp to get it out? He asks. "I'm going to drive it back, and that way, you have your truck back." He pulls the bottom of my neck to move my head closer to him.

"Thank you for letting me use your truck. Tomorrow, I will pick you up, and we will go riding. But no wheelies." He kisses me a little harder than earlier today. He reaches down and puts his hands right below my butt. He lifts me into the back of the truck. A

little out of breath, I pull out of the kiss.

"Will you pop the kickstand and roll it back to me towards the ramp." He instructs me.

I stand up and do as he asks. I jump down out of the truck as soon as he gets the bike on the ground. He slides the ramp back into the truck.

"Just leave that in there for now." He tells me as he closes the tailgate.

I nod. I watch him walk to the cab of the truck and pull out a helmet. He puts on some leather-looking gloves. He straddles the bike, puts his helmet on, and lifts the visor part of the helmet so I can see his eyes. I walk closer to him. He looks so good that I can hardly stand it. He puts his arm around my waist.

"I will see you tomorrow." He says with a smile.

"Maybe you can wear this helmet to bed sometime?" I say to him as I raise an eyebrow and close the visor down over his eyes.

He shakes his head a little, and I hear a slight chuckle. I kiss the helmet where his lips are behind it. I step back, and he starts the bike. He revs it a little, making it louder. I watch him leave and start to go down the road. I watch as he stops and turns the bike around to ride back towards me from the end of the street. He rides back down the road at a fast speed and pops a wheelie right in front of me as he motions that he is blowing me a kiss.

"Show off!" I yell down the street and smile at him. I feel butterflies inside every time I am with him. I watch him turn the corner, and I hear the sound of his bike fade away.

A little over an hour later. I walk into the café for my first shift. I walk up to Gavin, knowing he will be training me today.

"So, what's our plans tonight?" I ask.

He looks at me as if I said something that offended him. He puts his hand to his chest.

"Do you not know what day it is?" He asks me with disgust in his voice.

I try to think about whether I missed something important. I must have taken too long to answer him because he looked impatient.

"Um, It's the 30th. It's burn and cleanse day." He says.

I had forgotten entirely about Gavin's burn days. Ever since I met him, on the last day of the month, he has a small bonfire and burns things that he writes down that are bothering him or struggling with to cleanse himself from it. I learned so much about him in those days we used to have burn days. He would burn names or hateful words that harm him for being homosexual. People have been so cruel to him in the past. I got to where I had to burn their names, too, because I couldn't stand how they hurt him. We would always feel better after those fires.

"I have missed almost a year of burn days, so it better be a big one tonight." I say.

Gavin smiles at me.

I went through training as people came in. Thankfully it was slow right now. Gavin said it should pick up soon for lunch, then again after dinner, with a small rush on some days for dessert or coffee. Gavin went on break, so I was the only one up front for the next 15 minutes. I busied myself with cleaning.

I hear the door chime, letting me know someone walked in. I look up and see Julia walking towards the front counter. I look behind me looking to see if Gavin is coming back. I want to run. I don't want to face her right now. I am going through a panic attack on the inside. My heart is racing. I take a deep breath and, in my head, try to devise a plan. I will just keep it business-like.

"What can I get you?" I say, trying to be professional, although I am dying inside.

"I heard you were back in town. I almost didn't want to believe them until I saw you at the funeral the other day. And here you are. Got yourself a job and are sticking around for a bit, huh?" She leans on the counter to talk closer to me. "I know you live upstairs, too." She whispers.

I feel my face getting red. I feel the heat heating my whole body. I can't believe this woman is trying to take my sister. She can't have her. She doesn't deserve her.

"Are you trying to threaten me?" I ask as I lean on the counter and match her stance and eyes. Although I am screaming inside from anger and fear, I will not back down.

"Oh, of course not. I'm just letting you know what I know. I know a lot more, too. I know things about you, your family, your sister, your friends, your little boyfriend." She says with a hateful tone.

"Do you know I am contesting your adoption? You will not get Katie without a fight." I tell her, standing my ground.

I look her dead in the eyes. I refuse to look away first. Just then,

I hear the door chime again. I do not look over to see who it is. I continue to stare at Julia as if my life depends on it. She looks over and stands back up straight, moving away from me. I take a breath and look towards the door. I see Lucas' mom walking towards us.

I don't know if I can take on both of them. I look over towards the kitchen, and I see Gavin walking back towards the front. I give him a look of panic in the doorway, and he walks a little faster. When he gets back behind the counter, he sees the reason for my panic and walks towards them. He steps into action without me having the opportunity of stopping him.

"Oh, hell nah, we are not serving you two old skanks. You need to leave." He points towards the door.

"How dare you talk to us like that. We are customers." Lucas' mom says.

"I do not care if you are Santa Claus. I would rather be fired than serve either of you. You had better find a new place to go. You are no longer welcome in this establishment." He says firmly. He starts to walk them towards the front door.

As soon as they leave, he walks back towards me.

"You, okay?" He asks.

"Yeah. Gavin, you shouldn't have done that, and you really may get fired for that." I say, worried for him.

"Worth it, but I had better go call Carrie and give her a heads up." He says.

I watch him walk to the back. I head outside to clean an empty table and ensure they have left. I check on the ladies sitting at one of the tables before cleaning off the other table. I look down the street in both directions and do not see them.

I try to process everything that just happened. They know where I live, should I be worried? I also told them my plans. Should I have kept that a secret? I need to follow up with the lawyer thing, and get that process moving. I try to stop all the thoughts running through my head before I have an anxiety attack. I take a deep breath and hear ladies chatting next to me.

"I feel so bad for her. She lost her son, her husband moved on and got himself a new woman, and then did you hear her brother-in-law got shot by a girl he sexually assaulted, and now her sister Linda is in jail somewhere. Yeah, she has been through the wringer that one."

I drop the dishes I'm carrying, and the glass shatters everywhere.

Nineteen

Let it burn

I sit in front of Gavin's house with Beau. I am still in shock after discovering that Jared was Lucas' uncle. How can this even be? Linda is his aunt. I put my head on the steering wheel. Did Lucas know? When I told him what happened, was that even real news to him? Did he play me as a fool this whole time? Anger and tears well up inside me.

I feel that this whole damn town has something against me. Everyone knows or is related to everyone. I cannot stand it here. I am ready to move far away. I just need Katie, Gavin, and Josh. Beau starts whining. I look up and see Gavin on the front porch.

"Let's go, Beau." I grab my notebook and the police report I picked up after work. I'm ready to burn it all. I walk over to Gavin, waiting.

"You okay, sunshine?" He asks.

I gave him a weak smile. He put his arm around my shoulders.

We walk to the backyard where he has a small bonfire burning with two chairs and a small table with some drinks, popcorn, a speaker for music, and tissues. We sit in the chairs and stare into the fire.

"What a day, and on a burn day, too," Gavin says, looking into the flames. "You know this will be the first time in a long time I do not say your name and burn it. I tried to cleanse myself of you because losing you was so painful."He tells me with a little hurt to his voice.

I look over at him. I reach over and hold his hand. I used to believe it was just me trying to get through one day at a time. Feeling all lonely, this gem was right here, going through the same feelings, because I had left. I squeeze his hand.

"I'm so sorry. It will never happen again, I promise. We are soul mates and will forever be in each other's lives." I say to him, grateful to have him.

He looks over at me and smiles with tears in his eyes. I remember how much we cried at these things.

"I'll go first. You remember the rules. We write it, we say out loud one last time to get it out of us, and then we burn it and cleanse ourselves from it." He says. He gets his notebook and rips out some of the pages. He walks up to the fire.

"Dad. for saying I am not a true man. That I'm a disgrace, but you're mistaken because I am more of a man than you will ever be. I will never shame someone because they are different but damn amazing." He takes a small piece of paper with the name on it, squeezes it in his hand, and throws it in the fire." I have heard him burn his dad's name many times.

"Nathan, f- you." Paper in the fire.

I stare at the fire as he went on with different things and names. I was thinking about what I wanted to burn.

"Your turn. When you're ready," Gavin says as he sits beside me.

I stand up and put all my stuff on my chair.

"Wait, did you read that report?" He asks me.

"No, and I'm not going to. I lived it. There's nothing in there I need to relive." I say.

I open the police report folder, start pulling out page after page, and throw it in the fire.

"Jared. For everything you did to me, every touch, all the pain you inflicted on me. For what you turned me into. For whom you made me think I was." I grab the rest of the folder and throw it all in there. I watch the burning pieces of paper float up into the sky with the breeze.

"Linda." I crumble the paper in my hand. I think of all the pain she caused in so many lives. I throw it in the fire.

"Fear." I'm so done living in fear. "Oliver." I only said his name, but so many memories race through my mind. I close my eyes and just let them come. I turn back to my notebook, write on a sheet of paper, and rip it out.

"Lucas." I know you knew more than you told me. Why have all these secrets? "Lucas' mom. Julia and Seth Mates." I watch all the paper I throw in burn in the flames. I stand there and watch it turn into nothing but ash at the bottom of the fire.

I sit back down next to Gavin. He hands me the tissues. I shake my head. I have no tears. I'm not sad right now. I feel determined. There is a little fire in me. A strength I didn't have earlier today. I look over at Gavin. He was watching me.

"F them all, girl." He says. He grabs the popcorn, puts on some music, and offers me popcorn.

"Let's watch and celebrate all our ops burning." He says as he laughs.

He takes a handful of popcorn and sits back in the chair. I do the same. We sit there staring into the flames and feel our healing coming from the flames. But for me, there was more strength coming from the flames than healing tonight.

As I was leaving, Gavin hands me a little back bottle with a key chain on it.

"What's this?" I ask.

"Mace, just take it. I worry about you going home alone."

I grin at him.

"Thank you." I say, I give him a hug, then head out to my truck with Beau.

As soon as I get in, I start it up and look at my phone. I missed a call from Josh. I call him back.

"Hey there. Have a fun night?"He says as he answers.

"Yes, it was much needed. I am about to head home right now."

"Okay. I've had a long day. But I'm looking forward to seeing you tomorrow. What time should I pick you up?" He asks, sounding tired.

"I get off at four tomorrow," I tell him.

"I will be there around five then. When you get home, text me so I know you made it safely." He pleads.

"Alright." I agree.

Khloe," There is a pause before he continues. "I'll be thinking about you. Good night."

"Nite," I say before I end the call.

I sit the phone down on the seat, smiling. I thought he was going to tell me he loved me. I give a small chuckle.

I put the gear in drive. Do I love Josh? Maybe in some ways. A flicker grabs my attention as I look ahead about to take my foot off the brake. There is a white car sitting there. The person inside the car lit a cigarette, and I see the lighter flicker. I watch them as the black figure in the vehicle faces me. I see an arm go out the window with the cigarette. I can tell it's a man from the arm.

I take my foot off the brake, slowly roll up to the vehicle, and stop right in front of them. I turn on my brights to see into the car. I have never seen him before. I stay there for a minute. He did nothing, and neither did I. I want him to know whoever he is, I see him.

I back up, pull away, and head back toward home. My heart is racing. I look in the rearview mirror every few seconds to see if there is a car behind me. The short drive home, there was nothing. I back into the alley near my stairs. I turn the car off and sit there to see if the white car shows up. I hold the mace Gavin just gave me.

Still nothing. I slide over to open the passenger side door and let Beau out first, and I get out, taking the stairs two at a time. Rush to open the door. Rush in, lock the door, and turn on the lights. I look out the front window down at the street below, no white car. I take a long breath as if I were holding it for so long that my lungs are burning now.

"Maybe I am just freaking out, Beau," I say to him, trying to calm down.

He looks up at me.

"Let's make a snack and get ready for bed."

I text Josh to let him know I made it home safely. Make a sandwich and give Beau some lunchmeat.

I move the TV into my bedroom. I need the noise tonight. I also put a kitchen knife on my bedside table. I will not be a scared little girl anymore. I could call Josh or Gavin right now; they would come, I know it, but I need to be able to handle myself. How can I care for Katie if I must be saved, too?

"You will protect me, right Beau?"

He jumps up on the bed and puts his head on my stomach. I pet his head and slowly drift asleep.

Twenty

Reckless

I wake up still feeling tired. I didn't sleep well at all last night. I pull the covers over my eyes. Beau starts to bark from the doorway of the bedroom.

"No, Beau! Let's sleep a little longer." I plead,

He barks again with a little howl, then walks away. I can hear him going into the other room. He is not going to let me sleep any longer.

I pull the covers back and sit up. He comes back into the room, dragging his leash in his mouth.

"Okay, okay. Let's go out." I say, smiling at him. He is too cute.

I get out of bed, throw on some clothes, and head out the door with Beau wagging his tail. I didn't feel like walking on the main street in front of the café, so I went the other way along the alley towards the back street.

We walk down the street towards the grassy area at the end of the street. The street is lined with business offices. No one is outside at this time of day. I see my reflection in the glass of one of the offices, and I stop and look. I need to look in the mirror before I leave. I start combing my hair with my hands while looking at the reflection in the window.

"Khloe!"

I turn to look at who is calling my name.

"Naomi?" I say as a question, almost from the shock of seeing her.

"I knew it was you when you walked by." She runs up to me and wraps me in a hug before I can react.

"Oh, I have missed you and your family so much. How is your sister?" She asks.

"Katie is umm, she is away at camp right now."

"That sounds fun. How have you been?" She asks as she steps back, looking at me as if taking me in to see if I have changed.

I have changed more than she could ever know.

"I am okay. You?" I ask.

"Oh, so many changes. I am no longer at your dad's firm, as I am sure you know."

I think of her name missing off the desk at the office when Oliver and I broke in that night.

"I am working for this family lawyer right here downtown." She points to the building I was using as a mirror moments ago.

"A family lawyer, huh?" I ask.

"Yeah, she is great. I am so happy to be working with her. It got too hard to work with Seth." She looks down at her feet. "I am so sorry about your parents, Khloe. They were the absolute best. I was at the funeral, but you looked so heartbroken that day I couldn't face you. It broke my heart to see you looking like that." She reaches for my hand and continues to talk in a sweet loving tone. "I should have come up to you that day. You still have a family around here, and so many loved your parents. You and your sister will never be alone."

I study her for a minute and let that last statement sink in. I still have a family. I have felt alone so many times since my parents died. A void no one could ever fill. Maybe I do not need to fill the hole that is there, but plant friends all around it until it doesn't look so deep and dark. Little did I know that I still have a family. It just looks different.

"Thank you, Naomi. That means so much to me." I squeeze her hand back.

She reaches up and touches my cheek.

"I will always love you girls." She says with a twinkle in her eyes.

I smile at her and just feel the warmth from her hand.

"So, you work right here, huh?" I ask.

"Yup."

"And for a lawyer, you said," I confirm.

"I do."

"I am sort of in need of a lawyer right now. Do you think she could talk to me?" I ask.

"She is in court today, but I can schedule you this week if you want. Come in here, and let me get you a time set up."She holds the door for me.

I follow her into the office building. I look down at Beau as he pulls away from the door.

"Oh, can I come right back? I need to walk him real fast."

"Of course. Swing by on your way back this way. It is so good to see you." She says, smiling, kindness radiating off of her.

She smiles at me one last time before walking through the door. I look at the name on the door as it closes to read the name. Law Office of Shila Delgado. Beau and I start walking again, and I pull out my phone to text Dee to see if she has heard of her.

Khloe: Hey Dee, I hope things there are good there. Have you heard of the attorney Shila Delgado?

Beau and I walk around the grassy area for a while. I sit down under a tree as Beau lays down next to me. I just sit there and listen to the cars and birds. I rest my head back on the tree. I hear my phone go off.

Dee: HI Khloe, I am so sorry I haven't gotten back to you sooner. Things here have been a little crazy. Mom took a turn for the worse last week. She has been admitted back into the hospital. As for that attorney, I do know her. It would be great if you could attain her. She is hard to get due to her caseload.

The guilt I carry for Tara and her injuries hits me like a Mack truck. I take a deep breath and say a silent prayer for her. I need to get this all taken care of here and back there to help care for her. The obligation to her is such a strong force in me.

Khloe: Dee, I am so sorry to hear this news. I am praying for you both. I hope to get back there as soon as possible to help. If you need anything, please let me know and keep me posted.

I jump up and start walking back towards the office to get that appointment set with Naomi. I need to get all this moving and taken care of. I feel the urgency to get everything done, so I can return to North Carolina.

"Here is an appointment card for you to remember the date and time." Naomi hands me the business card.

"What type of matter will you be meeting with her on? So that I can put in a note on the appointment."

"Custody of Katie. Seth and Julia Mates are trying to get custody of her." I tell her.

Naomi looks up at me, and her face says it all.

"Oh, Khloe, we cannot let that happen. You know he hits Julia. She came into the office a few times after your parents were gone with marks on her. One day, I silently gave her a card to the women's shelter to help her, and after that, I was fired." She tells me.

I take in this new information. Anger wells inside me, if he lays one hand on Katie, I don't know what I would do. I grip Beau's leash tighter. I look up at Naomi.

"I will be a witness for you with your case." She says.

I put the appointment card in my pocket.

"Thank you, Naomi; I appreciate you. I will see you soon."

She smiles at me. I turn and leave the office. I look at my phone to check the time. I need to hurry my shift starts soon. I walk at a faster pace, my mind racing.

I was in a mood the whole shift. I just can't shake the feelings about Tara and the thought of Katie being hit by anyone. Gavin was off today, so I didn't have him to get me out of my funk. After my shift, I walk back up to my apartment to grab Beau and take him out before I get ready for my date with Josh.

As soon as I return from walking Beau, I jump into the shower. I am hoping that helps me feel better. I attempt to let the hot water wash away today's worries and get in a better mindset before Josh gets here. I know he will sense my mood right away. He is good at that.

I close my eyes and let the hot water run down my face. I picture Josh as though he is standing before me. I picture his hands, arms, and chest. I see him raising one eyebrow at me when he thinks I am trying to get him to give in to me. The hot water is almost getting too hot now. I wonder if tonight will be the night. I am feeling reckless.

I get dressed in a haze. I look in the mirror, wearing black leggings and a crop top. I braid my hair and lay it over one shoulder. I feel flushed from the thoughts that now replace the earlier ones. I walk to the front window and look out over the street. I hear a motorcycle.

I watch Josh ride up the street. My pulse picks up. He has a box strapped to the seat area behind him. I watch him get off the bike, take off his helmet, and run his hands through his hair. I bite my lower lip.

Gavin's voice comes to mind, singing and hyping me up.

I walk to open the door and wait for him to reach the top of the stairs. I lean against the door frame. Do I even know how to seduce him? How do women do it? I'm clueless about these things. Beau is sitting next to me, turning his head as if he is judging me.

"Stop that. I'm trying to get you a daddy here." I wink at him.

He turns his head the other way. I start to laugh at him and myself.

"What's so funny?" Josh says as he reaches the top of the stairs. He bends in to kiss my cheek.

"Oh, nothing, just laughing at Beau," I say, still smiling.

I move to let him in. He walks in and bends down to greet Beau.

"I brought you guys gifts." He stands up and hands me the box with a little black cloth bag on top.

I close the door and carry the box to the coffee table. I open the little bag first. I pull out a little metal tag in the shape of a bone. It says Beau on it. I flip it over, and my phone number is on the other side. He got Beau a dog tag.

"If this little guy gets lost, someone needs to know who his family is so he can get back home to you." He walks up behind me, wraps his arms around my waist, and kisses my neck where my shoulder and neck meet. He rests his chin on my shoulder.

"Now open the box." He pleads.

I hand Josh the dog tag before I open the box. Inside the box, there is a motorcycle helmet. It looks to be a custom one. It's white, with a black visor that slides over your face. On the white, there are light gray wildflowers with accents of rose gold. On the back, near the bottom in rose gold, it says KP.

"I thought you needed your own. I had it made for you. Do you like it?" He asks.

"I love it." I turn it to look at all the sides. I think back to when I took him to my parents' gravesite the first time. We went and picked wildflowers. I told him the story of my mom always picking them.

"Thank you," I say, so thankful to have him in my life. I turn to face him.

"Let's try it on." He says. He grabs it and places it on my head. He lifts the visor and smiles at me.

"You ready to go for a ride?" He asks.

"I am. Let me just put my shoes on." I take the helmet off and sit the helmet down. I walk into my bedroom.

Josh follows me.

"You move your TV?" He asks.

"Oh, yeah, I wanted to watch TV before I went to sleep last night," I tell him.

"Come here, Beau, let's put this on." He calls for Beau. He sits on the edge of my bed and bends down to put the tag on Beau's collar.

I go to my closet to get my shoes.

"What is this for?" He says in a deep voice.

I turn and see him holding up the knife I put on my bedside table last night.

"Umm?" I say, slightly embarrassed.

"Khloe, why are you sleeping with a knife beside your bed?" He demands.

Panic washes over me. Should I tell him? Will he be upset?

"I thought someone was watching me last night at Gavin's. So, I put it there to help me feel safer."

He sits the knife back on the table and walks over to me.

"Why didn't you call me?" He asks.

I shrug my shoulders. He puts his arms around my lower back.

"Khloe, you can tell me anything anytime. Just because you tell me something doesn't mean I need to come save you. I know you can take care of yourself. But if you are scared, I want you to let me know. You can lean on me if you need to. Okay?" He says softly.

I wrap my arms around his neck.

"I know you will be there when I need you," I tell him.

"Good." He says before he moves in to kiss me. He tightens his hold on me as the kiss deepens.

He backs me up into the wall behind me. His hands on my back move to my sides, pushing my arms above my head. He takes one of his hands and holds my hands above my head. He takes his other hand and places it on my neck, then slowly moves it down to my chest, just above my breasts.

He pulls away from the kiss that has left me breathing heavily. He moves his free hand down to the curve of my cleavage, then back down over my hip. I am so aware of everywhere he touches, and my body is on fire, my skin burning under his hands. I take a deep breath and breathe in his scent. He grabs the back of my thigh and lifts my leg as he presses his body into mine.

I hold my leg there as he rubs my thigh and kisses me again. I can feel his hips push into mine. I push my hips back against him, wanting to feel more of him. He moves both of his hands and cups my face. He pulls away from the kiss and rests his forehead against mine. Both of us were breathless. He takes a long breath and gives me a look of desire in his eyes.

"Let's go ride." He whispers breathlessly.

Twenty-One

The Plunge

The sun is setting as we drive through town. The sky is filled with colors like a beautiful painting. We hit the edge of town, and Josh starts to go faster. I hold on tighter. I think back to the riding lesson he gave me before we left.

"This bike is different than my other one back home. So, if you want to be my backpack, you need to know this."

"Backpack?" I ask him confused.

"That's what we call passengers. Here are your foot pegs." He puts down the pegs on each side of the bike.

I notice how much closer I will be to him on this bike. It makes my heart beat a little faster. He gets on the bike.

"Okay, now you get on, put your foot on the peg, and use my shoulders to get on." He taps his shoulders as he says this to me.

I do as he says.

"Now you hold on like this." He wraps my arms around his chest.

"Now, put your hands here when we are downshifting or stopping." He moves my hands to what I think is the gas tank in front of him. He starts up the bike and revs it up.

"When I lean, you lean with me." He puts his hand on mine, which is wrapped around him.

This bike is faster than the last one, or his mood may differ from the other times, and he is driving it faster. Sometimes, I move my hands around on his chest. I can feel the muscles through his shirt. My new favorite thing is when he drives with one hand and puts his free hand on top of my hands, holding his stomach.

We stop at a four-way. He puts his feet on the ground and leans back slightly into me. He put his hands on my knees on each side of him. I lean into him to talk so he can hear me, but I headbutt him with my helmet to the back of his. He begins to laugh.

"Can we go down by the river?" I ask.

He nods his head, and off we go.

I have an idea that just came to mind. I'm unsure if I'm bold enough to do it, but I hope I am. I'm trying to channel my inner baddie. I am eager to see what he does. The sun has set now and it's getting darker, but there is still enough light to see.

We drive by the river for a bit, and I can see the moon rising just above the river. The water looks almost black in the lighting. He pulls into a little cove area with no one around. It is nearly a picture-perfect setting.

I get off first and take off my helmet as he gets off. I sit it on the seat of the bike. I can still feel the vibration in my legs from the ride. My whole body is just full of sensations. It's hot outside, and now we are standing still, you can really feel it. I know Josh has to be hot in jeans. I walk down towards the bank of the water. Josh follows.

"I sure do miss the ocean." He says as he stands next to me.

"I do, too. But there is something beautiful about the river, too. I grew up on this river." I turn to look at him. I watch him as he looks out over the river.

"What are you thinking about?" I ask, curious.

"Thinking about you growing up and coming here to swim at different times of your life."

He looks at me and smiles. I reach for my braid, pull the hair tie out, and put it on my wrist. I run my fingers through the braid to loosen my hair, so it is hanging down now in waves. He watches me intensely as I do this.

"Let's go swimming," I suggest. I look at him and wait for him to respond.

"Now?" He asks.

"Yeah, now," I say, still keeping eye contact with him.

I start to take off my shoes. He backs up slightly but keeps his eyes on me. I take a deep breath, don't lose your confidence now, Khloe, I say in my head. I lift my foot, pull off my sock, and then the other one. I turn my back on him. I slide my leggings down my legs, bending over when I get near the lower half of my legs. I don't look back to see his reaction or if he is even looking.

I pull off my top and throw it down on the pile of clothing on the ground. I slide my panties off slowly and purposely. I reach around and undo my bra. I stand back up and cross one arm over my breasts. I turn my head to the side to see if I can see him looking.

The look on his face did not disappoint. It made me smile. I turn and start to walk into the water, keeping my back turned to him as I enter the water. I wait to see if he will follow me in or not. It seems like time stood still while I stand there waiting for any sound of him walking into the water.

I hear the water start to make a noise. I let out a long breath, unaware I was holding it. I turn to see him walking towards me. The water was already to his hips. I could see all the muscle lines on his stomach and chest. I notice how broad his shoulders are. It's almost like he has been working out since I last saw him without a shirt.

He stops right in front of me. Both of us are just looking at one another. He looks into my eyes; he holds my gaze. He reaches out for me. I move into his arms. Our bodies pressed together.

"I need to know something." He says to me. "I feel like I know this answer, but I need, or maybe I just want to hear you say it." He says as he moves my hair back off my shoulder. "Are we together?" He runs his thumbs over my cheeks on both sides of my face. "Am I yours, and you are mine?" He asks as he bends down, lightly kisses me, and pulls away."Is there anyone else in that little head of yours, or is it just you and me, baby?" He asks.

"Yes, I'm yours. It's only you." I tell him, being completely honest with him.

I kiss him now. I am feeling so happy and safe in this moment with this man. That is how I see Josh. He is a man, not a boy. He is my protector. He also lets me be who I want to be. There is no control over me. I feel free with him, no judgment.

He lifts me, and I wrap my legs around his waist. It feels like we kiss for hours, although I know it is not long. I'm just lost in the moment.

"We will not have our first time here at this river. You deserve better than that. But I can tell you what we will do is cool off." He says, laughing.

Without warning, he pulls us both underwater. We separate underwater, and both come up at different points. We swim around for a while. We float on our backs, looking up at the stars. It's crazy that I forget I'm naked. Everything feels so natural. I feel confident in my skin around him.

"You are the most beautiful person I have ever seen, Khloe. You have no idea how happy you made me tonight. I have been waiting for this." He whispers to me as he holds me in the water, smiles at me, and lightly chuckles."But I cannot wait to watch you try to get back into those leggings all wet. I think that may be my highlight of the night."

I splash him and laugh because I did not even think of that. I shake my head. I will have to wiggle and jump to get them back on.

"Well, the night is not over yet," I tell him winking.

By the time we make it back to the apartment, I'm freezing. I'm pretty sure Josh could feel me shivering all the way home. We pull in next to my truck in the alley. I get off, almost ready to run up the stairs, but something catches my attention. I see a white car parked across the street on the side of the road. I go stiff as I look at it. Josh follows my gaze as soon as he gets off the bike.

"What is it?"He asks.

"That white car. It's a white car that I think is following me." I tell him.

He looks at me, then at the car again.

"Go inside." He tells me firmly.

He walks towards the car. I slowly start to go up the stairs, still watching him. I get to the door when he reaches the car. I watch him look in the windows. He turns and walks back. I start to calm down. The car must be empty. What if they are still here somewhere? What if they are inside? I stop and look through the window on the door. I see Beau on the other side, just looking at me. Josh comes up the stairs two at a time.

"The car is empty," he says as he gets to the top of the stairs with me.

I finally get the key in the hole and open the door. I am trying not to look nervous, but I am. I go in and greet Beau. Josh locks the door and goes to the window to look at the street.

"I need to take Beau out," I say nervously.

He walks away from the window towards me.

"I can take him." He says.

He grabs the leash, and Beau jumps and dances, all excited. Josh walks over to me and kisses my cheek.

"Why don't you take a hot shower? I will take the key and lock the door behind me. I will be right back."

I nodded and gave him a small grin. He goes out the door, and I hear the door deadbolt lock.

I walk over to the window and look out. The car is still sitting there. I see Josh and Beau walk across the street, then down the sidewalk. I watch for a few minutes to ensure he is safe before I go to the bedroom to get some dry clothes.

I turn on the hot water in the shower. Steam starts to fill the room. I get in and feel the hot water warming me up. I keep thinking about the car and Josh being out there. Just then, I hear the door. I freeze and listen to see if I can hear Josh and Beau. Then I hear Josh's voice talking to Beau. I look up towards the ceiling and let out a sigh of relief. I start to wash my face and then rub shampoo in my hair. I hear a soft knock on the bathroom door.

"Khloe," He opens the door just a crack. "I just wanted to let you know we are back. The car belonged to someone that came out of one of the offices. They left."

"Thank you for letting me know," I say as I peek out of the shower. "Want to take a shower with me, boyfriend?" I ask.

He stands there, crosses his arms over his chest, looks at me, and smiles. He hesitates, but only for a moment.

I watch him pull his shirt over his head and start to undress. I go back to trying to wash the shampoo out of my hair. He slides the shower door back more and walks in. I stop washing my hair and take all of him in for the first time.

"Let me," he says. He takes a step towards me, closing the small space between us.

He starts to rub his hands through my hair and rubs my head, washing the remaining shampoo out of my hair. It feels so good. I feel so relaxed as the hot water runs over my head and his hands work the shampoo out of my hair. A moan almost escapes my lips. When I open my eyes and look at him, I see that he has hunger in his eyes.

"Khloe." He whispers.

I didn't let him say anything else before I crushed his mouth with mine. His desire matches mine instantly. His hands explore my whole body. I gasp as his hand goes between my legs. He moves my arms above my head again and holds them there. I feel his mouth on my neck, moving lower. My legs were getting weak. I'm starting to feel tingling all through my body as he pushes his fingers inside of me.

He lets go of my hands, unable to hold them as he moves his mouth lower. I move my hands to his hair and grab his hair as I let out a moan. He stands back up and looks me in the eyes before kissing me again. He lifts me and pushes me up against the shower wall. I wrap my legs around him as he slowly enters me.

He let out a small moan with me. He didn't move right away. I could feel him filling all of me. There was almost a pleasurable pain to it. I hold his shoulders tightly. He begins to move in and out of me as he did, I can't hold in the moans any longer. His hands are holding me up as he lifts me to match his movements of thrusts in and out of me. I felt sensations I had never experienced before. My whole body was stiffening but relaxing at the same time. My legs automatically start to tighten around him. I bite his shoulder with my hold on him, getting tighter as I let out one final scream before my whole body felt in a state of bliss like never before.

He holds me there, not moving for a moment. He lightly kisses my shoulder and neck. He makes a trail to my swollen lips. I start to chuckle a little.

"That was..." I trail off, trying to gain control of my breathing and not feel as lightheaded as I do at that moment. He slowly starts to let me down, and I'm getting my footing on my own feet again.

"I know, same," was all he said to my incomplete sentence and thought. I open my eyes to look at him and watch him. I wonder if he is feeling what I'm feeling at this moment.

As we both gain control again. He reaches over with one hand behind my neck, into my hair, and pulls my head back just a little. He brings his lips close to mine.

"Khloe Pierce, where did you come from?"

I smile at him.

"I guess us Midwest girls just do it better."

He puts his head back and laughs.

"I never even knew what I was missing until just now." He says in a raspy voice.

He brings his lips to mine and kisses me.

The water is starting to get cooler. We just now notice it as we back out of the water.

"You hungry?" He asks.

I smile and nod.

"Let's go make something together." He says.

Twenty-Two

Suffocating

I lay there with the light radiating into the room. I stare at Josh's back as he sleeps peacefully next to me. I bring my hand to my mouth as I notice the scratches I left on him last night. There is a small bite mark on his shoulder, too. I roll over onto my back and feel the soreness throughout my body. The night before comes back to mind, and I replay the memories after the shower.

We were in the kitchen making grilled cheese sandwiches. The pull that we had before has changed. It is somehow stronger now. We could not keep our hands off one another. We had a thirst that could not be filled last night, no matter how many times we tried to quench it. I smile, thinking about it. The shower, the kitchen, the bedroom, until we couldn't stay awake anymore.

I look down at the foot of the bed and see Beau sleeping. I smile and start to chuckle, looking at Beau. Josh rolls over and moves closer. He puts his arm around my waist and pulls me closer to him. He kisses my shoulder.

"What's so funny so early?"He asks.

"Beau saw some things last night," I say and turn to look at him. His eyes were still closed, but he starts to smile.

"Oh, I bet he did. I'm surprised he didn't think I was trying to hurt you with all that screaming."He says, smiling proudly.

"Hey, I tried hard not to make noise," I say, feeling the embarrassment turning my face red.

"You failed miserably." He laughs with a small glimpse of pride.

Beau perked his head up. I look at him like he knows we are talking about him. He starts to bark. Just then, there was a very loud knock at the door. It made us both jump. Josh was on his feet first. He was slipping on his jeans before I was even out of bed. I quickly slip a shirt and a pair of shorts on.

When I enter the living room, Josh opens the door. I look to see who it is. The detective on my parents' case stands there.

"Mr. Graham, please come in," I say as Josh moves to the side to let the man in. "This is my boyfriend, Josh."

"Nice to meet you, Josh. I am Detective Aaron Graham with the New Harmony Police Department." He extended his hand to shake Josh's hand.

"What's your last name, Josh?"

"Walker," Josh states as he shakes his extended hand.

"Please come sit down, Mr. Graham," I say as I sit down on the sofa.

He walks over and sits next to me. Josh takes a seat on one of the bar stools near the kitchen. He sits there with his arms crossed over his bare chest.

"Here are the files you shared with me, Ms. Pierce." He sat them on the coffee table.

"Thank you. Was there anything in there you could use for my parent's case?" I ask.

"Well, there was interesting information in there." He turns to face me. "You are aware that you and your sister are the owners of your father's firm? Your sister will have 50% as soon as she reaches the age of 18. Currently, you are the sole owner of the business and all the stocks and accounts related to that business." He tells me.

I look down at the papers on the table.

"If I am the owner, then how is Seth Mates running that business?" I ask.

"That is the question I have been investigating since you gave these to me. He has changed the business's name and fraudulently moved money from one account to another. His actual contract, where he was a temporary partner, was up just after your parents' accident. He has no rights to any of the funds within that business."

It all hits me so hard. I stand up and start to pace the floor, tears coming from my eyes. Josh gets up and walks over to me.

"We have a warrant for his arrest right now. We also believe he has a motive for tampering with your parents' vehicle the night of the accident. But as of right now, we will hold him on money laundering of the business you own." He says.

"He did it. He killed them." I start to feel the panic set in.

"We do not know just yet. We will be picking him up today, hopefully." He stands up. "Listen, Ms. Pierce, we will increase the detail on you and around your home."

"Detail?" Josh asks.

"We had an unmarked car watching you. We needed to see what you were up to as well to rule you out and protect you in case something was to happen. We also feel this may set some things in motion, and we do not want you to be harmed. Where is your sister located?" He asks.

"She's at Wonder Valley Camp," I tell him.

"Wait, was the person watching her in a white sedan?" Josh asks.

"I'm not sure what kind of car; I will follow up on that for you. I will get someone out there to keep an eye on your sister, too. Just want to make sure everyone is safe." He says.

"Thank you," Josh replies.

I am just hanging on, barely standing on my own feet. Josh is holding me up. I cannot stop the tears from falling. I feel like I cannot get enough air. I am suffocating as the room starts to spin.

"I will be in touch soon," the Detective says, showing himself to the door and leaving.

"They were murdered," I cry out as I sink to the floor and cry in Josh's arms.

Something about saying the words out loud makes the pain feel fresh. Josh did not say anything but held me until I was able to overcome the stabbing feeling in my chest. The concept of time was lost that morning.

"I'm so sorry," I say as I sit up.

"Don't; you have nothing to be sorry about," Josh says as he stands up and enters the kitchen. He gets a glass of water and hands it to me.

I take a drink, and I watch him slowly pace. He walks to the window. He runs his hand down his face.

"Khloe, tell me what you need or want me to do." He comes and kneels in front of me.

"I don't know what to do right now. I was going to ask you what you thought." I say.

He takes a deep breath.

"I think you still need to meet with this attorney. I would like to see if there is anything you can do with your parents' business, too. What are your legal rights when it comes to that? We need to get your sister. That needs to be the top priority." He says.

"We?" I ask.

He looks at me and holds my hands in my lap.

"Yes, we are a team. I am here for anything you need." He says and kisses my forehead. "I should call in today. So, I can stay with you." He says.

"No, I will be fine. You should go to work. You just started." I tell him.

"Can I at least call Gavin to come be with you today until I get off?" He asks. I smile at him.

"Okay, good. Do you want to come and stay with me tonight? You and Beau?" He asks me.

"Yeah, I'd like that," I tell him with a little smile. I haven't been to his work or place yet.

"Okay, I better get ready to go then. You want me to run downstairs to get you anything at the café before I go?" He asks.

I shake my head no. He helps me stand up. He wraps his arms around me. He moves my hair back from my face and kisses the tip of my nose. Then gives me a peck on my lips and each cheek.

"I will see you tonight. I will send a location pin. Please let me know if you need anything."

I nod. I hug him. I am feeling so thankful for this man to be in my life.

I watch him leave and hear the motorcycle sound fade outside as he goes down the street. I change and put on my running shoes.

"Come on, Beau, let's go for a run."

I cross the street and start at a soft jog until we get to the trail that goes through the town. I feel my muscles come to life as I push them harder. I look down at Beau. He is keeping pace with me but is starting to pant. I slow down, not wanting to overwork him since I have no water or anything for him. I slow down to a walk and turn to head back towards home.

I think about my parents. They knew Seth was up to something and were getting their affairs in order. They didn't do it fast enough. How could they be so stupid not to do more? Why didn't they call the police? I don't understand what they could have been thinking to be putting themselves at risk like that. Putting Katie and me at risk like that. By the time I get back to our street, I am angry, crying uncontrollably.

Twenty-Three

Appearances

I sit in front of the mirror, brushing my hair. I thought the shower would help me. It was a false hope. I wish you could wash away your worries in the shower like it was dirt. Watch them go down the drain, and never see that worry again. I hear my phone go off, pulling me away from my thoughts.

Gavin: Let me in, sunshine.

I walk into the living room to open the door. As soon as I open the door, he hugs me.

"Josh told me what happened. I am so sorry, sunshine." I let him hold me for a few moments. Just taking in that feeling and comfort.

"Thank you," I say.

He pulls away. He walks into the apartment.

I see him look into the bedroom as he passes by the doorway. I immediately regret not making the bed. I see the sheets pulled off, the blankets a mess, and the pillows on the floor. Beau was lying on one of them on the floor.

"Rough night sleeping?" he asks with some suspicion in his voice.

I do not even try to hide it.

"Josh spent the night," I say.

He turns to face me real fast.

"Oh, did he?" He asks with curiosity in his voice.

I shrug my shoulders at him.

"Oh, was he no good?" He says with disappointment.

"Gavin!" I yell.

"What, you shrugged your shoulders. I feel like, what a shame." He says.

"No, he was amazing," I tell him, shaking my head.

He smiles.

"Tell me what the Detective said and what is happening with the case with your parents. We will circle back around to the Josh thing." He says as he sits on the sofa.

I tell Gavin everything that happened with the Detective, about running into Naomi and the attorney appointment, and about the white car I thought it was following me, but now it may have been the police. I tell him about calling Dee and finding out Tara was back in the hospital.

"Okay, wow. Give me a minute to process all this information. I swear I do not see you for, like, what, 24 hours, and all this shit happens." He says.

I shake my head and put my face in my hands.

"The weight is so heavy, Gavin."

He moves closer to me and wraps his arm around me.

"We just have to break it down into small pieces and tackle them one by one." He suggests.

I look up at him.

"What is the most important right now?" He asks.

"Katie. Josh thinks so, too." I tell him.

"Okay, I think we can all agree on that one. You have the appointment set, so we are moving forward with that. That attorney could probably help you so much. Maybe you can write a letter to her and fill her in some if you want. Or maybe you do not want to worry her right now. But at least let her know you are working to intervene in the adoption."

"That's a good idea," I say.

"What's the next important thing you think?" He asks.

"I am hoping the attorney can help me on this business thing. I do not know how to run that thing. What does that entail for Katie and me? I wonder if we can cash out or sell it something?" I say, thinking out loud.

"Okay, possibly the same person can help with that. Let's keep going, what's next? He asks.

"I want Seth to pay for what he has done. I want to know if he played a part in my parents' accident."

"Okay, we will let the police handle that, Sherlock. We have done all we can do on that. We gave him all the papers and research we had."

"You're right. So, I guess I sit and wait." I say with a big sigh.

"We just need to keep you safe. I feel like we are dealing with some crazies." He says.

"Yeah, they will have police watching me for my safety."

"That's good. How about we write that letter?" He suggests.

We sit down and write a letter to Katie. I choose not to mention Mom and Dad's case or Seth's right now. I just went over the basics. I let her know I'm in New Harmony, and I saw Brittany briefly. I talk about how much I miss her and look forward to seeing her soon. I decide not to bring up the adoption yet since I have not spoken with the attorney yet.

"I will have my mom mail this out tomorrow," Gavin says as he takes the letter.

"Thank you." I sit back on the sofa and lie on Gavin's shoulder.

"Josh and I are official now," I tell him.

"It's about damn time you locked that down." He says with a chuckle.

I nudged him with my elbow.

"That man is the sexiest straight man I have ever seen." He says, fanning his face like he is hot and bothered.

I start laughing at him. He always knows how to make me laugh.

"I think he is worried. He wants me to come stay the night with him tonight." I tell Gavin.

"Or you laid it on him really well, and he doesn't want to be without now." He says.

We both laugh.

"I don't even know what I am doing when it comes to that," I confess.

"Does he, though?" He asks. He looks over at me, and I start to blush.

"Exactly," he says with a smile.

We sit there on the sofa all day. We watch videos on our phones. We talk and laugh, and he has changed my mood entirely by the time I get ready to meet Josh.

"Gavin, I don't know what I would do without you. Thank you for today, for every day. My life is just so much better with you in it." I say to him.

"Sunshine. I love you more than you know. I am always here for you." He kisses the top of my head.

"What is my little vixen going to wear tonight?" He asks with his eyebrows raised.

"This," I tell him, looking down at my attire.

He looks down at my clothing.

"Um, no, you're not. Let's get you ready. Come on." He stands and pulls me up off the sofa. "Girl, that man needs to be stumbling for his words and worship the ground you walk on."

"I don't think he cares what I wear; he would still like me," I tell him.

"You're probably a hundred percent right, but still, it's powerful for a woman when she feels like she looks fierce." He lifts my chin to look at him. "And you, my love, are fierce inside and out. He needs to know who he is messin' with." He tucks a strand of hair back behind my ear.

I pull up to the club where Josh works and lives. I don't know what I was expecting, but this was not what I had pictured in my head. It is a black building with a logo on it at the end of a long driveway lined with trees. Off to the side is a garage with three stalls and stairs on the side that leads up to a door. That must be where Josh stays, I think to myself.

I text Josh to let him know I'm here. I stay in the truck and wait for him to come outside or text me back. I see his motorcycle parked near the garage. I also see other motorcycles parked in random places all over the parking lot.

A man walks out of the black building, looking at me. He starts to walk towards me. I see Josh walking out of the garage and start walking towards me as he wipes his hands on a rag. He is wearing a pair of blue jeans and a white tee with what looks like to be grease on it.

The other person makes it to my truck first. I roll down the window. Beau starts to bark. I tell him to shh as I pet him.

"Hello there, gorgeous. Can I help you with something?"

I smile at him. Josh walks up behind him and pats him on the back.

"She's with me, Marcus."

"Oh, is this your ole' lady Josh?" Marcus asks.

"She sure is." Josh winks at me.

"Well, damn, Josh, she got any older sisters?" He looks back at me. "Or maybe some friends?"

"No older sisters but I don't know about friends. You can ask her once we get inside the clubhouse and out of this heat." Josh says, shaking his head at him and laughing slightly.

Marcus laughs and backs away from my door. Josh opens my door for me. I turn off the truck and get out. Beau jumps out after me.

"What about Beau?" I ask.

"We can take him up to my room, and then we can hang out in the clubhouse and eat." He reaches over to get Beau's leash from me. "If that's okay, of course?" He asks as we start to walk.

"Yeah, that's fine." I smile at him as I adjust the short shorts Gavin talked me into wearing.

Josh notices me pulling on them.

"I like your shorts." He says, smiling.

"Gavin," I tell him with a sigh.

He moves in close to my ear. As he does, he reaches behind me and puts his hand on my butt.

"Tell him thank you for me." He winks at me.

I roll my eyes. I continue to follow him towards the garage. How is Gavin always right?

I walk up the stairs to his place. As I walk in, I notice it's like a studio. It's one large room. There is a bed against one wall, a bathroom to my left, and a small kitchenette, like my room back at Tara's.

"I know it's not much, but it does the job for now." He says it with a self-conscious tone.

I look over at him, watching me. I walk over to him.

"It doesn't matter. We both found places at the last minute. We are just here temporarily. And it's not even that bad." It really wasn't that bad. I walk over to the bed and sit on it. I bounce on a bit, then lie down.

"How does the place look now?" I ask.

He walks over, bends down, and kisses me. I roll to my side and prop up my head with my hand.

“The place has never looked better. I gotta change real quick, then we can go eat.” He says with a smile that gives me butterflies.

I watch him change as I lay there. It smells like him. I took long, deep breaths to breathe his scent in.

After Josh got ready, we put out some food and water for Beau; we walk over to the clubhouse. It looks almost like a bar and restaurant. There were tables everywhere, with a long one in the middle. There was a pool table and dart boards. A bar with some TVs hanging behind it. Pictures, flags, and what looked like motorcycle parts hanging all over the walls.

Josh pulls out a chair for me at a small table. Some people were sitting in different places around the room. I sit down, and he sits across from me.

“They have burgers or burgers tonight.” He says with a chuckle.

“A burger sounds great,” I say with a smile.

“Want something to drink?” He asks as he hops out of his seat.

“Water is fine, thank you.”

“Okay, I’ll be right back.”

I smile at him and look at the photos on the wall I face. There are photos of men and women in leather vests in front of the Ronald McDonald House, and then there are other photos of people looking as if they are working at a food pantry.

“Hey there. I don’t think I was able to introduce myself properly. I’m Marcus, and this here is Maverick.” The two men sit with me in the two empty chairs at the table.

“Hi, I’m Khloe.” I smile at them.

“This here is Josh’s lady,” Marcus says to Maverick.

“Really,” Maverick says.

I look at him, confused about why he would say it like that.

“What’s your last name, Khloe? You from around here?” Marcus asks.

"It's Pierce. I grew up in New Harmony."

"Peirce, huh?" He asks.

"Yup." I smile at them.

Josh comes back to the table with water for me and a beer for him.

"You fellows over here trying to steal my girl?" He hands me my drink.

He pulls up another chair and takes a sip of his drink.

"Nah, we are just talking," Maverick says as he shakes Josh's hand.

"Khloe, what's your father's name?" Marcus asks.

"Thomas. Did you know him?" I ask with curiosity.

He starts to shake his head as he looks up at the ceiling.

"No, I don't think I do." He replies.

"So, you guys do a lot of charity work?" I ask.

"Yes, we do. I think motorcycle clubs have a bad reputation. Most of them do good things for their community. We are one of those clubs. We also run the dirt track out on the south side of town. Have you ever been to one of the races?" Marcus asks.

"I haven't."

"Well, you should come. They are a lot of fun. I think your fella here should race in one. He's pretty good."

I look over at Josh. I smile at him.

"Do you guys race too?" I ask, looking at them.

"We sure do," Maverick says, smiling big, showing his dimples.

"I am going to have to bet against you two. Josh is going to win that race." I wink at Josh.

He smiles before he takes another drink, raising an eyebrow.

"We will have to place some bets on that one then, won't we?" Marcus says, laughing. A lady with long brown hair walks up with two plates.

"Here are your burgers." She sits the plates down.

"We will leave you guys alone to eat. Josh, come see me before you go, would ya." Marcus says.

"Yes, Sir," Josh says as he nods at Marcus.

"I'm Rosa." The lady who brought our food says to me.

"Oh, sorry, where are my manners? Rosa, this is my girlfriend, Khloe." Josh says as he motions towards me.

I like it when he says that. It makes me smile.

"Hello, it's nice to meet you," I tell the lady. I watch her look at Josh. She doesn't look at me.

"We have been fortunate to have Josh here helping out. The clubhouse looks great. And he sure knows his way around that garage, too," she says as she runs her hand from his shoulder down his arm.

I stare at her doing this. It suddenly bothers me. It looks like it was almost intimate. I have not felt this type of jealousy before. It hits me a little hard. Harder than I feel with Blakeleigh sometimes. I shift in my seat, trying not to make a fool of myself.

I look at Josh, watching me. He tilts his head at me.

"Thank you for bringing the food over, Rosa," Josh says to her and looks away from me to her.

She smiles and walks away.

"You, okay?" He reaches over and puts his hand on the fist I'm making on the table.

I was not even aware I was making a fist until he put his hand on mine. I relax my hand.

"I'm not a fan of how she touched you," I say, irritated.

"Yeah, she can get a little touchy. I try to avoid her. She's the chapter's president's wife. Other young guys around here told me about her, too." He holds my hand now that it's relaxed.

"You have nothing to worry about, I promise you. I have such tunnel vision for you, Khloe."

I look into his eyes. I believe him. He has done nothing to show me otherwise.

"We may have to get used to a few things being in a relationship. When I returned to the table, I had to take a few deep breaths with the men surrounding you already. As long as we feel free to talk about anything that comes up and trust one another, we will always be good." He says as he squeezes my hand.

I smile at him and squeeze his hand back. He leans across the table and kisses me.

"Let's eat so we can get out of here and be alone." He says as he winks at me.

We eat and talk a little. Afterward, I head back to his room to take Beau out, and he goes to speak with Marcus. I was walking over behind the garage with Beau when Josh found us. He has a worried look on his face.

"What is it? What did he have to talk to you about?" I ask.

"Um, this is not an easy thing to tell you. Dale, the chapter president, made a police report a while back. Maybe almost a year ago, involving your father's name. Marcus was with him when he did it."

"What do you mean?" I ask, confused.

"I guess some man came around here talking to members, thinking this was a club that is into shady dealings and such. They were looking for someone to hire," he stops talking and looks at the ground.

"To kill my father?" I ask, shocked.

He nods.

"They did not get the man's name but went to the police to report it. They had no clue who your father was. They did look at some mugshot photos at the police station, but it was not the man that came by."

"I could pull up a photo of Seth, maybe from social media. We could show it to him to see if that was the man." I say to Josh as I pull my phone from my back pocket.

"Yeah, we can do that. I also think we should call the detective to let him know so we can investigate it, too." Josh says, still looking down at the ground.

After we get back to his room, we do just that. We call the detective and leave a voicemail. I also found a photo of Seth and send it to Josh to forward to Dale to see if it's him.

"Can we lay down? I feel so tired after today." I say to him as I move up into bed.

"Yeah, I am exhausted today too. You kept me up too late last night." He says jokingly.

"It was not just me," I say defensively.

He snuggles up to me. Beau jumps up and lays at our feet.

Twenty-Four

Good Days, Bad Days

I can't sleep. I gave up trying a while ago. I lie here watching the ceiling fan. It's moving so fast you can't see the blades, but if you really focus on one, you suddenly see that one blade goes around and around. If you try to see them all again, they all become a blur in the shuffle.

I feel like that's my life right now. So many things are happening. It's kind of a blur. I try to focus on something like Katie, my time with Josh, Gavin, or my parents, but it all becomes a whirlwind. I look over at Josh sleeping next to me. Suppose I can focus on just being in the moment. Concentrating on the day at that moment, I feel like my life is starting to spin out of control.

I have so much guilt inside me. For so many things, for so many people. I feel bad for having good days, laughing, and enjoying some of the pleasures in life. I should only have bad days because I don't have my parents or Katie with me. I have caused pain to others directly or indirectly. In times like this, my mind will just not stop, and it's a silent torture at times.

The sunlight is coming through the windows. I roll over towards Josh. Beau gets down off the bed and starts to whine a little. He runs out of the room and then back in with a leash in his mouth. I sigh, knowing he has to go out, but I can't crawl over Josh and not wake him up to take him out. Josh starts to move and make noises.

"Okay, Beau, I'll take you." He says with his back to me.

Maybe he doesn't realize I am awake.

"I can take him," I say.

He turns over in bed to face me.

"No, babe, you need to try to go back to sleep. I know you haven't slept much. I got him. Come on, Beau, let's go." He stands up in only his boxers.

I watch as he puts on a pair of sweatpants and a shirt over his head.

As they head out the door, I get up. I know I will not be able to go back to sleep. I walk into the kitchen to see if he has coffee or anything with caffeine. I do see a small coffee pot. I am looking in the cabinets for coffee when they come back.

"I thought you would be back asleep by now." He says.

"I can't sleep. I'm sorry." I say, feeling bad.

He walks over to me, jumps up, and sits on the counter where I'm looking for coffee.

"I was going to make us some coffee. Do you have any?" I ask.

"I have some in the freezer since I don't make it at home often."

I turn and go to the refrigerator. Thinking to myself how weird it is to keep it in there.

"Hey, you know what," he says as he jumps off the counter and approaches me. "How about we get some breakfast and eat by the river? Since I don't think I can convince you to return to bed." He moves the hair out of my face. I look into his eyes.

"I mean, I never said you couldn't convince me," I say, putting my arms around his shoulders and my hands on his neck. I move my fingertips into his hair.

"Well, in that case, I want both," he says, picking me up and carrying me back to the bed.

He lays me down on the bed. He straddles me, holding his weight off me with his hands and knees on the side of me. He moves his mouth down to my waiting lips. As soon as he kisses me, I reach up and start pulling on his shirt to pull it over his head.

Our kiss broke long enough to pull his shirt off him. I run my hands down his back, feeling all the muscles. He moves his lips from mine. He starts to kiss my neck, giving me chills. I could feel his hand moving up my thigh, then to my shirt, pulling it up. I grab the shirt and pull it the rest of the way off.

He moves his mouth down to my breasts while pulling the bra down, exposing my nipple. The feeling of the cooler air makes my nipple harden. He flicks one with his tongue before putting it in his mouth. The sensation takes me by surprise. I'm getting lost in his touch, absorbing how he is making my body feel as I try to pay attention to where his hands and mouth are on my body.

Time stops. The world stops when I am with him. He consumes my mind and body. He is quickly becoming my favorite distraction. Who am I kidding? He is so much more to me than a distraction. I bring my hand to my head. My thoughts are starting to race. I take a deep breath and close my eyes.

My eyes pop open with a surprising sensation of his mouth between my legs. I look down at him. He is looking up at me. He lifts his head just a little, grabs the sides of my panties, and starts to pull them down my legs.

"You need to get out of that head of yours." He says. He licks me.

My hips involuntarily move off the bed a little towards his mouth.

"Close your eyes and just feel what I am about to do. Keep those thoughts here with me." He says in a husky whisper.

He reaches for one of my hands and intertwines his fingers with mine. He slides a finger from the other hand inside me and brings his mouth back down to my clit. He works his fingers and mouth in a way I have never felt. He has my whole body starting to buck. I squeeze the hand he is holding tighter. My other is grabbing the sheets on the bed.

My whole body feels relaxed and tense at the same time. I can feel the sensation all the way to my toes. He moves away from me for a quick second before I feel him push against me to enter me. That sensation takes me over the edge. I can no longer keep quiet. I open my eyes. I want to watch him. He was standing on the floor at the edge of the bed. He's holding my legs, as he moves in and out of me. Sometimes, he would go harder and faster, then slow back down.

I am completely out of body. I don't even feel like myself when he finishes. He lays down next to me, smiling.

"Are you proud of yourself?" I ask him as I regain control of my body and limbs, coming back down from the high.

He starts to chuckle.

"Damn, proud. But also, on my own rush over here." He says as he rolls over and kisses me.

"I will ruin you, where you will only want me," he says confidently.

"After that, I believe you." I smile at him and kiss him.

"Okay, where is this breakfast? I am starving now." I say as I try to get up but fall back down. My body is still weak.

He proudly laughs.

We get some food and coffee and ride down to the river. We sit on a grass bank, eating and talking. It's absolutely a perfect day I think to myself. I lay my head on him as we ride back. He holds my leg as he drives. I just take in the moment. I can get used to this. I would be happy if this was my life. One day, I want just this, none of the other drama.

We pull back into the clubhouse. He pulls in near my truck.

"Josh," I say as his back is turned to me.

He turns and looks at me. I just stare at him for a moment. I smile as I grab his hand. I just want to tell him I am starting to have stronger feelings for him. I'm not able to say the words, though. I plead with him with my eyes. He moves the hand I'm holding to his lips and kisses it.

"Me too, baby," he says to me. He pulls me into him. He wraps his arms around me.

"I'm not going anywhere. I feel the same. We don't have to rush it, but I think we are both on the same page with our feelings. I know it is hard to talk about it with all that is happening." He says as he kisses my cheek.

"I am yours, as long as you want me." He says to me before he kisses my lips.

I somehow feel that I do not deserve this man. But I will do all I can to keep him.

"I gotta get Beau and go before I'm late for work," I say when he pulls away from our kiss.

"Okay, will you let me know how the meeting with the attorney goes?" He asks.

"Of course, I will call you right after." I smile at him.

I rush home to get ready for my short shift at the café. Today is my last day of training. I will be on longer shifts after today. I feel bad for leaving Beau, but he seems to be exhausted. He is snoring on the sofa as I get ready to walk out the door. I smile at him and close the door softly to avoid disturbing him.

I see Gavin and Blakeleigh behind the counter dancing when I walk into the café. As soon as they see me, they start hollering. I begin to dance my way over to them.

"Where were you this morning?" Gavin asks as he raises an eyebrow.

I just smile at them.

"My girl is gonna make him want to marry her. She is putting it on him in a bad way," Gavin says as he starts twerking.

I feel my face and ears turning red. I hide my face in my hands.

"Girl, I must know. Is he as good as he looks?" Blakeleigh asks.

"Better," I reply.

Blakeleigh starts to fan her face.

Carrie walks in from the kitchen.

"Okay, you three, start doing something productive," she says as she chuckles.

Just then, we have a small group walk into the café, and we all get to work.

Gavin and I were walking through and wiping tables off near the end of my shift. I was going through the things I need to remember to go over with the attorney. Gavin has been quiet since I told him about someone coming to the clubhouse asking about harming my dad.

"You're going to make me feel nervous if you don't start talking. You are always talking, Gavin. What are you thinking?" I ask, feeling the panic coming.

"I wonder if it was Jared who went to the clubhouse." I stop cleaning the table and stand up straight.

"How crazy is my life that it could have been. I have not heard back from the Detective yet or the person who met with them to see if it was Seth." I say.

"What if your dad was laundering money for the cartel?" He says suspiciously.

"Gavin!" I yell.

"What? I mean, at this point, you could tell me some crazy stuff, and I would probably believe you. Your life is like a TV show." He says.

"I miss my old simple life," I say with a sigh. I put the rag down and sit at one of the tables.

"I know you do. But there are many things you have to be thankful for in life." He comes over and kisses the top of my head. "You better get your fierce face on and get to that appointment. It's time for you to go. Don't forget your files in the back."

I pull out my phone and look at the time. I stand up.

"I'll text you after. Love you." I say, rushing.

He makes a heart shape with his hands and blows me an air kiss.

I cut through the back alley to the back street. As I'm walking, I call the Detective again.

"Detective Graham." He answers.

"Hello, this is Khloe Pierce. I was just wondering if you found out about that information I left on your voicemail?" I ask.

"I am looking into it. I do not have all the information yet to give you any answers at this moment. We picked up Mr. Mates last night. He is in our custody."

I take a long breath and stop walking, standing in front of the law office.

"Okay, thank you for letting me know. Maybe it could have been Jared Coffman who went to the motorcycle club. If you could let me know if you find anything out." I say as I turn and see a white car parked along the curb. I watch an arm go out the car's window with a cigarette.

"Also, did you find out about the white car? I think there is a white car following me." I stare at the car, waiting for him to answer me. Silently praying, he says it's them.

"I did ask around about that, and we have no unmarked white cars at this station. We will have more patrol where you live, but they will be in regular marked police cars."

My heart sinks as I look at them staring back at me.

"Ms. Pierce, the FBI, is also in on this case due to money laundering. I can check with them as well. If you do see someone following, please do not engage with them. Can you get a plate for me so I can run it?" He asks.

"Yeah, I will try to get that for you. Thank you." I tell him.

The call ends. I look at the car, there's no front plate. I need to get behind them. I look at my phone and see it's time for my appointment. I walk into the office.

"Khloe. It's so great to see you again. I hope your day is going well." Naomi says, all cheery.

I turn to look out the window to see if the car is still there before turning to face her.

"Hello, Naomi. Yes, it has been good, thank you." I say, trying to slow down my breathing.

"Here, let me lead you to the conference room. Would you like anything to drink?" She asks.

"No, I'm fine, thank you." I start to follow her.

She opens a door to a room with a glass interior wall. There is a long table in the center of the room and tall leather desk chairs all around it. There are black and white photos on the walls of different places in town. I look at the one of the river.

"She will be with you in a moment, Khloe."

I turn and nod at her, watch her close the door, and walk back down the hall through the glass.

I sit in one of the chairs at the side of the table. I lay my papers on the table. I close my eyes and think of Katie. It has been so long since I've seen her. I can't wait to tell her about this meeting. I know this is going to work. I feel hopeful.

"Ms. Pierce?"

I turn to look behind me. A woman walks into the room with a strong presence. She has jet-black hair that is pulled up and away from her face. She is wearing a white button-up blouse with black slacks. I can hear her heels tap on the floor as she walks closer to me. She extends her hand to me; I stand and shake her hand, suddenly feeling like a child in her presence.

"Hello, Ms. Delgado; please call me Khloe."

"Hello, Khloe; it is nice to meet you. You can call me Shila. Naomi has wonderful things to say about you. Please take a seat." She motions towards the chair.

She sits in the chair at the head of the table. She sits her notebook down. I sit down to her left and move closer to the table.

"Khloe, how can I assist you? I hope you don't mind that Naomi has filled me in a little on some of your concerns and your parents' passing. My condolences."

"Thank you." I say as I look down.

"I knew your parents. I'm not sure if you knew that or not. I did some work with your father." She says.

"I did not. I am finding out pretty much everyone knew my parents in town." I say with a chuckle.

"That is how it is around here." She softly chuckles.

"I am not sure if you knew, but we didn't have any family or anywhere to go when my parents died. So, we went into the system, so to speak. I was living in a foster home, and well, things did not go well there." I look down and away from her eyes.

"Khloe, I already know all that information. I did my research before you came in today. I also know that is not true. I wrote your parents will for them. We had clear orders in there if there was something to happen to both your parents. What my confusion is, is why that was not followed for you and your sister Katie."

I look at her with so much confusion. I pull out the papers that include my parents will. I now wish I had read through all the information. I slide the papers to her.

"This will?" I ask.

She looks at it for what feels like forever.

"This is the one." She puts it down in front of me and points to a section. "See here. You girls were supposed to go live with Tara E. Jenkins in Southern Shores, North Carolina."

I hear what she says. I stare at the name on the paper. The room spins a little. I stand up and start to pace.

"How did my parents know Tara? We never even vacationed on the coast?" I ask, I pace more while I talk out loud, trying to wrap my mind around all this. I sit back down.

"Did they tell you why they chose Tara? I ended up living with Tara after her daughter Dee pulled some strings for me to go there. I'm sorry, but I have so many questions and am so confused right now."I say, none of this makes any sense.

"I actually do know why they picked this home for you girls. I remember they told me a story about a girl they were friends in college. That girl grew up in that home, and your parents remembered her all these years later. When we wrote this will, we called Tara Jenkins, and she said she was still taking girls in the home. She stated that her family would take over the home, so it would always be available for girls to come and live. Your parents did not know the woman running this home. Your parents donated to that home every year after we added her to this will." She says with a soft smile.

"I'm sorry, but I am just slightly shocked by this information. I ended up where they wanted." I feel the tears welling up in my eyes.

She hands me a tissue.

"Thank you." I tell her as I take the tissue and wipe under my eyes.

"I also wrote your trust. That was not done very long ago. Your parents wanted it done very quickly, which I thought was odd at the time with the urgency. It was about a year or so ago now. That money should have started for you by now."

"It has thank you."

"Naomi was the one to send that info to the Southern Shores address for me. We just assumed you both were there. I was unaware your sister was not with you." She says.

"So, since my sister is supposed to be there now, this adoption thing should be easy to stop, right?" I ask.

"I can petition the court on this matter. I will have to get back to you on everything. We could file for you to have guardianship, too, though. If we are unable to get the adaption stopped."

"Please, thank you. I hope this can be worked out quickly now." I say optimistically.

"I think we can get this all cleared up." She says as she smiles at me.

"I have these other papers my parents left me. Can you help me understand them?" I slide them over to her.

"Can you give me a little time? I can go through them, and we can meet again next week after I put in the petition." She asks.

"Yes, of course. Did you know Seth Mates was arrested? That should help our case, right?" I say.

"Definitely." She says as she writes something down in her notebook.

"Thank you. It means so much to me. How much do I owe you for this?" I ask.

"Nothing. I will be helping you pro bono. I knew your parents. I will help you get all these legal matters worked out." She says as she puts her hand on mine and gives a little squeeze.

We both stand up, and I can't help it; I hug her. She softly hugs me back. I walk out of the room with a new excitement. I stop and hug Naomi, too, and kiss her cheek.

"Thank you!" I tell her.

"I will call you for your next appointment. I am so happy it will work out. I always had faith it would." She says, giving me a warm smile.

I walk out of the office feeling so happy and light. Weight has been lifted off my shoulders. I don't know how this worked out, but it's crazy. I was where my parents wanted the whole time, and now Katie will be too. Everything is working out just as planned. I check the street and start to walk back to the alley. The white car is gone. I pull out my phone to text Josh.

Khloe: The attorney visit was amazing. I cannot wait to tell you everything. Want to go Ride or hang out tonight?

Josh: I can be there in an hour. Looking forward to hearing all about it.

I text Gavin.

Khloe: You will not even believe how great the appointment with the attorney went. I'm going out with Josh tonight btw.

Gavin: Yay! Call me tomorrow. Take it easy on that man, at least feed him.

Khloe: You know I can't cook.

Gavin: I never said food girl.

Khloe: OMG! LOL!

Gavin: Love you sunshine.

Khloe: Love you.

I'm still laughing and rolling my eyes as I call Dee. It went to voicemail.

"Hey Dee, it's Khloe. When you get this, please call me. I met with Ms. Delgado. You will not believe me when I tell you what I found out. It's the most amazing news. I have so many questions for you. Talk to you soon. Bye"

I take my stairs two at a time. I go inside, love on Beau, and take him for a walk with a pep in step that I have not felt in a long time.

Twenty-Five

Faded

It's been a couple of days since I met with the attorney. I have the whole day off. I sit on the sofa with Beau.

"What should we do today, fella?" I scratch his belly as he rolls over.

I continue to pet him as I look outside. Maybe we can go to the river. I text Gavin to see what he is doing today. I know he has the day off, too. I know Josh is working until later this afternoon.

I think back to the conversation I had with Gavin yesterday. He leaves in a few weeks to attend the University of Miami. He is so excited he has already started to pack. I am going to miss him so much.

I pick up my phone as it rings. I didn't look, assuming it was Gavin.

"Hello."

"Khloe?" The voice was small and almost a whisper.

"Sidney?" I pull the phone away from my ear to confirm it was Sidney calling me. I haven't heard her voice in a little while.

"Yeah, It's me, Khloe." She pauses.

I hear sobs come through the phone. I sit up straight on the sofa and begin to stand up. I start to feel the anxiety take over.

"Sidney, what is it? Is the baby okay? Are you okay?" I ask frantically.

"It's Tara." She pauses again. "She died early this morning."

I stand there numb. I know Sidney was still talking and saying something about a blood clot. But none of it is registering with me. I'm lost in my internal hell at the moment.

She's gone. The guilt hits me hard. This is my fault. I instantly see Katie's face. Did I just lose Katie, too? Everyone I care about leaves. I have been surrounded by death so much this last year.

"Khloe, the service is in three days. If you can make it, it would mean a lot to all of us."

"I will be there," I whisper.

"Love you, Khloe."

"Love you, Sidney." I end the call.

I don't know how long I sit there on the floor. I cry until I have no more tears. I must have fallen asleep because I woke up to someone knocking on my door. I slowly get up and go to the door.

"Girl, I know you did not text me, but then ghost me," Gavin says dramatically.

I just stand there. He looks at me, and the smile fades from his face.

"What happened, sunshine? If he hurt, you..." I shake my head no.

"Tara died."

He brings his hand to his mouth. He steps into the doorway and wraps me in his arms. I hold on to him and cry more.

Gavin sits with me and lets me cry, listening to me rambling on and on as he strokes my hair. He is trying to reassure me that the Katie thing would still work out and that I had nothing to do with Tara's death. But I literally brought Linda to her door. We both look up at the sound of a motorcycle.

"Did you text him?" I ask him.

"I did not." He says.

Beau got up as soon as he heard him coming up the stairs. He's waiting at the door for him when he opens the door. Josh walks into the room and sees us sitting there on the sofa. He sits his helmet down and walks over to us. He kneels in front of me.

"I am so sorry, Khloe. Nicole called me and told me." He says softly.

I wrap my arms around him. He hugs me back tightly. I move over and make room for him to sit on the sofa with us. I rest my head on Josh's shoulder.

I sit there with some of the most important people in my life. They are both here when I need them. They show up for me every time and time again. I need them both for something else right now. I need them to be there for me to get through this.

"Will you both go to North Carolina with me for the service?" I watch Gavin and Josh look at one another.

"We will both be there for you," Josh says.

"I could use a vacation, to be honest; although this is not ideal, you know I will make this trip a lot less sad," Gavin says.

I watch Josh smile just a little and put his head down to hide it.

"Gavin," I say, not even surprised, really.

"You know I am right." He says matter-of-factly.

"I will book the flights for us," I tell them. "We should probably try to leave tomorrow. Can you call Carrie to get our schedules taken care of? And do you think Blakeleigh would keep Beau?" I ask Gavin.

"I will get all the small details worked out. I'm going to go and start on all that. I think you are in good hands for tonight." Gavin says as he winks at Josh.

"Okay, we will text you the times." I say.

He kisses my head and stands up to leave. He opens the door.

"Gavin, thank you." I tell him.

"Love you, sunshine." Then he closes the door.

"How about we go take Beau for a walk?" Josh suggests.

Beau gets up and goes to sit by the door.

We walk in silence. Josh holds my hand and on to Beau's leash with the other hand. We walk down through downtown towards a grassy area. There's a small bench, and we sit down, as Beau sniffs around as far as his leash would reach.

I cross my leg over the other and lean towards Josh. I rest my head on his shoulder, and he rest his hand on my thigh.

"I wasn't as close to Tara as you were. But I have known her my whole life, I feel. She was always at local gatherings, and I think we went to a few of the new girl welcome parties when my mom was around. I don't feel the pain that you are feeling. I am sorry, hon. Is there anything I can do?" He turns just a little and kisses my forehead while he squeezes my leg softly.

"Going back with me and being here is all I could ask for." I say lovingly.

"I cannot think of any place I would rather be." He replies.

I pull out my phone to look at flights.

"I would like to pay for my own." He says as he watches me.

"No, I got it." I say as he turns to face me.

"I know I don't have much right now, but I want to show you at least, that I can take care of us. I will work so hard to build a life for us." He lifts my chin with his finger and kisses me.

"You know I will not have to worry about money unless I am just foolish with it." I tell him to hopefully help with his worries.

"I was raised that you work and take care of your family, and I have every intention of doing just that. I know your parents were very smart when it came to finances, and I see that in you, too. Just think about all you can do with that money though. You can attend college without worry and focus on your studies. You can give to charities and back to your community, like your family did. I want to be like that, too. I admire them for what they did, giving to Tara all those years." He says with admiration.

I feel the tears well up in my eyes.

"Sometimes the most amazing people are taken from us too soon. I think there is a higher power at work. Although we see no reason for it, I believe everything happens for a reason. I think with my mom, she was just in so much pain every day, fighting for us at the end. I saw it in her eyes. She was tired. She had no fight left in her. She was fighting for us. It helped to know she was no longer suffering."

I look at this man before me. The strongest feeling is that, somehow, he is meant to be in my life. In a weird way, maybe I am grateful for my past, as it led me to him. I reach up and hold his face in my hands. I kiss him with all the love I could give him in that kiss. I know with everything in me, I am falling in love with him.

Later that night, I follow Josh back to his place so he could pack for tomorrow's trip and leave his bike there. I wait in the truck as he ran to get his things. There is a light tap on the driver's side window. I look over and see Marcus with another man standing there. Marcus flashes me a smile, and I roll down the window.

"Hello, beautiful," Marcus says, and he winks at me.

"Hey, Marcus. How are you?" I smile back at them.

"I'm good, sweetheart; this here is Dale, the chapter president. I wanted to bring him over here to introduce you." Marcus says.

"Hello," Dale says as he puts his hand through the open window to shake mine.

"I know Josh told you about a man coming here askin' about your pops. Dale, here is the one who talked to him." Marcus says.

"He told me his name was Jack, and no last name was given. Do you know anyone by that name? Honestly, he probably used an alias. I looked at the photos that Josh sent over. That's not the guy. The man was younger and the scruffy type. I gave him an earful after I found out what he wanted. To think we were a club like that insulted me and the guys." Dale retorts.

"I'm sorry they thought that I don't know any Jacks," I say, putting my head down. To think someone wanted to hurt my dad that bad.

I look up and see Josh walking back towards us. The men back up from the truck. Josh walks to the driver's side.

"Hey Josh, we will see you when you get back. Don't forget we have that race coming up." Marcus says.

"Oh, I haven't forgotten. I will be there to show you, old fellas, how it's done." Josh says with sarcasm in his voice.

They all start to laugh and slap Josh's back. He gets in the truck as I slid over to the middle of the seat.

"Should I be worried about this race?" I ask him as we start to drive off.

"No, babe. I'll be safe." He reaches over, puts his hand on my thigh, and squeezes it.

Twenty-Six

Southern Shores

We pull up to Gavin's house early in the morning. I get out with Beau. I have been giving him extra love all morning. I feel bad leaving him, although I know he will be in good hands. Josh grabs both our backpacks.

Beau runs straight to the door as soon as Blakeleigh opens it. She bends down, pets Beau, and lets him in the house.

"Blakeleigh, thank you for taking us to the airport and watching Beau for me." I say thankfully.

"Oh, don't sweat it. I'm excited to have Beau. I may not give him back." She lets out a little laugh.

"Where's Gavin?" I ask her.

"Oh, he's coming." She says with a laugh.

She opens the trunk of her car. Josh puts the backpacks in there and stands on the side of the car next to me. Gavin comes out the door, pulling a giant suitcase and bumping it into everything. He is wearing a neck pillow and has a sleeping mask on, slid up on his forehead. I look over and see Josh chuckle and shake his head before he walks to help Gavin with his suitcase.

"Gavin, we will be back in three days. Why do you need so much stuff?" I ask.

He looks at me and puts his pointer finger up at me.

"First off, I don't know what I will need, what vibe it will be there, if I'm swimming, tanning, or if there will be humidity. There is a lot you need when there are so many unknowns."

I start to laugh, and I see Josh smiling as he opens my door so I can get in the backseat with him.

We have an uneventful flight and layover. Gavin slept most of the time. Josh's dad is picking us up from the airport. We walk out of the airport, and the heat hits us. It's warm in Indiana, but not like the South. The heat and humidity are just different. I look over at Gavin.

"I told you. I know more than just how to be a passenger princess." He says as he starts to fan his face with his sleeping mask. I laugh as we wait on the sidewalk outside the door. Josh is on the phone with his dad.

"I know we are here to lay your dear friend to rest, but girl, I have been needing a little vacation. So can we at least go to the beach once while we are here?" He pleads.

"I think we can do that." I smile at him. He has no idea what the house is on the beach.

Mr. Walker pulls up in Nicole's car. I look and see Nicole in the front seat with him. I cannot help it, but it makes me smile. As soon as they stop, she jumps out and hugs me.

"Khloe! I have missed you." She says excitedly.

"I have missed you too." I genuinely mean that. I sort of forgot how much of a friend she has been to me.

"Nicole this is my best friend from home, Gavin. Gavin, this is

Nicole." Gavin is looking at her, almost seeing if she measures up.

Nicole did not notice and went over to him and hugged him, too. I see him hug her back and smile.

"What, no hug for me?" Josh says.

Nicole turns to Josh. She walks up to him and hits him on the shoulder, then smiles at him before giving him a hug.

"Well, kids, let's get out of here before they ask me to move my car." Mr. Walker says.

Josh puts all the bags in the trunk. Then walks to open the car door for me.

"Thank you, Mr. Walker, for taking the time today to pick us up." I tell him.

"Please call me Ed, sweetie. And not a problem at all. The house is so quiet with Josh gone. I sure have missed you, son." He tells Josh.

"Awe, Dad, don't go getting all emotional. How's the new place?" Josh asks.

"It's good. Close to everyone, pretty much across the street from your cousins." Ed says.

Nicole turns around in the front seat and looks back at us, all crammed in the back seat.

"Too close if you ask me. Josh will still be around to be a pain in the ass." She sticks her tongue out at him.

"Nicole, watch your mouth," Ed says, chuckling.

Josh grabs my hand and squeezes it. Nicole watches the motion, then looks back up at me. I give her a little smile. She then turns back to face forward. Is she upset? Does she even know we are together? I get a little lost in my worried thoughts over our relationship, and I didn't notice his dad was talking to me. Josh nudges me.

"I'm sorry, I must be tired. Can you repeat that?" I ask him.

"Do you know where you guys are staying while you are in town?" Ed asks.

"I was not able to get in touch with Dee, but I am assuming I will be there at the house, at Tara's house," I tell him. Saying her name out loud has a pinch in my heart.

The car went quiet for a moment.

"I know Dee has been busy. I ran into her yesterday. She looked tired. I think she said she was staying with Jake. From what I heard around, she has not been back to the house since her mom passed. That one girl is still there, though. I'm sorry, but I do not remember her name." Ed says.

"Danielle?" I ask.

"That could be it. I'm sorry, sweetie, I am not good with names. I probably would've forgotten yours if I had not heard everything about you whenever I talk to Josh." Ed says, laughing a little.

Josh reaches up and squeezes his dad's shoulders.

"Thanks, pops," Josh says, chuckling but blushing a little.

His dad starts to laugh harder. He has the same laugh Josh did when he really laughs hard. I blush and look down. Gavin nudges me. I look over at him. He winks at me and smiles. He makes the motion of putting a ring on a finger. I roll my eyes at him. It feels good somehow, the banter with everyone in the car. It makes me feel like I'm at home.

"In all seriousness, if you cannot stay at Tara's, you are all welcome to stay with Josh and me at the new house." Ed offers.

"Or you can stay with me." Nicole chimes in.

"Thank you, both of you," I say.

I take out my phone and text Danielle again to see if she is home. She replies that she is. I check to see if Dee has texted me back yet, but still nothing. She has ghosted me for days. I keep thinking it's just because of what is going on. Josh has told me to give her some time. I just hope she doesn't hate me for what happened.

I look out the window as we pass the landmarks I remember. Josh turns and puts his face in my hair near my ear.

"Welcome home, baby." He whispers.

I let that sink in. I'm torn between two places. Here and back, where I grew up. I always assumed Katie and I would come back to Tara's. Now, that may not be an option. Where will I go? Will Katie even want to come here? Would Josh be willing to stay up north with me? So many questions.

We pull up in front of the house. I look at the sign on the edge of the yard. Jenkins Fresh Start in dark blue letters with a whitewash background. It's the same sign that has always been there, but looks different now. Will someone buy it and take it down?

I look over at Gavin's reaction. It makes me smile. It was my reaction the first time I saw it, too. Josh opens the car door once we stop, he puts his hand out to help me out. I take his hand. He gets our bags for us.

"Do you want me to come with you? He asks me.

"No, spend some time with your dad. I think he missed you." I stand on my toes and kiss him. I walk over to the driver's side door.

"Thank you again, Ed. I will see you soon, I'm sure. Nicole, text me." I tell her.

His dad reaches out the window, grabs my hand, and squeezes it with a little smile. Nicole grins but faces forward not looking at me.

Josh gets back in the car. I watch them drive away. I turn to Gavin. He was still staring at the house.

"You lived here?" He asks.

"I did." I did, smiling.

"Damn girl, I wouldn't want to go back to New Harmony either." He says.

"It's right on the beach, too," I tell him.

"I cannot wait. I need a beach day in my life." He says with a sigh.

"We can go down there here in a little while. That's exactly what I did when I first got here." I think back to that night.

The night I met Oliver. I haven't thought of him in a while. I bet he is sad with all this going on. He just lost his aunt. My heart starts to hurt for him a little. I also know I will probably see him soon. I take a deep breath.

"Let's go," I say, walking up the walkway to the front porch.

I knock on the door. There's no answer. I ring the doorbell. I try to look into the windows. I see Danielle's car parked next to the house. I get my phone out, then the door opens. I see Danielle standing there with a swollen red face. As soon as our eyes meet, she rushes to me, and we wrap our arms around one another.

"Danielle, this is my best friend from back home, Gavin," I say, hugging her.

She lets me go and turns to Gavin while wiping her face. I have never seen her so broken. She is always full of life. It breaks my heart to see her like this.

"Hey Gavin. Thank you for coming." She says as her voice cracks a little.

"I am so sorry for your loss," Gavin says as he puts his hand on his chest.

She is affecting him, too. I can see it on his face.

"Come on in. It's just me here." She says.

We walk into the foyer. Everything looks the same. I sit my bag down on the floor near the staircase. We follow Danielle into the kitchen. She goes to get a bottle of water for everyone. She hands Gavin and me one. I stare at the back door. The door where Linda caught back up to me. I feel the pain in the pit of my stomach.

"Thank you," Gavin says.

I keep looking at the door.

"Khloe? You, okay?" Gavin asks.

I turn to see they are both staring at me.

"Yeah, sorry, I'm fine." I sit at the little table.

"Have you seen Dee? I have been trying to get in touch with her, but I have had no reply." I ask Danielle.

"She lost her phone with all this craziness. You can text Jake to get in touch with her." She says.

"Will you excuse me? I am going to try and call her." I pull out my phone, I walk back to the dining room area as the phone starts to ring.

"Hello?" Jake answers.

"Jake? It's Khloe."

"Oh, hey, Khloe. Everything okay?" He asks.

"Yes, I'm in town, over at Tara's. I found out the news from Sidney. I came back as soon as I could for the service." I tell him.

"That will mean so much to Dee. She's asleep right now. I can have her call you, or if you want, we can come by as soon as she wakes up. I hate to wake her up; she's just not sleeping, and she keeps going." He says concerned.

"Yeah, don't wake her. That's fine I will see you both when you get here. Hey Jake, it's good to hear your voice." I tell him. I've missed him.

"You too, Khloe. We have missed you around here." He says before ending the call.

I walk into the living room and look at the sofa. I think back to sitting there with Lucas. How are there more memories in this house than back home? I feel like my whole life is here, even though I was not here that long.

"You get in touch with her?" Danielle asks.

"I did. She's sleeping. They will come by later." I tell her. "Danielle, I am so sorry about Lucas. I know you would have been there if you could have."

She sits down on the sofa. I sit down next to her.

"It's just so much so close together. I am having a hard time here. I am supposed to be happy right now, and instead, I'm wandering around this house all alone, losing my mind." She says.

I reach over and hold her hand.

"I got accepted to an art school in New York City. When you called me about Lucas, I was packing up to go out there. Now, this is all just too much." She says sniffling.

I squeeze her hand. It was one of those times I felt I just needed to listen to her. She did not need a reply.

"I'm sorry, you two must be exhausted. I have to run out anyways." She puts her hand on top of mine, holding hers. "I will see you tonight." She says.

"Yes, we will be here. Would it be okay if Gavin takes one of the empty rooms for a few days?"

"I don't see why not," she says with a grin. She gets up and walks out of the room.

I walk back into the kitchen, but Gavin is not there. I look out the back window over the sink and see him outside. I walk out to him, standing on the beach. I stand next to him and cross my arms over my chest. I look out over the ocean and watch the waves come in.

"I could get used to this." He says.

"Yeah, me too," I reply.

Twenty-Seven

Rumors

I show Gavin around the house and where he will be staying when I hear the door open.

"Hello, Khloe?"

I turn and start to go down the stairs. Dee and Jake are standing there in the entryway. I begin to go down the stairs at a faster pace. I run into her arms. Somehow, she comforts me when I should be doing that for her. She rubs my hair back as I let tears fall.

"Dee, I am so sorry," I say.

"Thank you. I know you will miss her too. We all will." She says in a soft voice.

"I know the pain of losing your mom," I tell her. Tears come harder.

"I know, sweetheart." She pulls back to look at me. "But we will always have one another." She says.

I nodded in agreement. I see Jake looking up the stairs. I turn to see Gavin waiting at the top of the staircase.

"Oh, this is Gavin, my very best friend from back home. He traveled here with me and Josh. I hope it's okay that I said he could stay here in one of the empty rooms." I say, hoping it's okay.

"Of course. I have been having a hard time being here. I have been staying with Jake." Dee says.

I smile. It warms my heart to see them together. Gavin came down the stairs.

"It's nice to meet you, Gavin. I wish it were better circumstances," Dee says.

"Same here. I am sorry for your loss to the both of you." He give them a small grin and puts his hand on his chest.

"Why don't we have a seat," Jake says.

We all follow him into the living room.

"We have missed you around the restaurant. Mindy is driving me crazy," Jake says as he chuckles.

"How is Mindy? I miss you all so much." I ask.

"She's good. I'm sure you will see her tomorrow." He looks down.

"Do you need me to do anything? We can help with anything." I say as I look at Gavin.

"No, everything has been taken care of. Mom had this all planned out, I guess. There really is not much for us to do." Dee says.

I reach over and put my hand on hers and hold it.

"Dee, I found out my parents knew someone who stayed here. They met her in college. They donated to Tara for years. Would you know anything about that? My parents wanted Katie and I to stay here if something happened to them. I would love to know who it was they knew." I plead.

"We had a lot of donations over the years. I can look through the records to see if they were not anonymous. What college did your parents go to?" Dee asks.

"University of Pennsylvania," I tell her.

"It had to be Andi. She got a scholarship there when I was starting high school. Her real name is not Andi, but that's just what everyone called her. I will have to go back through records to see if I can get her information." She turns and squeezes my hands. "You were meant to be here." She says with a smile.

"Are you going to be taking over?" I gave her a little smile. All I can think about is Katie. If the house is still running, then we should be able to get Katie here with no issues.

"I really don't know. It was never my dream. It was my mom's. Danielle will be leaving soon, and then it will just be a big ole' empty house. I don't think I have it in me to do what my mom did." She says sadly.

She looks down and pulls her hands away from me. I knew what she was telling me at that moment. Panic was overcoming me. I was trying to sort out the racing thoughts in my head. I may not be as sure as I thought I was at getting Katie. I stand up and walk over to the big window. I turn back towards them.

"Are you going to sell the home?" I ask.

"Most likely, I will in time. It will take time to go through everything."Dee says as she turns to look at me.

"Can you offer me the opportunity to see if I could purchase it before you list it? I would need to figure out if I could even afford it." I ask.

"Of course. I will let you know first." She says.

I let out a sigh of relief. I turn back to the window. Can I even afford this place? I need to try. Katie was supposed to be here. I want to make that happen. Gavin came to stand next to me. In hushed tones, he starts to talk to me.

"Girl, this place will be so expensive. How can you afford this?" He questions me.

"I have to try." I shrug my shoulders.

"Well, if you find a way, I get the room on the left twice a year." He puts his arm around my shoulders.

Later that evening, Josh came by to pick us up for dinner at Nicole's house. On the way over, I thought back to how Nicole had acted in the car when she had seen Josh touching me. It was making me a little uneasy. Maybe she doesn't want me with her cousin.

Josh must sense my tension as he drives. He reaches over and puts his hand on my thigh.

"You, okay?" He asks.

I just turn and smile at him with a little nod.

We pull up to the house. Gavin gets out and starts taking selfies with the beach in the background. Nicole's house is closer to the water than Tara's. Josh walks over to my side of the car. He puts his arm on the car in front of me, stopping me from walking or moving toward the house.

"Let's do a little check-in. What's wrong? Do not say everything is fine. Trust me when I say I know it's something."He says in hushed tones for only me to hear. He takes his other hand and caresses the side of my face as I look at him. I take a deep breath.

"Well, Dee is going to sell the house. I asked her to tell me first. And I think Nicole hates that we are together, so I am super anxious to walk into that house right now." I tell him.

He removes his arm from the car and steps closer to me. His body against mine, pushing my back into the car a little. He puts his hands on both sides of my face and holds my face so that I must look up at him. He brings his face close to mine.

"First off, I do not care what Nicole thinks of us being together. I am not going to base my decisions on someone else. You are mine, and I am yours. That is what matters. All that other noise from others is just that, noise. We are the music, the song. They can either listen to it with us, or we will play it alone." He brings his mouth down to mine and kisses me as he moves his hands into my hair, pulling me tightly to him. When he pulls away, I'm a little blushed and winded.

"Okay, lovers, can we go inside now? I'm starving. Or I am about to record you two and post it to my Only Fans and make a dollar off you, hey," he says it as he makes the motions with his hands like he is throwing dollars.

Josh started to laugh.

"How much we talkin' Gavin? My girl over here is giving me she wants to buy a house on the beach vibes." Josh says, laughing.

"Hey!" I say as I push him a little.

We are all laughing as we walk to the door.

We walk into the house; you can hear talking and laughter. It's such a different feeling in this house than at Tara's right now. It's so gloomy there. Here, there is life everywhere. I close the door behind me. I look up and see the staircase. I instantly think about seeing Oliver and Avery at the top of the stairs. I roll my eyes and follow Josh into the back of the house. I try not to think about that memory. This is also the house where I saw Josh for the first time.

"Khloe, Gavin, I'm so glad you guys made it. Dinner is ready, so make yourself a plate." Ed chirps.

"Don't mind if I do," Gavin says as he walks over to the food.

I'm standing there next to Josh. Ed walks over to me and puts his arm around my shoulders.

"I am so happy Josh met you. Even if you sorta stole our truck from us." He says as he laughs.

"I mean, could you blame me? She walked up with $1500. I couldn't tell her no." Josh says as he winks at me.

"I mean, if she met with me on it, I would have given it to her for free," his dad jokes.

"Hey, old man, you know if I came back with no money for it, you would have my neck," Josh says, laughing.

"Probably right," Ed says with a smile. "In all honestly, though, I'm happy you came for dinner tonight. Now go get something to eat."

He walks away. Josh motions for me to go first. We make our plates, then go into the dining room and sit down next to Gavin, already eating. Nicole was already in there with her plate almost finished.

"Hey Nicole," I say, trying to start a conversation with her.

She looks up at me, smiles, and then takes another bite. I look at Josh. She stands up.

"Excuse me," Nicole says as she walks behind us and leaves the room.

I look at Gavin to see if he caught that; he is looking at his phone and eating. Maybe I am just overreacting. I start to eat the food on my plate. Am I really okay with Nicole being upset with me?

After dinner, we are all back in the kitchen. Gavin has probably drunk a gallon of sweet tea by now, and looks like he is enjoying the coastal vibes.

"I'm going to slip out and look at my bike in the garage. It's been sitting for a while. Want to come?" Josh leans into me to talk near my ear.

I look over and see Nicole sitting on the back deck.

"I think I will go and try to talk to Nicole," I tell him.

He kisses my cheek and slips out.

"Gavin, another one?" I ask him as he pours another cup.

"Look, we live in an unsweet tea area. I have missed some southern sweet tea." He says with sass.

"Well, come with me to talk with Nicole, please," I beg.

He follows me out the back door.

I walk out and take a seat next to Nicole. Gavin sits on the other side of me. He starts taking pictures of the sun setting over the water in the distance.

"Nicole, what's wrong? Why are you acting like you are upset with me? Is it because of Josh?" I ask.

"I just did not see you as a person who would play two men at the same time, one of them being my cousin." She puts her phone down and turns towards me.

"Excuse me?" Gavin chimes in, irritated.

I put my hand on him to calm him down.

"What are you talking about? What two men?" I ask.

"Khloe, Oliver! Does Josh know you two are together? I'm not going to tell him, but I don't like seeing it." She barks back at me.

"Together? Oliver and I are not together. I asked him to leave and come back here to leave me alone." I explain to her.

"Khloe, he told us all you two are together still, when he got back." Her face changes.

Gavin spit out his drink. I could feel some of the spray on my arm. I turn towards him and wipe my arm. He starts coughing. I pat his back.

"No, we're not together. Why would he say that?" I feel the anger rise inside me. I stand up and pace a little. How could he do that? Why would he?

"Khloe, there's more." She says.

I stop pacing and turn to face her. Gavin is now facing her, too. She looks down. I can tell whatever it is she does not want to tell me.

"What?"I ask.

"Avery is pregnant."

I hear Gavin make an oh-drawn-out noise.

He lied to me. He said they didn't go all the way. He is going to be a father. I turn and look over at the ocean. How do I really feel about this? I stare out as I try to get my emotions in check. I conclude I am more upset that he is lying and saying we are together than I am about Avery being pregnant. Although that does shock me too, but moreso that he lied to me.

Nicole comes up to me and put her arm around me.

"I'm sorry, Khloe." She says.

"Sorry? You don't have to be sorry. You didn't do anything wrong.

Thank you for telling me." I tell her.

"But I did. I shouldn't have acted that way towards you when I saw that you two may have something going on. I'm happy for you guys if that's what you want." She says sweetly.

"It's okay, Nicole. I understand. I really do care for Josh. Like a lot." I tell her.

Gavin walks up to us.

"I am witnessing them falling in love this summer." Gavin chimes in.

Nicole smiles at me.

"I have a question, though: where does this clown live? I have things to say to him." Gavin asks.

"Down, Gavin," I say and laugh a little.

"The boy needs to realize he ain't shit, for real." He says.

Nicole and I both laugh out loud.

We all walk down the beach and kick off our shoes as soon as we hit the sand. We walk into the water and let it wash up on our feet. I stop and look up at the moon. I close my eyes and just listen to the waves. I let the moon and sea calm my soul. I feel so rooted here. Gavin walks over to me and holds my hand. I rest my head on his shoulder.

Josh drives us back to the house. Gavin goes in after saying his goodbyes. I sit on the porch steps with Josh. I put my head on his shoulder. He wraps his arm around me.

"You get everything worked out with Nicole? I saw you guys on the beach laughing. So, I just assumed." He asks with worry in his voice.

"Yeah, we did. She is a little protective of you." I smile at him.

"We have always been close growing up. So, what was her deal?" He asks.

"Well, apparently, Oliver is running his mouth around that he and I are still together," I tell him.

I feel his arm tighten slightly around me.

"Also, Avery is pregnant. So, he is about to be a father, I guess saying it's his." I say, still slightly shocked.

"Would you let me handle this one? I would really like to talk to Oliver myself." He pleads.

"Yeah, but you better let him hear it." I nudged him.

"Promise." He leans over and kisses my cheek.

"I will pick you up in the morning. Go get some sleep; it's been a long day." He says sweetly.

"Night." I turn and kiss him on the lips before he stands up to leave.

I walk inside the house, there is something about this house that just feels lonely now. I look over at Tara's door. I look around to see if anyone is around. I walk into her private area. A room in the house I have never entered before.

The room is a little sitting room with an office area. I see a large wooden desk. I walk over to it and run my fingertips over the surface. There are framed photos on the desk. I look at them. One is a photo of Dee and Jake holding a baby. This must be their baby boy.I have always felt bad for Dee on the loss of her child, but Tara lost her only grandchild. I also see a photo of a younger Tara holding a little girl who looks like Dee as a child.

I look to my right and see another room. I look inside and see Tara's bedroom. I see her bed made; everything is as she left it, all tidy and put together, just like her. I go back to her desk, and sit in the desk chair. I stare at the photos and try to imagine the life Tara lived as the tears fall onto my lap.

Twenty-Eight

In Mourning

It feels weird sleeping in this room again. I roll over and look out the window and look out over the beach. The sun was starting to rise. If I move back here, I can't stay in this room. This room has too many memories, and I have been battling them all night. Feeling frustrated, I get up. I start the shower.

After the shower, I look in the closet at my clothing. There was nothing I saw that I wanted to wear today. I slip on a robe, leave the room, and go to the attic. As soon as I walk in, I hear crying. I look to the other side of the racks of clothing. I see Danielle sitting in a chair, holding a dress, crying. I walk to her and kneel next to the chair she is sitting in. I start to rub her back as she cries.

"Only a few of us are lucky enough to have two moms. And now we have lost our second mom. The pain of losing someone you love is not just something you feel once. You feel it over and over again. It hurts less as time goes on, but it still hurts every time you think about them or that loss." She says to me in between sobs.

I knew exactly what she meant. We sit there and cry together. We hold hands and pull ourselves together in time. I was unsure how long we just sat there together. I stood as she stood.

"Let's find something to wear and get ready. We got all our tears out, so now we can be strong for Dee. She needs us today."She says, determined.

I nod in agreement.

I walk down the aisles of clothing. I didn't feel like wearing a dress. Then I found black dress pants with a black blazer. I also grabbed a pair of black strappy heels. I take the items back to my room and start to get ready.

I hear a soft knock on my door as I look in the mirror. I paired the slim-fitting pants with a white crop top and slightly pushed the blazer sleeves up on my arms.

"Come in," I yell as I still look in the mirror. I braided my hair, and it lays over one shoulder, and there are loose strands hanging around my face.

Gavin comes in and stands behind me. I can see him in the mirror. He raises his eyebrows at me.

"You look fierce. I love it."

"Too much?"I turn to face him.

"Not at all." He says.

"So, what are you going to do today?" I ask him.

"I'm going to hang out at the beach. I may borrow a book if you think that's okay." He asks.

"Oh, yeah, pick one out. I think everyone is meeting here afterward. How about I join you on the beach then?" I suggest.

"Perfect." He says excited. "Oh, Josh is waiting for you on the front porch."

"Why didn't he come in?" I ask.

"I offered when I answered the door, but he said he would wait out there for you." He says shrugging his shoulders.

"Okay, I better run then." I kiss him on the cheek, and leave the room, go down the stairs.

I open the front door and see Josh sitting on the front porch step. He turns as soon as he hears the door open. He stands up and brushes off his pants with his hands. He's wearing black slacks, a black button-up shirt with a couple of buttons unbuttoned at the top and a black dress jacket, he's also wearing aviator sunglasses. I am definitely drooling over this man. It should be a crime to look that good I think to myself.

"Look at you," he says as he walks over to me. He puts his arm around my lower back.

"I think we clean up nicely," I says.

"I think you are right." He gaves me a small kiss. "You ready for this?" He asks me.

"I guess as much as I will be." I feel a slightly hollow feeling in my stomach.

"Where's Gavin?" He asks.

"Oh, he's having a beach day. I thought maybe we could join him later." I suggest.

He smiles at me. He takes my hand, brings it to his lips, and kisses it.

"Let's go, hon." He says softly.

We drive with his dad to the graveside service. The number of people at the service was impressive. We worked our way through the crowd to go stand near Dee, Sidney, and Danielle. I put my hand on Dee's shoulder as I stand behind her. She reaches up and puts her hand on top of mine. I think back to when she made that same gesture to me at my parents' funeral.

They start the service. I was halfway listening as I look at the ground. I have a hard time looking at the coffin. I feel Josh put his arm around my lower back and rests his hand on my hip, slightly pulling me closer to him. I look over at him. He is not looking at me. I follow his gaze. My eyes met Oliver's.

His eyes are swollen and red. He looks as if he has not slept in a few days. I have never seen him look that before. I stare at him for longer than I wanted to.. I was just pulled in a way I can't explain. My empathy was replaced with anger as I think of him telling everyone we were together.

I lean into Josh, putting more of my body weight on his side. His hand tightens on me. I look up at him, and this time, he is looking at me. Was he watching me stare at Oliver? What is he thinking? It hit me hard at that moment that my actions may speak louder than my actual thoughts. I don't want to ever hurt this him. He doesn't deserve that. I reach up and put my hand on his face. I rub his cheek with my thumb. I move my hand, and he reaches up to hold my hand.

I rest my head on his chest. I then dare to look at the coffin. I think of all the times Tara was there for me. She would share her experience and wisdom with me when I thought my life was falling apart. I remember how she would hug me, and the love of a mother would come through that embrace. The world lost a real savior when her time came. This town is a little dimmer now without her light shining. I close my eyes and say a silent prayer for her.

After the service, everyone gathered back at Tara's house to show their last respects to this amazing woman. So many of the girls who once lived here came to pay their respects. All are in different stages of life. Some came with their families, some alone. As I walk through the house and hear them share stories.

"Khloe, can you come here for a moment?" Dee calls for me.

I walk towards where I thought I heard her call for me. I see her sitting near the large window in the living room. She has another woman sitting with her. She reaches up and takes my hand as I got close.

"Khloe, this is Andi. She is the one I was telling you about who went off to Pennsylvania for school." I look at the woman in front of me. She has dark hair and light eyes.

"Hello, Khloe. Dee was telling me how you are the daughter of Tom and Jenna." She smiles at me.

"I am. So, you knew my parents in college?" I ask, curious.

"I did. My boyfriend at the time was best friends with your father. We did everything together. Your mom and I got close. Wow, you look so much like them. You are a good mix of them both." She says as if she is remembering them.

I smile at her. It makes me happy to hear that.

"What were they like?" I say, hopeful I will learn more about their past and who they were.

"They were so much fun. They were an adorable couple that everyone envied. My relationship ended in our junior year, and we all went our separate ways. I heard they got married and moved out to the Midwest. I haven't heard from them in so long. But those times we spent together in college were amazing. Looking at you makes me miss them more, though." She says.

"They picked this home for my sister and me in their will because of you, I think. They also donated to Tara for years." I tell her.

"Your mother was a real activist back in the day. She was a powerful force in women's rights stuff. It does not surprise me that she would help a home like this for young women. I would sit with her for hours talking about life and this place." She smiles, and it's almost like she is reliving those moments as her eyes glaze over.

I reach for her hand and squeeze it. I know if she lived here, something had to of happened that would be painful to go through.

"Thank you. Thank you for being brave to tell her your life story. Your life impacted her, my sister, and mine. I am forever grateful." I as to her.

She squeezes my hand back. I look over at Dee, smile at her, and walk away.

I didn't need to drill her for all the details. It didn't matter; she made an impact on my parents, and that was all that mattered. I walk through the crowd of people, looking for Josh.

Hearing my mom was such a person standing up for women's rights was news to me. I am learning more daily that your parents are not who you think they are by the perception they let you see. They had whole lives I knew nothing about.

I turn towards the kitchen and see Josh outside through the back door window. I walk towards the door. I stop when I see him talking to Oliver. I watch to see if I can tell what's being said. I watch Josh's body language to see if I can see anything. I can't tell anything by looking at him, but I can tell Oliver is upset by his body language. I debate if I should walk away or go out there. I take a deep breath, open the door, and walk towards Josh. Oliver immediately turns and stares at me.

"Oliver, why are you telling everyone, my cousin included, that you and Khloe are together?" I hear Josh ask Oliver.

"In my eyes, we are together. We are just having a little disagreement right now. And here you are, sliding in, trying to take her from me. What kind of friend are you?" Oliver questions Josh.

"Oliver, are you delusional?" Josh snaps back at Oliver.

"We were together in Indiana. We went on a date. We had sex. We are together." Oliver states his reasoning.

Josh lets out a small laugh. I feel my face getting hot. I stop walking. Josh turns to see what Oliver was looking at and see's me. He turns back to Oliver.

"You think a date is love? Do you think sex is love? That's not love, Oliver." Josh turns to look at me as he continues to talk. "No, it's showing up every day, being there when things are hard and messy. It's being uncomfortable and pushing past it. It's growing in who you are and helping them grow without forcing it. It's trust, it's knowing one touch from them can completely change your thoughts or mood." He turns back to Oliver as he continues. "It's knowing no matter how hard it may be, I will let her choose her path every day and not force her into deciding because I want her to."

I stand next to Josh and put my hand on his back. He puts his hand around my shoulders and squeezes one shoulder a little.

"I hear you are going to be a father soon, Oliver. I think it's time to grow up and get your priorities straight. Stop the gossiping and trying to hurt others, including Khloe because you didn't get your way. It's time to be a man; no longer act like a child." Josh tells him as he turns us to walk away from him.

I fight the urge to turn and look back at him. I want to see Oliver's face so bad after Josh said that. I was processing everything I heard Josh say back there. The difference between Josh and Oliver is night and day. I never looked back. I didn't need to, my future was right here.

Twenty-Nine

Past Creeps In

Josh and I walk up to my room. I'm ready to hang out with Gavin. Josh walks over to the patio. I go into my bedroom to change, then join him on the patio. He laid his jacket over the railing. I put my back on the rail next to him.

"You want to go to the beach with me?" I ask.

"I will definitely go if you want me to. But if you want to spend some time with Gavin and have a bestie day, I will go for a ride with the ole' man. He got a new bike."

"No, you should go be with your dad," I tell him.

He moves to stand in front of me. He put his hands on the rail, leaning in towards me.

"Let me know if you need me." He says.

"I will," I say softly, smiling at him.

He leans in and kisses me. The kiss deepens and he moves one of his hands from the rail and wraps his arm around my back to pull me in closer.

"Josh, what you said earlier," I trail off and look away from his eyes. "I believe that too," I whisper.

He lifts my face to look at him. He kisses the end of my nose.

"It's exactly what I believe and want." He tells me.

"Do you think we could be like that?" I ask him.

"We are baby." He tells me sweetly.

"Do you think you would want to live here with me, like in this house?" I ask.

"I honestly think I could live anywhere you are. I have faith in you and me that we could make a life worth living in a thousand different places. So, the place doesn't matter; it's us who does. I also feel like we are not ready to make such big leaps yet." He leans in and kisses me, then continues. "Doesn't mean I don't dream about it or want it."

I smile at him. He's right, we are still so new in our relationship. He kisses my forehead, grabs his jacket, and turns to walk away.

"See you later, beautiful." He says as he passes me.

"Bye," I blew him a kiss.

I watch him walk back inside through the glass doors and walk out the door. I turn and lean on the rail and look out over the beach. I start to look if I can see Gavin. I see Oliver sitting on the boardwalk edge. He has his head in his hands. I devise a plan to walk out the front of the house and down to bypass him to get to the beach. I grab my bag and head downstairs.

Just as I'm about to walk out the front door, I hear my name.

"Khole!"

I turn to see Sidney. I hug her.

"Look at your baby bump," I say, noticing how pretty she looks. She really is glowing.

"Yeah, it is starting to get noticeable." She rubs her stomach as she talks. "How are you? I miss you around here. Do you think you will come back?" She asks.

"I'm okay. Just trying to get everything squared away back home, and I plan to come back here." I tell her.

"Good. I wanted to talk to you privately briefly before you leave." She requests.

I nod my head, and she opens the front door for me, and we step out onto the front porch.

"Look, I know things are not working out for you and Oliver, but I need you to know that even though he is like my brother, you will forever be my sister. All of Tara's girls will be forever sisters. I was hopeful Oliver would not be an idiot, but it seems he still is." She smiles at me.

"I hear you may be an aunt soon, too," I say to her.

"Who knows if that baby is even his? Avery has been known to be a little promiscuous around town." She lets out a little laugh.

This is news to me, but then again, I don't really know her. I just nod in agreement to Sidney.

"I will let you run; just don't be a stranger." She pulls me into a hug. "Love you, Khloe."

"Love you, Sid." I hug her back.

I walk down the street a little to the public access point, then head down to the beach. Once I get to the sand, I take off my shoes and carry them. I scan the beach, looking for Gavin. I spot him talking to a small group. Of course, he already made friends. I smile, roll my eyes, and walk towards him.

"Khloe!" He yells as soon as he notices me. "These lovely people were just telling me about a beach slash pool party with a DJ down that way tonight."

"Brad's?" I ask.

"Yeah, you know him?" One of the people standing next to us smiles and asks.

"I've met him. I've been to one of the parties before." I tell them.

"Let's go. I have never been to a party on the beach. Please, please?" Gavin says getting all excited.

"I will think about it." I tell him.

"That's not a no, so I will see you guys later tonight then." He tells the group.

The group smiles at him and starts to walk back down the beach. I look over at Gavin, who is clapping his hands a little. I take a deep breath and close my eyes. I don't want to go to Brad's tonight, but Gavin looks so happy, and I already know I'm going. I pull out my phone to text Josh.

Khloe: Gavin wants to go to Brad's party tonight. Please at least make an appearance to hang out with us.

Josh: I can do that. Have fun, see you soon.

We hung out on the beach for the rest of the afternoon. We swam and laid out on the beach, soaking in all the sun we could handle. I told him what Josh had said to Oliver and what he had said to me when I asked him if he would live there with me. Gavin was telling me about his opinions on all of it. He thinks I should be happy Josh is the way he is and takes things slower. He thinks about things, not just reacting or moving into things too fast.

I'm waiting in the kitchen for Gavin later that evening to head out to Brad's. I keep myself busy by putting food that was left out away. Danielle walks into the kitchen and sits down heavily in a chair at the table.

"You want to go to Brad's with us tonight?" I ask.

"It's my party. He is throwing that party as my goodbye party. I just don't know if I can do it." She says.

I sit down next to her at the table.

"You know Tara would want you to keep living. That's how we honor her legacy. She gave us all a new life; she would hate for us to waste it away, depressed. You should come with Gavin and me." I plead with her.

"I will go change." She gives me a half grin.

I smile at her as she stands and goes back upstairs. I grab the trash and take it out the backdoor towards the trashcan outside.

"I'm never getting you back, huh?"

The voice startled me and made me jump in the dark. I turn to see Oliver sitting in the corner of the patio. He stands and walks towards me. The darkness hides his face. I set the trash down.

"I'm never going to come on this porch and climb up to your room to lay with you again." He reaches up and touches my face.

I jerked out of his touch.

"Do you love him?" He asks me.

"I am not even sure if I know what love is, Oliver. I thought I loved you, but I was completely wrong about that." I tell him harshly.

"I messed up one time." He says with a sigh.

"No! You keep screwing up. The bonfire, the river, and now I come back here to find out you are telling everyone we are together. Why?" I yell.

"I don't want to accept we are over, I guess." He says sadly.

"Well, you better get over it. Your life is going on a whole new path with the choices you made." I tell him firmly.

He starts yelling and hitting his head with his fists. He takes a step towards me, and I back up too fast and trip over the trash bag; I fall backward onto the decking.

"Oh, hell no!" Gavin comes out the door yelling. He stands in front of me, facing Oliver.

"Are you okay, Khloe? Did he touch you?" He asks, still facing Oliver.

"No, I tripped," I say as I get to my feet.

"I don't know what you are trying to do here, Oliver, but you better go before things get out of hand. And that is me being generous before I beat your face into a pulp for even stepping towards my girl like that. Don't you ever come at her like that again!" Gavin is getting louder as he talks to him.

Oliver took a step towards Gavin. Gavin did not back down and takes a step towards him to match his stance. I thought they were about to come to blows any second. I stand in front of Gavin; he grabs my wrist to pull me out of the way if needed. I face Oliver and push his chest until he backs up.

"Go!" I yell at him.

He takes a step back one at a time. Finally, he leaves and walks down the beach towards his house. I let out a long breath that I was holding. Gavin put his hands on my shoulders.

"You sure you're okay?" He asks.

"Yeah, I'm fine; he just scared me," I say, getting control of my breathing.

"You and me both." He says."You need to tell Josh."

"No, I don't want to worry him. He is out with his dad." I tell him.

"Well, then I am telling him." He says defiantly.

"Gavin, no, let's at least wait until he gets to the party tonight. He's riding. I don't want to upset him while he's on the motorcycle." I beg.

"Okay, but I will tell him later if you don't. He needs to put that little boy in his place." He says as he puts his hand on his hip, fed up with Oliver.

I turn and pick up the trash and continue to take it to the can. I go back to the kitchen with Gavin.

"Is that what you are wearing?" Gavin asks me.

I look down at myself. I'm wearing a bikini top and shorts. I let my braid out, and my hair lays in small waves down my back.

"Yeah, it's hot out. I may want to swim with this heat." I explain to him.

He smacks his lips. I take in what he is wearing. He has on a pair of tan khaki-colored board shorts and a short-sleeved white button-up shirt.

"You look like you are about to get on your yacht." I tell him.

"Exactly, classy baby. I'm on the hunt for a captain of this boat," he says as he flips his collar up on his shirt and starts to twerk.

I roll my eyes at him but laugh.

We can hear the music before we even walk into the house. I can see Gavin getting noticeably more excited with each step. This is so his scene. I look over at Danielle. She glances back at me. I give her a smile for encouragement. This is so out of character for her to act like this.

Almost immediately, Gavin kisses my cheek and takes off. I wave at him as he goes off. I walk with Danielle up to Brad. She hugs him, and he hugs her back. I look at them. I see the way he looks at her. I wonder if he has feelings for her. They start talking. I look around for anyone I know or a small corner to hide in.

I start to walk towards the back, thinking I will go sit on the beach and listen to the music. I weave in and out of people. I am suddenly picked up from behind and swung around. I'm startled, and my heart starts racing. Once I am back on my feet, I turn to see Tristan laughing.

"Khloe, dance with me." He says happily.

I smile at him as I catch my breath. I see Nicole with him and a few others from school.

"Hey cousin," Nicole says as she hugs me.

"Tristan, Khloe, and Josh are together." She tells him.

"Oh, shit you're with Josh? He looks around over me. "Where is he?" He asks.

"He's coming later," I tell him.

"Josh is a good dude. I have always looked up to him. Where's that punk Oliver at?" He asks me, laughing.

I shrug my shoulders. I hope I don't see him again tonight, I think to myself.

"I'm going to go out to the beach. If you see Josh, tell him I'm over there." I tell Nicole, she nods.

I continue walking out to the beach. I find a little spot away from everyone where I can still hear the music. I sit down, lean back on my hands, and stretch out my legs. I sit there for a few songs, then lie down, feeling the long day catching up with me. I start to doze off. I can't fall asleep out here. I get up and think I will head back to the house.

"Let me help you up." Josh puts out a hand towards me. I look up and take his hand. He pulls me up into his arms.

"How was your ride?" I ask.

"It was good." He says as he watches me carefully.

I start to knock the sand off my behind and legs.

"Gavin stopped me when I came in and told me what happened back at the house." He says frustration in his voice.

I feel frustrated with Gavin.

"Yeah, I tripped," I tell him.

"Um-hm," is all he said.

I can't see too well in this lighting, but I could see him clenching his jaw, and it pops out a little from the outside.

"He did scare me a little. I stepped back and fell over the trash I was taking out." I say to him as I put my hands on his chest.

I feel his whole body tense up under my hands.

"You want to get out of here?" He asks me.

"Yeah," I reply, thankful he wants to leave.

He takes my hand and led us out through the people. I'm looking down, not paying much attention as we walk; I text Gavin to let him know that I am going back home with Josh. I also messaged Danielle to let her know too.

"Josh!" A female yells.

We stop walking. I look up at a small group of girls standing in front of us.

"I thought that was you. How are you sexy?" She says as she gets closer to him.

Who is this? She looks around his age. I feel the jealousy creeping in for no reason. She is beautiful. She touches his chest. I squeeze his hand. He takes his other free and removes her hand from him.

"Hello, Abby; this is my girlfriend, Khloe." He pulls me lightly forward so I am not behind him.

"Oh, sorry. Nice to meet you, Khloe." She steps back away from him.

"Sorry, we were just leaving," he replies and continues to walk past the small group.

"Who is Abby?" I ask with a grin.

"An ex-girlfriend."

I turn to look back at her. I know, of course, he must have exes, but I have never actually met one.

We exit out in front of the house, and I see the bike parked. We walk towards it. He hands me a helmet. I start to put mine on while he puts his on. I am still trying to buckle it when he finishes. He reaches over and does it for me. He smiles at me. He gets on the bike, and I get on behind him. He starts it up, and the sensation somehow relaxes me.

"A little late-night ride?" He asks me.

"Yes," I tell him, feeling the frustration we both are carrying.

We start to ride through the streets of the town. Both our moods are changing. We both were tense as it seemed our past had been creeping up in today.

I start to rub my hands on his back. I move them down to his legs; I move forward and reach and rub his thighs. He moves one of his hands and rubs one of my legs. We stop at a light. I move my hands to his stomach and rub his stomach and chest. He takes a hand, puts it on mine, and holds it. He squeezes my hand. He leans back a little into me.

The light changes, and he revs the bike before he pulls off from the white line on the road. We go a little faster. I rub on his chest and stomach. I inch closer. I feel as if I cannot get close enough to him.

His hand is still rubbing my leg. I move my hands to his inner thighs. I am so close to him that I can feel him adjust a little in his seat. I watch him look down at my hands, still moving and rubbing him. I start to rub between his legs. I feel him get harder under my hand. He removes his hand from my leg and puts it on the handlebar of the bike to drive with both hands. He pulls off to a side street and parks on the side of the road that doesn't have any houses. He turns the bike off and hops off. He gets back on the bike but facing me now. He pulls me closer to him, my legs over his. I am now partly straddling his lap on the bike. He takes off his helmet, then mine.

"You want to get a little handsy on the ride, huh?" He says to me with a grin.

I smile at him, and he kisses me as he holds me tightly to him.

Thirty

Closure

I wake up to Beau kissing my face. I push him away a little.

"Okay, okay, I'm awake."

He walks out of the room. I look at my phone to check the time. I need to get up anyway. I meet Ms. Delgado in an hour. Beau walks into the room with his leash in his mouth. I smile at him. I missed him.

We got back into town late last night. I let Josh take the truck home. I was just too tired to drive him. I start to get dressed. I think back to saying goodbye to Danielle. She should be on her way to NYC by now. She will do great there. I smile, just feeling so happy for her. I start to chuckle, thinking back to Gavin telling me all about the party after we left, and how he met the love of his life.

I put on my shoes and see the scratches on my legs. I think back to the sticks poking me on the ground in the field Josh and I rolled around in after he carried me off the bike. I smile and blush just thinking about it.

"Okay, boy, let's go."

We walk down in front of the café to the grassy area. I sit on the bench and watch videos on my phone as Beau sniffs around. I look up and see a white car. I stare at it to see if it is the same one from before. As soon as I see the hand with a cigarette go out the window, I know it is.

"Come on, Beau, time to go."

I keep my phone out and walk towards the car since it's parked in my path back home. I make eye contact with the man as I walk past him. I have never seen him before. He has light-colored hair and facial hair, and he may be in his thirties. I walked past the car, put my hand down with my phone, and took a picture of the license plate. I pull my hand up to make sure I got it. I text the photo to Detective Graham.

I walk faster and keep looking back, making sure he is not following me. I take the stairs two at a time. Once I get inside, I look out the window to see if he is out there. I know I need to leave again for my meeting, but I want to make sure the coast is clear. I leave through the backside of the alley.

I feel the blood pumping fast in my veins. I am almost jogging to the office. I feel so paranoid, constantly looking back, I almost ran into a lady with a stroller. I open the door fast to get inside the office safely.

"Khloe, everything okay?" Naomi asks me with concern in her voice.

"Yeah, probably just me freaking out." I look out the front windows, still nothing. I walk to her desk.

"She's ready for you right this way," Naomi says.

I follow her as I try to control my pulse and breathing.

"Khloe, it is good to see you again." Ms. Delgado says.

"Hi, you too." I reply.

"Please have a seat." She motions for me to sit.

I sit in the same chair I sat in in the meeting room last time. She slides over a folder to me.

“Here are your files back. I made some copies, hope that is okay.” She asks. “So, I attempted to file with the court per the decree of the will. We have a little problem; the home is no longer operating with the owner passing. I was able to put in an injunction for the adoption, though. With Mr. Mates being arrested, we have a high chance of getting at least a legal guardianship.” She says with a smile.

“Thank you,” I say with gratitude.

“Of course. I will let you know the court date as soon as I am notified. There are a few other items I wanted to discuss with you as well. The financial documents, I reached out to a realtor in case you would like to sell the business. Everything is written to be split evenly fifty-fifty between your sister and yourself. You would both profit from the sale of the business, the sale of the home, their bonds and stocks, and the trust that. You both would likely receive half a million dollars when it’s all said and done.”

I try to wrap my head around the words she just spoke to me.

“I don’t see how that is possible. We did not live a fancy life. We were not rich at all. How can it all be worth that much?” I ask, confused.

“Your parents were investors and savers. They lived a very frugal life, and that is what you know about your parents. They were handling their finances in a very modest fashion. They were easily worth a million dollars, possibly more.” She says matter-of-factly.

I just sit there staring at her.

“I can help you get all that worked out and managed as well.” She says.

“That’s why they wanted them gone. That’s why they want Katie.” I say.

“Money will sometimes bring out the worst in some individuals.” She tells me.

I walk back home, thinking I have just been given some of the best news. I will get Katie, and I am basically rich. All I can think of is I want my parents back. In a daze, I get ready for work. I cannot shake the feeling he did all this over money.

I work my shift on autopilot. Evan Gavin was not able to cheer me up. I told him about the meeting with the attorney. I just was not in the mood for the jokes on the money. He just hugged me. It's not worth it. I don't even want it after what it cost me.

I want to talk to him. I want to see him. I want to ask him why. I want him to look me in the eyes and tell me the truth. I pull out my phone, text Josh, and ask if he can take me to the police station once he is off work. He agrees to take me. I walk outside to sit outside for my break. I sit at one of the tables away from any customers.

"Khloe?"

I look up and see Brittany standing there.

"Hey, Brittany," I say, surprised to see her.

"Can we talk?" I see her look around as she asks.

"Is everything okay? Is it Katie?" I ask.

"I would just feel more comfortable if we were somewhere private," I say.

"Yeah, okay, let's go upstairs to my place." I walk to the side of the building and go up the stairs she follows.

Once inside, we sit down on the sofa. I can tell she is nervous. It makes me feel nervous. I start to fidget a little.

"What is it, Brittany? I'm getting nervous." I tell her.

"Your letters are not getting to Katie. She wrote to me and told me she found out they were being taken. She said she's fine. Just wanted to let you know that you may have to write her through me."

"Okay, thank you for coming to tell me. I will write one later, and maybe you can send it to her for me." I ask her,

"I can't do that, though, Khloe. I'm moving. My dad is leaving, and

I have to go with him. I cannot stay here with my mom." She looks down at her hands in her lap.

"She's not a good person, Khloe. I would tell you everything I know, but it doesn't make it any easier accepting your own parent is a bad person." She takes a deep breath, and I see the tears falling down her face.

I scoot closer to her, put my arm on her back, and start to rub it a little.

"I am so sorry. Just know you are nothing like her." I tell her, my heart breaking for her.

"I am just going to start from the beginning. My mom and Julia Mates are best friends. I have known them my whole life. Lucas used to tell me never to trust them. He must have sensed they were not good people. One night, Mom was talking to Julia, and they were talking about how much money your family was worth and how they were going to get rid of Seth, and he would be jobless if this partnership thing didn't work out at your dad's office. They came up with this crazy plan to kill them and just take it over. Lucas overheard this conversation. He thought they were talking crazy talk while they were drinking wine." She looks up at me with tears still falling down her face.

"He was wrong. They continued to plan. He told me about it. He knew Katie and I were close friends. He overheard them planning to do it with all of you. You all needed to go when Seth found out that everything was going to transfer to you guys if something happened to your parents. They planned to kill all of you in some crazy freak accident."

"Why didn't you go to the police?" I ask her, confused that if they knew all this, why didn't they do something?

She looks away from me.

"She's my mom. I was scared. We were scared. We were in shock they were going to follow through with this. So, Lucas and I were going to try to step in and at least save you and Katie. Lucas was trying to get closer to you at school. We heard it may happen that night; your dad told Seth you were going to the movies, and the plan went into motion. That day, Lucas purposely picked up a shift at the movies to be there. He knew the plan to make you two somehow not get in that car." She stands up and starts to pace the floor.

"It worked; we saved you both. I know it came with a huge cost. Looking back, we should have done something like the police or told our parents. This was the plan we came up with, though."

Beau starts to whine a little. I call him over to me.

"We had no idea you had no family to take you. You girls ended up in that home. Then, the plans started again. Julia and Seth would take Katie, and my aunt and uncle would take you. Lucas about lost it. He knew our uncle was a creep. He stopped going to school and took online classes. He felt he saved you from a situation and then fed you to the wolves when you went to live with our aunt and uncle." She tells me, crying.

I try to process all this information.

"We then heard you shot our uncle. Lucas knew something had happened to drive you to that point. It was eating away at him. He started drinking. Then you moved to the coast, and my aunt was crazier than my mom. She wanted vengeance. Lucas had my mom believe he would help them get to you. But he was just trying to save you. He felt if he could get you to fall in love with him, he could save you. He could run away with you and keep you safe forever. He felt that obligation to you to make your life better since he blamed himself for ruining it." She came back and sat down next to me.

"Khloe, I cannot be part of this anymore. It drove my brother to his death. I'm convinced of it. They will do anything to get you and your sister and take all they can from you, including your lives. I know they arrested Seth, but it's not over; I know it. Trust me, please be careful. You need to get Katie and disappear." Her phone went off.

"I gotta go. I am so sorry, Khloe. We were trying to save you, and we made more of a mess of things." She stands up and walks out the door.

I sat there, losing all track of time, replaying all the events that had happened and trying to see Lucas' part in all of it. Am I mad at him or thankful for him? I hear my phone going off. I ignore it. I stand up, go into my bedroom, and just collapse on my bed and cry.

There is a loud knock on my door, and I hear it open and close. I don't move. Beau didn't bark, so I didn't move. Gavin walks into the room.

"Hey, hey, what's the matter? You never returned from your break, and Josh is blowing me up since you didn't get back to him." He pulls out his phone and starts to make a call. I can only hear one side of the conversation.

"Hello, yeah, I found her. She was in her apartment. I'm not sure. Okay, I will see you soon."

"I'm going to text Carrie and tell her you are sick and cannot come back for the rest of your shift." He tells me as he is typing. He starts to rub my leg as I lay there, just not saying anything.

"I'm going to go get you some water and a cool cloth." He gets up and leaves the room. I think he is just getting uncomfortable sitting there in silence with me.

I hear the door open again. I hear Josh and Gavin talking in the kitchen.

"What happened?" Josh asks Gavin.

"She's not talking, I don't know," Gavin tells Josh.

I get up, open the side bed table drawer, pull out a piece of paper, slip it into my back pocket, and walk into the room where they are. Gavin brings me a cup of ice water and a wet washcloth.

"Here sweetie, you can use this to wipe your face," Gavin tells me.

I take it and sit on the sofa. Josh comes over to me and kisses the top of my head. He sits next to me; he puts his hand on my thigh. I look up at him, knowing I look like a wreck. He just looks back at me with concern. He reaches up and moves my hair, which is stuck to my face from tears drying on my face. Gavin sits in the chair across from us.

"Tell us what happened." Gavin pleads.

I take a deep breath and tell them everything Brittany told me.

Josh walks into the police station with me. I head to the front and ask for Detective Graham. We sit in the waiting room area and wait for him. Josh reaches over and holds my hand.

"You sure you want to do this?" He asks me.

I look at him and nod.

"Ms. Pierce?" Detective Graham calls.

I turn and stand up to meet the detective walking towards us.

"Thank you for meeting with me at the last minute," I tell him.

"Of course, let's go into a room to talk." He leads us to a little room down the hall.

"Did you get the photo of the plate I sent you?" I ask.

"I did. I ran the plate. It came back registered to Jared Coffman." He says.

Hearing that name will forever affect me.

"He is deceased, so we don't know who is driving that car. I did have dispatch put a lookout for it. If they are spotted, we will pull them over and find out who the driver is." He tells me.

"Thank you," I say with a grin.

I already know it's someone connected to Linda. I feel a sickening feeling deep in my stomach.

"Are you sure you want to see him?" He asks me.

"I am," I say, determined.

"There will be glass between you, and we will keep a guard in there.

Also, anything you two talk about will be recorded."

I nod. I look over and see Josh making a tight fist as his hand lays on his leg under the table. I place my hand on his. He looks over at me and relaxes it.

"Okay, let's go." The Detective says as he stands.

I get up and follow him.

I walk into a room with chairs next to what looks like little desks with a piece of glass separating us from the other side. I see the guard enter the room. He leads me to a chair in the middle of the room. I sit down and wait. I see a door on the other side of the glass open. A guard is holding Seth Mates' arm, and he sits him down in the chair across from me.

We just stare at one another for what feels like an eternity. He points to the phone's hanging receiver on the wall. He picks it up. I look to my right, pick up the one on my end, and place it to my ear.

"Khloe Pierce, what do I owe the pleasure? Sorry, I would offer you a refreshment, but it seems we are fresh out in my new establishment." He says with a smirk. His sarcasm makes me sick and mad.

"I hate to break it to you, but you look horrible in orange. And from what I can tell, you will be wearing it for a very long time." I smile as I say it.

"Cut the shit. What do you want, you little bitch?" He laughs.

"I want to hear it from your lips; why did you do it? Why did you kill my parents?" I ask.

"I didn't do anything. I have no idea what you are talking about." He says. He just stares at me.

"Was it all for money? Was it worth it?" I continue.

"Like I said, I know nothing." He turns his head to look behind him and yells. "Guard!"

"Was it too much to know he would get rid of you? You would never be as good as him. You knew you would lose everything you worked so hard for. You would never make partner." I ask with sarcasm.

"Too bad. While you sat at his desk, pretending to be the top guy, all the papers were hidden in that desk for me. For me to take it all." I tell him, watching him turn red.

"I knew where they were the whole time. I bet you tore the place apart trying to find all the stocks and investments." I sit back in my chair a little as I continue to talk. "I guess you can call me your boss now. It looks like you will be late tomorrow, as well as the days, months, and years after that." I lean forward as close as I can to the glass.

"Guard!" He yells again.

"By the way, you and Julia are fired; neither of you are nor ever will be worthy to work for Thomas Pierce Investments," I tell him, almost touching the glass with my nose.

He leans in. Our faces are so close to one another. Just that glass was separating us.

"I would do it again; the only thing I would do differently is make sure you two little brats were in that car, too."

I sat back in my chair. I smile at him.

"Thank you for the recording, Seth. See you never." I hang up the phone.

I give him a little wave as they pull him from the seat and escort him back out of the room, and rest my head on my arm on the little desk area. I cry but also feel proud I got him to admit it. I help get his confession. I helped get that closure.

Josh and I pull up to the cemetery. He turns off the truck and gets out to walk around to my door. He opens my door for me. I lean against the bed of the truck next to the door. He stands in front of me after he closes the door.

"I am so proud of you." He says proudly.

"I was so scared," I tell him as I smile at him.

"But you still did it. You're brave and so much stronger than you even know." He bends down and kisses me.

"I won't be long," I tell him.

"I will be waiting right here." He tells me with a wink.

I watch him walk to the back of the truck, put the tailgate down, and jump up to sit. I walk over to Lucas' grave first. I kneel next to his name. I brush it off. I kiss my fingers and place them on his name.

"I'm sorry for the burden you felt you had to carry. I also forgive you; I understand you were trying to help. Thank you."

I stand and walk to my parents. I lay down with their gravestone at the top of my head. I lean to the side and pull out the paper from my pocket. I open my dad's letter and begin to read it out loud.

Hello, my sweet Khloe,

From the moment I first saw you, my life has been forever changed. I never knew I could love someone so much at first sight. I knew I would never want to leave you and miss any moment of your life. I wish I could live forever and always be here for you, but that was not what was written in the stars for me or you, love. I know you are strong. I know your mother and I are making a good choice when considering your future, if it is to continue without us. We want you to go live in this incredible home in Southern Shores, North Carolina. There is a family there that takes in girls and helps them reach their potential in life. We have seen firsthand what she can do. We don't have a family to care for you girls, so this is our solution for you. Stay close to your sister. In the end, you will always have one another. Be happy and smile often, take risks, and learn from your mistakes. Forgive often, and never have too much pride in saying you're sorry. We have set a plan that money will never

have to be a stress for either of you. One day, when you fall in love, make sure they are worthy of the amazing woman you will be. Make this world a better place for my grandchildren that will come one day. We will always be watching over you.
Feel us when the wind blows, when you smell the scent of wildflowers, or step into the ocean.
Love,
Dad

Thirty-One

Linda

I try to get comfortable on this thing they call a bed in here. There is always noise in this place. Even at night, there is noise. I haven't had a good night's sleep in so long. I feel on edge, like I am about to snap. I think of why I'm even in this place, that little whore. I close my eyes and try to go back to sleep. I think back to the first time I met her.

"I have an idea, Jared." I think this will be the perfect time to bring up the topic. I have been making plans all week long. He has just been his normal depressed self since we moved here.

He moves the food around on his plate of food. I study him. He doesn't even look up at me as I speak. I know all he thinks about is the little girl from the old school he worked at. I have an idea of the monsters he battles. He tries to be strong and fight them. He tries not to give in to obsessions and desires when it comes to the girls.

I think back to the first time I found out. I tried to overlook it when we were dating, thinking he would learn to control it or overcome his desires. I will change him. I will show him what love is, and he will only desire me. I was proven wrong again and again. Yet here I am, staying with him. Now, the demon he is may pay off for me.

"Yeah, what's your idea, Linda?" He asks with no interest.

"I was thinking we could be foster parents. Since we cannot have our own children, maybe we could foster and adopt in time." I knew he would perk up with this information.

All the pain I went through was unnoticed about not having children. We could have children. We almost did once. I was pregnant, but I lost the child. I thought it was better that we didn't. The fear of him hurting our child was a constant worry for me. I had an implant since that miscarriage. I know having children with this man would only end in despair.

"I'm listening." He says as he lays down the fork on the plate.

"See, my sister Kristin knows of this family of sisters in a girl's home. Their parents were killed in a car accident. We could go help one of them." I am not telling him that I also know these girls will be cash cows. My money worries will be over if I could adopt one. The one left will be taken by my sister's friend Julia.

"When will we go to meet them? Is there a screening we need to do?" He asks.

"Yes, there is a process we can get started if you are ready to move forward." I see him smile. It almost gives me a sick feeling. I know this girl will one day be harmed by this man across from me. I only want her for the money, so in a way, we both have our reasons to move quickly on this.

A few weeks pass by. We are approved to move forward with visits to the home. We are driving there now. In the past weeks, Jared's mood has changed. He even got an offer to teach again at a middle school nearby. He has been volunteering in the community. He's just going around this new little town, fooling everyone from who he really is. I look over at him singing as he drives. I only see the monster he is or is about to be. I must get away from him. I just need the funds to disappear.

We walk in, hand in hand. We both have our parts to play today. We get a tour of the facility. The girls come and go doing various things around the home. We sit at a table in a common area.

"We are so happy to have you come in today. Do you see anyone you would like to foster? We can give you more information on any of the girls." The sweet-looking older lady states.

"You see, we are looking for a certain family friend's daughters. Their last name is Pierce."

"Oh, you mean Khloe or Katie Pierce?" She replies.

I see Jared look at me. I turn to look at him, but I cannot read his expression.

"We are interested in Khloe he tells the lady with a big smile." He chirps.

I look at him in confusion about how he would know her name.

"She is sitting right over there." The lady points behind us.

I turn to see a girl sitting near a window. Her knees are pulled in, and she has her arms wrapped around them in the chair. She is looking out the window. She has beautiful blond hair. I feel the urge to walk away right then when I see Jared look at her. I look back at her. I feel sick to my stomach.

"Yes, that is her," Jared says.

"Khloe! Can you come over here a moment?" The lady calls to her.

I watch her walk slowly over to us. Her face is so sad, almost emotionless. I study her. She is a beautiful young woman. The pain in her eyes sticks with me. It draws me in. I look away. I cannot falter on this. I cannot get an attachment to this girl. Jared stands up eager to meet her.

The jealousy that runs through me is shocking. It was not something I thought I would feel. I thought I was over the emotional connection when it came to Jared. I am filled with anger at this very moment. I look back at this young girl standing there, looking down at her feet. I feel the hatred welling deep inside me. I try to control it.

I go out into the rec room that is filled with tables. All the females in here have some sort of drama or another. I head to the phones. I call my sister Kristin.

"Hello," her voice sounds different.

"Hey, it's me. How are things?" I ask.

"We picked up the, um, package today. Me and Julia have it." She tells me.

"Oh, that's the best thing I have heard all day," I tell her, getting excited.

"We are going to deliver the package in a couple of days. It's not been a smooth process. Feisty this one is. We had measures to keep it calm." She tells me.

"Just keep the flower alive until delivery. We all will be paid generously." I tell her firmly.

"Yeah, okay." She replies anxiously.

"What about the other one?" I ask.

"That package has not been picked up yet. We are working on it." She replies.

"Well, work faster; I will run out of time here. My trial is coming up before we know it." I hung up the phone, feeling frustrated. I should have known better than having those two to care for this. They had already made a mess of things, and my niece and nephew mixed themselves into this mess. I pick up the phone and make one more call.

"Hey, it's me. I am calling to collect on that one favor you still owe me. I need you to strike and do it fast."

Also by Bobbie Hamlett

Dark Roads will be a three-book series,

Dark Roads

Dark Skies

Dark Waters - Coming 2025

Possible spin off about Dee and Jake coming .

Dark Roads

Book one of the Dark Roads Series

Made in the USA
Columbia, SC
31 October 2024